LOVE I
THE (

Barbara Cartland

Barbara Cartland Ebooks Ltd

This edition © 2017

Copyright Cartland Promotions 1965

ISBNs
9781782139478 ~ EPUB
9781782139485 ~ PAPERBACK

Book design by M-Y Books
m-ybooks.co.uk

THE BARBARA CARTLAND ETERNAL COLLECTION

The Barbara Cartland Eternal Collection is the unique opportunity to collect all five hundred of the timeless beautiful romantic novels written by the world's most celebrated and enduring romantic author.

Named the Eternal Collection because Barbara's inspiring stories of pure love, just the same as love itself, the books will be published on the internet at the rate of four titles per month until all five hundred are available.

The Eternal Collection, classic pure romance available worldwide for all time .

THE LATE DAME BARBARA CARTLAND

Barbara Cartland, who sadly died in May 2000 at the grand age of ninety eight, remains one of the world's most famous romantic novelists. With worldwide sales of over one billion, her outstanding 723 books have been translated into thirty six different languages, to be enjoyed by readers of romance globally.

Writing her first book 'Jigsaw' at the age of 21, Barbara became an immediate bestseller. Building upon this initial success, she wrote continuously throughout her life, producing bestsellers for an astonishing 76 years. In addition to Barbara Cartland's legion of fans in the UK and across Europe, her books have always been immensely popular in the USA. In 1976 she achieved the unprecedented feat of having books at numbers 1 & 2 in the prestigious B. Dalton Bookseller bestsellers list.

Although she is often referred to as the 'Queen of Romance', Barbara Cartland also wrote several historical biographies, six autobiographies and numerous theatrical plays as well as books on life, love, health and cookery. Becoming one of Britain's most popular media personalities and dressed in her trademark pink, Barbara spoke on radio and television about social and political issues, as well as making many public appearances.

In 1991 she became a Dame of the Order of the British Empire for her contribution to literature and her work for humanitarian and charitable causes.

Known for her glamour, style, and vitality Barbara Cartland became a legend in her own lifetime. Best remembered for her wonderful romantic novels and loved by millions of readers worldwide, her books remain treasured for their heroic heroes, plucky heroines and traditional values. But above all, it was Barbara Cartland's overriding belief in the positive power of love to help, heal and improve the quality of life for everyone that made her truly unique.

CHAPTER ONE
1784

"Then what shall I do?"

The question was plaintive, the voice shrill with anger.

The Earl of Wynchingham turned on his heel.

"You can go to the devil," he said in a voice that seemed to cut through the air like a whip and on the way you can find some other cork-brained idiot to pay your bills."

He walked from the room with dignity, crossed the hall, waited for the footman to open the door and stepped across the pavement into his coach that was waiting outside.

He flung himself back against the cushioned seat.

"Where to, my Lord?"

For a moment it seemed as though he had not heard the footman's question. There was a deep frown between his eyes and his mouth was set in a hard line.

"Where to, my Lord?" the footman repeated the question a trifle nervously.

"Home."

The word came out like a pistol shot.

The footman sprang up onto the box.

"'Ome," he whispered to the coachman, "and 'is Nibs be in a rare tantrum."

The coach had already begun to move and the driver turned his head to wink at the footman.

"I bet you she wouldn't last long," he said. "Not but what she's cost 'im a pretty penny."

"'E can afford it," the footman countered laconically.

Inside the coach Lord Wynchingham put his hand up to his forehead and then covered his eyes as though they hurt. In fact he felt exceedingly ill.

The brandy he had drunk last night in large quantities, the rich food he had consumed and above all the tension of the evening had all combined, when he did get to bed, to make sleep impossible and as soon as it had been decently possible he had risen and called for his coach so that he could visit his mistress.

He had no idea why he turned to her in his trouble, except that there seemed no one else and perhaps at the very back of his mind, behind the cynical facade that was so characteristic of him, was some youthful fantasy that believed that her continually voiced expressions of love had some basis in reality.

He was to be speedily disillusioned. He had no sooner begun an explanation of his gaming losses the night before than Cleo de Castile, who incidentally had been christened 'Maisie Smith', produced a sheaf of bills, which she declared were his responsibility.

He would not have minded so much had he not been convinced in his own mind that he had paid those self-same bills only a fortnight earlier or at least he had given Cleo the money to do so.

What had started as a half-expressed appeal on his part for a little sympathy and understanding had ended in a furious quarrel with Cleo de Castile making threatening demands and Lord Wynchingham's final decision to be rid of her once and for all.

Now, sitting back in the coach with his eyes closed, he wondered how he could ever have been so besotted as to have wasted so much of his money on such a particularly common and unpleasant strumpet.

But Cleo was the fashion and the fact that he had beaten two of his greatest friends in a race for her affection and carried her off from under the very nose of one of the richest and most powerful men at Court had added both flavour and piquancy to the affair.

Now he saw her for what she was, a loud-mouthed, hard-headed creature whose only interest in any man was what she could get out of him. He counted up how much he had spent on her during these past six months and clenched his teeth in a sudden fury.

'God! What I could not do with that money now!'

Through the fumes that still seemed to be in possession of his head and the throbbing of his temples the scene last night came back to him in all its vividness.

He had not been too foxed to know what he was doing. He realised that his luck was out, but like every gambler since the beginning of creation he had believed that his luck would turn and the next card would be in his favour – the next or the next –

But Lampton had gone on winning and winning and, because they were old enemies across the green baize tables, he had not hesitated to taunt Lord Wynchingham, needling him into making more and more extravagant bids until, finally, one hundred thousand pounds had waited on the turn of a card.

Lord Wynchingham could see his own six of diamonds staring up at him and he thought now that he had known, even before Lampton's long thin fingers very slowly turned his own card over, what it would be in the split second before he actually saw what the card was, he had known that he was beaten.

And, drunk though he was, he knew exactly what it meant.

It was almost as though he saw a procession of his possessions passing away from him into Lampton's keeping. His house, his estate, the pictures his father had set so much store by, his horses and last of all, because she was the least important, Cleo de Castile.

The card was there blinking up at him from the green baize, the ten of spades, black as his luck, dark as the sudden despondency that gripped his heart until he felt himself almost squeezed of breath.

Yet he managed with a superb effort to give a little laugh.

"My pockets are now definitely to let, Lampton," he had said lightly and as though it was not of the least consequence. "I must drink to your good fortune as it is too late for any further play."

He had known by the expression of the faces of those who had been standing round the table that his sportsmanship appealed to them. He gulped down the brandy that the waiter had brought him and then turned towards the door.

He was surprised to find Lampton at his side. For a moment he had thought the older man was going to taunt him, but Lampton had said in a quiet, almost commiserating tone,

"I know that this is going to knock you a trifle, Wynchingham. Shall we say payment in a month?"

Just for a moment rage had surged up in Lord Wynchingham. He had longed to be able to retort that the money should be in Lampton's hands first thing the following morning and yet, even as he moved his lips, he knew that it was impossible. But because he was embarrassed, furious, hating both himself and his opponent, he merely muttered ungraciously,

"I shall not default, you may be sure of that."

He had walked from the Club without looking back. His coach was waiting outside, the horses and the coachman half-asleep.

A drunken fop was protesting to the nightwatchman that he had been robbed by footpads.

"It's a dish-grace!" he slobbered, " – that's what it is – a stinking dishgrace that a gentleman cannot move about the streets without being ash-aulted! What I asks ish – ish this 1784 or ish it not?"

Unsteadily he brushed against Lord Wynchingham who swore at him.

Lord Wynchingham flung himself into his coach and slammed the door without waiting for his footman to do it for him.

It was only a short distance to Berkeley Square, but it seemed to him that he had time to review the whole of his life as the carriage carried him home.

God! What a fool he had been! He cursed himself as he climbed out and glanced for a moment at the fine exterior of the house and at the massive silver door handle and knocker that shone in the light from the linkman's lantern.

He cursed himself as he moved across the marble hall with its ghost-like busts of his ancestors and he cursed again as he went up the softly carpeted stairs where the pictures of previous Earls stared back at him with what seemed to be accusing eyes.

He had never before appreciated the elegance of his bedchamber, his valet waiting up to undress him, the fire burning brightly in the hearth and the heavy silken curtains blotting out the dawn which was just beginning to creep over the rooftops.

He waited until his valet had left and then he strode up and down his room remembering, too late, an interview only three days ago with his Solicitor.

"You are spending too much, my Lord," he had been told then.

"Gracious!" he exclaimed. "What is money for but to be spent and why this sudden parsimony? There has always been plenty in the past and to spare."

"Not to spare, my Lord," the Solicitor corrected. "We've managed, with I think commendable administration, to keep what one might call a steady balance. In fact, to put it clearly, the rents from your Lordship's estate have been able to offset the majority of your expenditure, but now things are different."

"How different?"

He had known the answer even before his Solicitor had enumerated his increased expenditures, his racing stables at Newmarket, the improvements he had made to his house in the country before the Prince of Wales's visit six months earlier, but these were almost paltry beside the sums of money that he had been expending in London on the entertainment of his friends and to satisfy the extravagance of his mistress.

Cleo de Castile had not been the only one. Before her he had been the protector of a more flamboyant and even more expensive 'lady', who was not only French by name but French by birth. She had succeeded an opera dancer and further into the past were innumerable little 'bits of muslin' whom he had allowed to fleece him, only because money appeared to give them so much pleasure and he had so much of it.

He was not so stupid that he did not realise that one hundred thousand pounds to be found in cash in thirty days from now would mean his selling almost everything that he held of value.

His horses must go, the house in London, a great deal of the land around Wynch and perhaps even the house itself.

What a fool he had been and all because he had been too proud to refuse Lampton's challenge and too stupid not to stop when he realised what the man was doing.

They said in the Club that Lampton never forgot.

Lord Wynchingham could remember now enticing away a pretty little actress whom Mr. Lampton had already installed at some expense in a house by Chelsea Hospital. It seemed an amusing bit of piracy at the time and Lampton had shrugged his shoulders and taken his loss with apparent good humour.

But Lord Wynchingham had known that behind that smile there was an angry and bitter opponent. Lampton had not the temperament to be a loser and certainly not to a younger man who had neither his authority nor his prestige.

Once or twice Lord Wynchingham had had the uneasy feeling that Lampton was a merciless enemy!

Now he could see all too clearly how the trap had been baited for him and that Lampton had waited a long time to get his revenge.

'One hundred thousand! *One hundred thousand!*'

The words seemed to burn themselves into his brain until he had thrown himself down on his bed with his hands over his ears as if to shut out voices from the outside rather than those that cried and cried again within him.

*

Now, as his coach turned from Piccadilly down Berkeley Street, he thought dully that he must send for his Solicitor and tell him to put up a bill of sale.

It was too late now to think of his family, of the generations of Wynchinghams who had lived at Wynch.

To recall how his great-grandfather had bought the house in Berkeley Square and how much of the history of

England had been decided in the quiet library at the back of the house where the Wynchinghams, who had served their country better than he had tried to do, had conferred with their fellow Peers and wielded their power as Statesmen with ability and sometimes with brilliance.

'Fool! Fool! *Fool*!' the words seemed to repeat themselves over and over again to the sound of the wheels and clop-clop of the horses' hoofs.

The footman opened the door and Lord Wynchingham stepped out on the pavement. For a moment he hesitated. Should he send the coachman for his Solicitor or should he wait a little while?

His head was still throbbing and he decided that first he would breakfast, a meal he had refused with some violence before he had left the house earlier in the morning.

He walked into the marble hall noticing that the butler and three footmen were in attendance. It was something that would not have occurred to him on other days and it was because he knew now that he was unlikely to see such an array in the future that he counted them, wondering vaguely what their wages were and how much they actually cost him during the year.

"Bring me some breakfast."

The words coming from his lips sounded harsher than he intended simply because he was so disturbed.

"Your pardon, my Lord," the butler replied, "there is a young lady to see you in the library."

"A young lady?" Lord Wynchingham repeated the question almost stupidly.

For a moment he thought that Cleo must be waiting for him.

The thought was incredible, but it crossed his mind that possibly she intended to give him back some of the money that he had spent so freely on her – the emerald and diamond necklace that had lost him eight thousand pounds, a diamond bracelet at five thousand pounds, pearls at three thousand pounds and at least ten thousand pounds on her carriages and horses.

He pulled himself together.

"A young lady," he repeated. "What is her name?"

"She didn't say, my Lord. She merely said that it was imperative she should see your Lordship."

Lord Wynchingham turned towards the stairs.

"Tell her I am indisposed," he began and then checked himself.

Perhaps, although it was a forlorn hope, this woman, whoever she might be, had news for him. It was unheard of that anyone should call at such an early hour, especially a member of the opposite sex, and there must be a reason for it.

He would see her.

He walked along the passage to the library, which lay at the back of the house. The footman hurried to open the door.

As he entered the long book-lined room, which looked on to the small but exquisite private garden with its Grecian Temple and ornamental sundial, it seemed to Lord Wynchingham that the room was empty.

Then, at the far end and almost obscured by the chair she was sitting in, he saw a tiny figure.

For a moment he thought that it was a child who was waiting for him. But she rose from the chair and he saw she was in fact a girl wearing a muslin fichu around her shoulders and a chip straw bonnet over her fair hair.

Lord Wynchingham, walking towards her, realised that he had never seen her before in his life. She was a complete stranger.

Pretty. there was no mistaking that, but certainly no one of any consequence. His experienced eyes took in the full-skirted grey poplin dress that, unless he was much mistaken, had been home-made. The ribbons on her bonnet certainly owed nothing to Bond Street and the gloves her tiny hands were covered with were of the cheapest cotton.

"Are you Lord Wynchingham?"

The voice that asked the question was low and almost breathless. It was surprisingly a woman's voice and had a quality about it that commanded attention.

"That is my name," Lord Wynchingham replied. "You wish to see me?"

The girl curtseyed.

"I came especially to see you, my Lord," she said simply. "I am Tina Croome."

She paused, looking at him, and he realised that she had expected him to recognise the name, but it evoked no response.

"Tina Croome," he repeated. "I am sorry. Should I know who you are?"

She made a little sound, half a laugh, half a sigh.

"Of course you should," she answered. "I was christened 'Christina', but everyone has always called me 'Tina' because I am so tiny. But surely, surely you know who I am?"

She had the bluest eyes that he had ever seen in a woman. They were not the blue one expected to find allied with fair hair and a complexion of milk and roses. Instead they were dark blue, almost the colour, he thought, of the enamel that decorated some diamond and gold snuffboxes that his mother had collected and which stood in a cabinet in. the drawing room.

'They will have to go,' an inner voice taunted him.

~10~

"I apologise," he said almost harshly, "but I am very occupied this morning, perhaps you will be more explicit. I am not very good at riddles."

To his astonishment a suspicion of tears came into her eyes.

"Please, oh, please, don't be angry with me. I know it was wrong, but I wrote and wrote and you never answered my letters."

"You wrote to me?" he asked astonished.

"Of course," she answered. "I have always written to you every Sunday. It was the day we were told to write letters home and, as I had no home, I naturally wrote to your Lordship."

Lord Wynchingham put his hand to his head.

"I regret to inform you," he said, "that I have not the slightest understanding of what you are saying. You are, I suppose, sure that you have come to the right house and that I am the person you are looking for?"

"If you are the Earl of Wynchingham, then I am looking for *you*," Tina Croome replied. "Surely you realise, my Lord, that I am your Ward and that you have been paying for me to be at school for the last five years."

Something stirred at the back of Lord Wynchingham's mind.

"Croome," he said. And then again, "*Croome!*"

The child in front of him, because she seemed little more, clapped her hands.

"You have remembered!" she exclaimed. "My father was Charles Croome and he saved your life. Do you recall that?"

Once again Lord Wynchingham put his hand to his aching head.

"Of course, I remember," he said. "There was that skirmish in America, it was not really a battle, my horse was shot under me and I was knocked unconscious. If your father had not stood over me and kept the enemy at bay, I would not be here at this moment."

"Oh, we discussed it so often," Tina cried. "My father told me how brave you were, how you struggled to your feet and the two of you fought your way back to join the rest of the Company. My father admired and respected your Lordship which was why, when he was dying, he made me your Ward and left me in your care."

"Yes, of course, I remember now!"

Lord Wynchingham could remember a letter arriving. He had read it through and then thrown it across the desk to his secretary.

"Do what you can for the child," he had said. "I gather Colonel Croome has left her no money. She had best go to school. Anyway don't bother me with the details."

His Solicitor had looked worried.

"I would just like to know, my Lord, how much."

Lord Wynchingham had interrupted sharply.

"I told you, I want no details. Do what you think best. God knows, it's bad enough that other people must saddle me with their children without my having to play Nanny to them."

His instructions had evidently been carried out to the letter.

"I understood that you were at school," he said slowly. "Those were the instructions I gave."

"I have been at school for the last five years," Tina replied, "but I cannot stay there indefinitely. Surely you must see that. I am too old – they don't want me there any more."

"You are too old?" Lord Wynchingham repeated.
Tina nodded.
"I am seventeen and a half."

She said it as though it was indeed a prodigious age.

"And they can't keep you any longer," Lord Wynchingham echoed almost stupidly.

"Even if they would, I would not wish to stay," Tina replied. "I am grown up. I want to see the world. I wanted very much to come to London and, of course – to get married."

"Of course."

Lord Wynchingham sat down suddenly in one of the wing armchairs. Tina sat herself opposite him arranging the folds of her full skirt with tiny meticulous fingers.

Lord Wynchingham cleared his throat.

"The position is a little difficult," he began.

"Oh, I know that," Tina interrupted. "I knew you might be angry at my coming without permission, but what could I do? I have been writing to you for the past six months explaining the whole situation. The only replies I received were from your secretary who always made excuses – 'his Lordship is away' – 'his Lordship is very preoccupied with other affairs'."

She mimicked the pompous tone, which was so like that used by his secretary that Lord Wynchingham could not repress a smile.

"So at last I decided to wait no longer," Tina said. "I told the Headmistress that I had heard from your Lordship and you were willing for me to come to London. They were all very kind. In fact, in a way, I think they were sorry to see me go. I took the stagecoach and here I am."

She paused a moment and then with her eyes shining and her hands clasped together, she said,

"It's so exciting to be in London. And this house is magnificent, just the sort of place I thought you would own!"

She had the enthusiasm and excitement of a child.

Lord Wynchingham had the uncomfortable feeling that he was about to destroy a butterfly or shoot a songbird as he said,

"Unfortunately you cannot stay."

Tina's face fell.

"Oh, please," she said, "please don't send me back."

She moved from her chair, crossed to where Lord Wynchingham was sitting and slipped down on her knees beside him.

"I beg you not to send me away," she pleaded. "I am too old. The other girls will laugh when I tell them. I know it was a lie, but I could not help it. I told them that you had planned to introduce me to Society. In actual fact – "

She hesitated for a moment and a soft blush stole over her cheeks.

" – I even told them that you would present me to the Prince of Wales."

Her skin was transparent and the colour came and went in a manner that he had never noticed before in any woman's face. But it was her eyes that held him, those vivid deep blue eyes, which he saw now were surrounded by thick dark lashes, a strange and unexpected contrast to the ripening corn of her hair.

Almost as if she knew what was surprising him, she took off her bonnet and flung it onto the floor beside her,

"Look at me," she said. "I will not disgrace you. I am not beautiful, I know that, but I am pretty, indeed prettier than many of the other girls and, if I had fine clothes and my hair powdered, you would not be ashamed of me, I assure you, my Lord."

Her small red mouth trembled and the blue eyes were suddenly suffused with tears.

"Your Lordship loved my father," Tina whispered. "I always believed that you would wish to repay your debt of gratitude by helping me."

Lord Wynchingham rose to his feet.

Never had he imagined in the whole of his life that anything could be so difficult to say.

Never had he thought that an explanation would seem as if he deliberately killed something that was beautiful and helpless.

"Get up, Tina," he said.

There was a tenseness in his voice that surprised even himself.

"I have to talk to you and to talk sensibly."

For a moment she remained kneeling, her little fingers clasped together, her face raised to his.

Then with a movement that he recognised as being as exquisitely graceful as anything he had ever seen on the stage, she rose to her feet and came towards him where he stood with his back to the fireplace.

"You are worried about something," she said softly. "It's not me, is it?"

"No, it's not you," Lord Wynchingham replied and then added as an afterthought, "You merely add to the troubles that are already in existence."

"I am sorry," she replied simply. "Tell me about them, perhaps I can help."

"You?"

"I used to be able to help Daddy when he was quite desperate." she answered. "I may not be clever. The Headmistress always said that I was not in the least clever, but I had ingenuity. Yes, ingenuity, my Lord, that is what she said about me."

"It would need more than ingenuity to help me out of my difficulties," Lord Wynchingham said wryly.

"My mother said two heads were better than one," Tina remarked and made it sound as though indeed it was the wisdom of the ages.

"Your mother is not alive?" Lord Wynchingham enquired.

Tina shook her head.

"She died long before my father, when I was only nine. But I can remember her quite clearly."

She paused for a moment and then, as Lord Wynchingham said nothing, she went on,

"Pray let's not talk about me. I can tell you all about myself later. Let's talk about you. What is wrong? What has happened to upset you."

"It's quite simple." Lord Wynchingham said. "I am completely and absolutely broke. I have no money and I have a debt of honour, a gambling debt of one hundred thousand pounds that has to be met in a month's time."

Tina put her hand up to her mouth to stifle an exclamation of horror.

"One hundred thousand pounds!"

She hardly breathed the words.

"My father was always in debt, but never for a sum like that!"

"Well, now you know the truth," Lord Wynchingham said harshly. "Now you understand why you could not have arrived at a more inopportune moment. Although I have paid your school fees in the past, I am very unlikely to be able to do so in the future."

"Do you mean that everything you own will have to be sold?" Tina enquired.

"Practically everything," Lord Wynchingham answered. "I might be able to keep my house in the country, because large houses are not fetching very good prices at the moment. This house will have to go, my property in

London, my horses at Newmarket, they ought to bring in a bit. But there's always a great deal of crookery over horse sales. The person who is selling seldom receives what he expects and those who are interested in what he has to sell get together beforehand and decide what they will buy, so that they don't bid against each other."

"That is mean, is it not?" Tina asked.

"I have done it myself," Lord Wynchingham replied.

He remembered a pair of chestnuts he had persuaded two of his friends not to bid for because he had wanted to buy them at a reasonable price.

"You have no other assets?" Tina asked.

"I have some pictures," Lord Wynchingham answered, "but they are merely family ones and who wants other people's ancestors? There's my mother's jewellery, of course." He sighed even as he said it. "I had hoped that it would have been heirloomed to my children when I had any."

Tina sat bolt upright in her chair.

He could see that she was thinking and it struck him suddenly what an extraordinary situation it was. Here he was talking to this child, quite frankly and openly as he had been afraid to speak to anyone else.

He knew that he had gone to see Cleo simply because he dared not face his Solicitor. He had put off sending for the man when he returned home for the same reason.

He could not bear to face up to the fact and could not tell anybody what a damned fool he had made of himself. And yet here he was confessing quite easily to this chit of a girl whom he had never seen before and who bore no resemblance whatsoever to the rather rough, good-natured, not particularly handsome man whom he remembered as her father.

~17~

It was a pity, he thought, that he could not give her the money to dress herself well and let her burst upon the *Beau Monde*. She might have been a success.

She had, he felt sure from long experience, the makings of a beauty about her. No, she would have to suffer, as a great many other people would have to suffer, for his foolhardiness.

It was too late to remember now the tenants at Wynch, the old pensioners who relied on him for their houses and the pensions that kept them alive.

Too late to remember those who had served Wynch all their lives, the old gardener he had known as a boy, the Head Groom who had been there nearly forty years, the butler who had come there first as a pantry boy. How could he face them, how could he tell them that they, like everything else, had got to go?

For the first time in his life Lord Wynchingham was aware of his responsibilities and saw them for what they were, a heritage handed down to him from generations that were past.

But, although he could now see them all too clearly, it was too late.

Suddenly he walked across to the window where he stood gazing out with unseeing eyes at the daffodils stirring in the breeze, the lilacs just coming into bud and the crocuses mauve and white surrounding the sundial in a fairy circle.

"It's all got to be sold," he said harshly. "All of it. And I will not stay here to creep around the haunts that I used to patronise to be laughed at or commiserated with by my friends."

"Have you any real friends?" Tina asked in that soft voice which somehow was strangely penetrating.

Lord Wynchingham was silent for a moment.

"If you had asked me that question yesterday, I would have told you that I have dozens, no, hundreds of friends. Today I am not sure. In fact, I am not sure of anything."

He heard Tina give a little sigh and then she said in a voice that had a sudden note of excitement,

"I have an idea!"

"What is it?" he asked, not because he was interested, but simply because he thought that it was expected of him.

"Come back here, my Lord," she said. "I cannot talk to the back of your head. There is something very disconcerting about talking to someone without seeing their face."

He turned immediately and walked back to the fireplace. She was sitting in the big high-backed armchair and the sunshine coming through the window illuminated her, the little pointed chin, the big eyes and the fair hair.

'Yes, she will be a beauty,' he thought.

It was indeed a pity that she was not going to have the chance. She was a casualty of his carelessness, something else that had been run over by the wheels of his selfishness and stupidity.

"What are you going to do with yourself?" he asked, "now that I can no longer help you? Will you become a Governess or a companion?"

They were the only two positions he could think of.

Vaguely at the back of his mind he recalled that they were in fact the only employment open to young gentlewomen.

"I am going to do neither of those things," Tina said.

"Then what?" he asked.

"I am going to get married," she said, "and you are going to help me."

Lord Wynchingham raised his eyebrows.

"I thought I had explained," he said gently, "that I can give you no help. There will not be enough money for one person, let alone two. It's hard, I know, but you are going to have to manage on your own."

Tina shook her head.

"You don't understand," she said. "I have an idea and I know it is the only possible one. I am your Ward, remember? You can present me in Society, just as you might have done if all this had not occurred, and we have a month – one whole month in which you can find me a really rich husband."

"What on earth are you talking about?" Lord Wynchingham asked in a bewildered voice.

"Can you not see it is the only way?" Tina asked. "There are many, many rich men in London. Everyone says so. One hundred thousand pounds would matter little to one of them. It could be my marriage dowry. You, as my Guardian, will arrange the terms and then I can give it to you."

Lord Wynchingham stared at her.

"Are you seriously suggesting this as a sensible proposition?" he asked.

"Can you think of anything better?" Tina enquired.

"I can think of nothing worse," Lord Wynchingham retorted. "Do you really believe that I would take your money, your dowry?"

"Pray don't be stupid!" Tina exclaimed almost sharply. "I know all the arguments you are going to put forward. But you cannot at this moment afford to be high-souled and, if you think that you are doing something wrong to me or something that is not gentlemanlike, look at it from this point of view. If you refuse, I shall become a Governess or companion."

She paused for a moment and then he saw an expression almost of horror on her face.

"I should hate it," she said passionately. "I have dreamed about many things, but never of becoming the paid servant of people who would despise me. And yet that is what you will be forcing me into unless you agree to my suggestion. If you say 'yes', everything will be so different."

"But it's impossible," Lord Wynchingham asserted.

"Why?" she asked. "If I had come to you earlier, you would, I think, have been prepared to sponsor my debut and to arrange a Season in London, and I promise you that I had already made up my mind to find a husband and get married so that I could have a home of my own."

She closed her eyes for a moment.

"I cannot tell you what it would mean to me to belong to someone I love and who loves me."

"It would be very different if I could have done that," Lord Wynchingham said.

"Why would it be any different?" Tina queried. "You would have introduced me to your friends and I might have found somebody to offer for me within a week, two weeks or perhaps two or three months. In the circumstances I suspect that I would have prevaricated a little and looked round! That is the only difference. Now there will be no time to prevaricate and the suitor for my hand must be a very rich man."

"Even so, I could not take the money that was yours," Lord Wynchingham said firmly.

"Of course you could," Tina contradicted him. "How can you be so bird-witted? If you can pay this debt in the time agreed, then you will have the opportunity to retrench, to save a little here, to save a little there, to put your affairs in order so that this disaster will never happen again. In time you could pay me back. What you have not, at this moment, is time."

Lord Wynchingham stared at her.

"In a crazed sort of way you are making sense," he muttered.

"But, of course, I am," she answered. "Do you suppose that I have not dealt with my father's debts before he died without understanding how the most important thing is to play for time? Oh, we had no money, we were not rich like you, but in our own little way our debts were just as pressing and just as frightening."

"I think 'frightening' is the right word," Lord Wynchingham said.

"That is why you have to accept my plan," Tina insisted.

"Can you not see it means everything to me? At least I will have a chance to meet Society, to be in London and to be married. If you refuse, then I become a Governess. I will never meet anyone who is in the least eligible, my whole life will be ruined."

Lord Wynchingham brought his clenched fist down with a bang on the mantelshelf.

"Stop!" he cried. "You are trying to coerce me into this. It is wrong and you know it is wrong. Even supposing a rich man did offer you his hand, how could I possibly think of behaving like a cad and outsider?"

Tina bent down and picked up her bonnet from the floor.

"Very well," she said with a little sigh, "I see that your Lordship is determined to make yourself and everybody else unhappy and uncomfortable."

She walked towards the door.

"Where are you going?" Lord Wynchingham enquired.

She had reached the centre of the room and turned to face him.

"To look for a post as a Governess, my Lord," she said, "and to hate you for the rest of my life."

Lord Wynchingham stared after her.

For a moment nothing was said. Their eyes met across the intervening space.

It seemed as though it was a battle of wills and then quite suddenly Lord Wynchingham capitulated.

"Come here, you little fool," he said sharply. "It's a mad crazy, impossible idea and I must still be foxed even to consider it, but God knows, there is no alternative."

CHAPTER TWO

"It's impossible!"

"It is not!"

They had argued for nearly two hours. The butler had brought in breakfast and had set down in front of the fire a table laden with silver dishes containing every sort of delicacy, which had made Tina exclaim with delight,

"This is very different from school!"

Lord Wynchingham would have waved everything away distastefully, but finally he had been persuaded to partake of a lamb cutlet and to wash it down with a glass of brandy.

The servants removed the remains of the meal and then they were at it once again,

Tina putting forward her plan of campaign, Lord Wynchingham objecting and then finally capitulating with a bad grace.

He might have argued more forcibly if he had not, during their conversation, sat down at his desk in the centre of the room. Without thinking what he was doing he opened the middle drawer. It was filled with bills of every sort and description.

For a moment he stared down at them, not really taking in what he saw. Then the figures seemed to jump out at him – five thousand pounds, two thousand five hundred pounds, ten thousand guineas. The last item had been for the house he had bought for Cleo.

For a moment he felt only a blind rage at himself that he had been so stupid as to give it to her magnanimously as a present, putting the deeds in her name.

Remembering now the huge sum he owed Mr. Lampton, he knew that, if he forced himself to add up all the bills that he had pushed so carelessly into the drawer of his desk, he would find that they would total as much as, if not more than, his debt of honour.

The words that he had been contradicting and opposing Tina with died on his lips. He knew that the very moment his creditors realised that he was in financial straits the duns would be at the door, demanding payment of these and perhaps dozens of other bills which had for the moment escaped his notice or had not yet been presented.

It was only a question of time before the hounds were after him and for a moment he felt quite sick at the mess that he had made of his life. Everything that made for position and comfort he had lost at the turn of a card.

He slammed to the drawer in the desk and jumped to his feet.

"All right, have it your own way," he said angrily. "You have convinced me and I have little to lose one way or the other. How do we start?"

Tina looked back at him helplessly, her eyes a little bewildered in her tiny pointed face.

"Your Lordship will have to tell me that," she replied. "I know little about Society, having been incarcerated in a young ladies' Seminary. Of course I have listened to the chatter of the other pupils. Some of them came from very genteel families."

"And you really imagine that I know how to present a *debutante* to the *Beau Monde*!" Lord Wynchingham asked and added with a twist to his lips, "My knowledge of that particular species of womanhood has been confined to hearing them mentioned casually by their mothers."

The innuendo of his remark escaped Tina.

"As we are both ignorant," she sighed, "we had better find someone to advise us."

"You will have to have a chaperone at any rate," Lord Wynchingham pointed out.

Tina looked at him in distress.

"Must I really?" she asked. "It will complicate things considerably always having another woman with us."

"You cannot stay here in this house without one," Lord Wynchingham replied.

"I thought as I am your Ward and – you are so old – " she faltered.

"Old?"

The question seemed to explode across the room like a pistol shot.

"Old?" he repeated. "I would have you know that I have not yet celebrated my twenty-ninth birthday."

It seemed to him that Tina looked up at him in astonishment.

He walked to the mantelshelf and stood staring at himself in the gold-framed mirror above it.

"Old indeed!" he repeated and then saw, almost as though he had never looked at himself before, the reflected face of a dissipated man who certainly sported no youthful air.

There were deep lines of dissipation under his eyes, some of them, he told himself, were due to lack of sleep, but a great many more were the result of the brandy he had consumed, the smoke in the gaming rooms and the wild parties which he had indulged in with Cleo and her like for the past five years.

Lord Wynchingham stared at himself in disgust.

Then surprisingly he had a sudden longing for Wynch, for the wind blowing across the green Parkland, rippling the silver water of the lake and stirring the flag flying high above the chimneypots.

What a fool he had been to spend so much time in London when he could have been in the country exercising his horses, hunting or taking part in the local steeplechases!

Behind him he heard a soft voice saying,

"I am sorry if I offended you, my Lord. I suppose because you are my Guardian it made me think of you as old and, of course, you have so many worries at the moment."

"There is no need to apologise," Lord Wynchingham said harshly, angry not with Tina but with himself. "But let me make it clear. A chaperone is necessary and must be procured at once."

He thought, with a wry smile, how little chance Tina would have of shining in the *Beau Monde* if it were known that she had spent even a few hours alone in his company.

He was well aware of his reputation – it was neither worse nor better than that of any of the gay set in attendance on the Prince of Wales, but no young unmarried woman seen in his company would be given the benefit of the doubt and Tina would certainly not be entitled to enter the best houses unless a chaperone was found with all possible speed.

Without looking at Tina, he rang the bell furiously.

"What do you require?" she asked a little apprehensively.

He did not answer her as almost immediately the door opened and a footman stood awaiting his command.

"Fetch Mrs. Browning," he ordered.

"Very good, my Lord."

The door closed and Tina asked,

"Who is Mrs. Browning?"

"My housekeeper," Lord Wynchingham replied. "She has been in the service of my family for over twenty-five years. I have a feeling that she will be of assistance to us. Be careful what you say in front of her. 'Browny', as I called her as a child, has the eyes of a hawk and a way of nosing out the truth however carefully one tries to keep it hidden."

"She sounds frightening," Tina murmured.

Lord Wynchingham looked down at her with amusement in his eyes.

"Does anything frighten you?" he asked. "You were not afraid to come here by yourself by stagecoach or afraid to demand that I should launch you into Society. You are not afraid to embark on the maddest, craziest, most fantastic plan I have ever listened to, but now you say that you are afraid of my housekeeper."

She smiled up at him engagingly.

"I think perhaps I am a trifle scared of women," she admitted.

He could not help laughing. There was no doubt that the child had perception and was quite different from the average maiden he had always in the past given a wide berth to.

He could understand that she spoke the truth about her fear of women. Men would always be far friendlier than women where Tina Croome was concerned.

There was something appealing in her tininess, in her big liquid eyes and the soft, almost childish mouth, but perhaps, he thought with a sudden and for him unusual perceptiveness, women would sense that Tina had a will of her own despite her apparent helplessness.

Tina had not been mistaken about Mrs. Browning.

She was, in fact, very formidable in her rustling black silken dress, with a chatelaine of keys hanging from her waist and her severe, wrinkled unsmiling face.

She came into the room and curtseyed politely but with dignity.

"Browny, I need your help," Lord Wynchingham began.

If her heart was softened by his affectionate nickname, she gave no sign of it.

"I am always prepared to serve your Lordship to the best of my ability," she said.

"Stop being formal, Browny," he said, "and try and be a little more human. We're in the devil of a fix. Here is Miss Tina Croome, my Ward, come all the way from Yorkshire to stay with me and the letters announcing her arrival have not arrived and so we have to procure a chaperone immediately. Whom do you suggest?"

"Your Ward, my Lord?"

There was surprise in the quiet question, but Tina knew exactly what Mrs. Browning had been thinking when she entered the room and she felt the colour rise hotly to her cheeks.

"Yes, my Ward," Lord Wynchingham repeated. "Surely, Browny, you who remember everything have not forgotten Colonel Croome and the fact that he saved my life when I was taking part in the War with America. I remember distinctly telling you about it when I returned home."

"Colonel Croome, my Lord? Of course I recall the incident. Your Lordship related it to your father immediately on your return. And this is his daughter?"

She turned towards Tina with a very different expression on her face.

"Tina, may I present Mrs. Browning, my housekeeper," Lord Wynchingham said formally.

There was a twinkle in his eyes as he noticed how fervently Mrs. Browning clasped the hand that Tina held out to her.

"We shall always be grateful, miss, for your father's courage and gallantry," Mrs. Browning said.

"Thank you," Tina answered softly. "He was wounded in the same battle, but he often spoke of his Lordship and how glad he was that he was able to save his friend."

"We were all glad, miss. His Lordship insisted on going with his Regiment to America despite his father's protests and very thankful we were to see him return."

"You are making me feel quite sentimental about myself," Lord Wynchingham said. "Now, come along, Browny, think! Who will make a suitable chaperone for Miss Croome? Have I any relations who will fill the bill? As far as I can recall they are all hatchet-faced old harridans who consider themselves doomed to eternal hellfire if they so much as cross the threshold of this house."

"Now, my Lord, there is no need to speak in such a manner," Mrs. Browning remonstrated. "You have not been particularly kind or considerate to your relatives, as well you know. Your aunt, Lady Harrogate, was deeply incensed last time she came here and found that you had not only forgotten her intimation that she intended to call upon you, but were keeping the most – unconventional – company."

Lord Wynchingham threw back his head.

"I remember my aunt's face when she saw the company, as you call her," he said. "Well, I have no wish to ask her to chaperone Miss Croome."

"I am afraid that it would be hopeless even to consider her Ladyship," Mrs. Browning replied. "Now let me think. What about your Lordship's cousin, the Countess of Lazonby? She has been a widow these past two years."

Lord Wynchingham put his hand up to his head.

"Not Sybil Lazonby, I beg of you. If anyone has expressed in terms of the utmost vehemence the way she both dislikes and despises me, it is my Lady Lazonby. Indeed, on the last occasion we met, I informed her that it was not surprising that her husband had died. It was, I was convinced, the only way he could find a little peace."

Tina giggled.

"Did you really say that?" she asked.

"I regret to say, miss," Mrs. Browning interposed, "that his Lordship has an unfortunate way of incensing his relatives against him."

"There must be somebody," insisted Lord Wynchingham, "someone whom I have not insulted. Browny, you know the lot."

"I have it, your Lordship! What about Mistress Lovell?"

"Anne?" Lord Wynchingham said.

"Yes, indeed, my Lord. Your cousin Anne. She is a sweet gentle lady. She was married off when she was still very young to Colonel Lovell, a contemporary of her father's. She was, I believe, extremely unhappy with him. There were no children of the marriage and, when he was killed in a street brawl, I doubt if anyone mourned his demise."

"Yes, Anne. I remember her vaguely," Lord Wynchingham said. "Surely she is very young?"

"No, indeed, my Lord, she must be on the wrong side of thirty-five years of age."

"I have not seen her for over ten years. Have you any idea where she is?" Lord Wynchingham enquired.

"Mistress Lovell sometimes honours me by a visit," Mrs. Browning said. "She is interested in the family and has need to occupy her mind since her husband's death. She has been left in poor circumstances and manages by doing needlework to eke out a slender income, most of which had been dissipated by her husband. She has, in fact, repaired some of the curtains in this house. I did not mention it to your Lordship, but I felt that it would meet with your approval."

"Anne getting a living by her needle!" Lord Wynchingham exclaimed. "You should have told me, Browny, I would have helped her."

"I think, my Lord, Mistress Lovell is too proud to accept charity," Mrs. Browning said repressively, "but if you required to employ a chaperone, that would be an entirely different matter."

"Browny, you are a genius!" Lord Wynchingham exclaimed. "Send the carriage for her immediately. Better still go yourself. Explain that the matter is of the utmost urgency. Does she live far away?"

"Only in Chelsea, my Lord."

She saw by his Lordship's face that this was not a district that he particularly wished to remember at the moment and she continued,

"I will, as your Lordship suggests, go myself and explain the circumstances to Mistress Lovell. I hope I can persuade her to return with me."

"Tell her she must do so," Lord Wynchingham said imperviously. "Offer her any salary you think fit or, if she will not accept a salary, agree to any conditions she likes to name, but bring her back with you."

"I will do my best, my Lord."

Mrs. Browning curtseyed and then said to Tina,

"If you would like to come upstairs, miss, and wash after your journey, I shall be pleased to show you the way before I leave."

"Yes, I should like that above all things," Tina answered quickly. "It was certainly very dusty in the stagecoach and, although we stopped at various Posting houses, the accommodation was not what one might call luxurious."

She paused a moment and looked around the room.

"I never thought anything could be as beautiful as this house."

"You should see Wynch, miss," Mrs. Browning said proudly. "As I often said to his Lordship's mother, it is in my opinion one of the most beautiful houses in the whole country."

Lord Wynchingham watched them move together from the room.

As the door closed behind them, he wanted to cry out,

'Unless a miracle happens, Wynch will have to be sold!'

The full force of what that meant swept over him like a flood tide. Could it really be true that because he had been such a fool it meant that the tradition of centuries could be swept away overnight?

Because he could not bear to think about it, he strode across the room and stood staring through the open window that looked on to the garden.

The spring air was soft and mellow, a faint wind was stirring the daffodils, the sunshine had quite a lot of warmth in it and he thought of the lawns at Wynch sloping down to the lake and how soon the miracle of spring would bring the lilacs, rhododendrons and azaleas into flower.

He could almost see their reflection in the silver water and the white and black swans moving beneath the bridge that led into the Park beyond.

How happy he had been there as a child. How much it had meant to him.

Although, as he grew older, London seemed so desirable and so enticing, he saw himself becoming more and more bemused and entangled with the social whirl. He could watch himself flinging away his money as though it came from an inexhaustible source.

The Prince of Wales was always in debt and it was fashionable to ape his extravagance and cry in tones of mock dismay that the duns were at the door.

Horses, women, gambling, they were all ways of spending money, of leading a life of riotous extravagance and now suddenly he had come to a full stop.

He had reached a fence that was too high for him to jump. As far as he was concerned the race had ended.

He thought of Tina almost with exasperation.

She was only delaying the final moment when he must either blow out his brains or creep away to the obscurity of the Continent.

He had spoken the truth when he had told her that he could not hang about being patronised by the people whom he had previously treated with condescension.

Perhaps, after all, it would be best if he was man enough to put his duelling pistol to his head here and now.

A soft voice behind him broke in on his reverie.

"Do I look a trifle more modish?" she asked.

He turned to see Tina smiling at him.

He saw that her golden hair had been rearranged by skilful fingers, one of Mrs. Browning's maids undoubtedly. There was a clean muslin fichu round her white shoulders and a pink camellia, doubtless from the greenhouse, was tucked into a brooch at her breast.

"Your house is magnificent!" she exclaimed before he could speak. "Mrs. Browning let me peep into the salon upstairs. How I long to see the tapers lit and couples dancing on that beautifully polished floor."

"Entertaining costs money," Lord Wynchingham said sourly, "and we have no time to rhapsodise."

"A month's grace," Tina said, "that is all I ask."

"Damn you, I believe you came from the Devil to tempt me!" Lord Wynchingham exclaimed angrily. "Nothing will come of this but further debts and, if you find yourself a husband, he is more than likely to hang onto his purse strings and to refuse to part with a penny."

"You are being unduly pessimistic, my Lord," Tina smiled.

"And your optimism has about as much substance as a will o' the wisp," Lord Wynchingham retorted.

A voice at the door made them both start.

"Am I interrupting a private mill?" it enquired, "or may anyone join in?"

A young man advanced across the room.

His face was painted, and he was dressed in the height of fashion. His embroidered waistcoat was a blaze of colour, his azure-blue coat almost too dazzling to behold and, as affected by Frenchmen on the Continent, he carried a small fur muff.

Lord Wynchingham looked at him sourly.

"Good morning, Claude," he said. "Is there anything you require of me?"

The newcomer gave a little giggle of laughter.

"You are not very gracious, my dear coz," he remarked, "and certainly not very hospitable. I have called to see you and what do I get – black looks and not even an extended hand in welcome. As the Head of the Family, you should be more approachable."

"I am afraid that I am not in the right mood for your witticisms," Lord Wynchingham said sternly, "and, if you have called for the reasons I suspect, I can save you the trouble by telling you that the answer is 'no'."

The young man held up his muff in horror.

"Pray, my dear coz," he protested, "don't live up to your name. I always thought that Stern did not become you, it was inappropriate. Today I am not too sure. I have, it is true, private matters to discuss with you, but I see that you are already engaged."

He turned, looked at Tina and fumbling among the lace of his cravat found a diamond-framed quizzing glass and raised it to his right eye.

Reluctantly, because there was nothing else he could do, Lord Wynchingham said,

"Tina, may I present my cousin Claude Wynchingham. This, Claude, is Tina Croome, my Ward, who has just arrived in London."

"Your Ward!" Claude exclaimed, "And I never knew that you had one! Your servant, ma'am."

He made an elaborate bow while Tina curtseyed.

"And where have you come from, if I may ask?" he enquired in a tone of lively curiosity.

"You may not ask," Lord Wynchingham said. "I have told you, Claude, that I am engaged and find it impossible to concern myself with your affairs. If you want to see me, come back in a week or so's time and kindly make an appointment before you do so."

"Now, now, my dear coz, don't take that tone with me," Claude pleaded. "I must see you now, it is of the utmost urgency."

"I have heard that expression before," Lord Wynchingham said sharply, "and I know exactly what it means. The answer is 'no'! I have not a guinea to spare you and, if I had, I would not proceed to drop it down the bottomless pit of your idiotic extravagance."

"You would not like to see me in the Fleet, dear coz," Claude said, "for that is what I am afraid may happen."

He broke off to turn towards Tina.

"Forgive us for speaking so intimately, but I have no alternative. My dear coz is very harsh! If he turns me from the door, as indeed he is quite capable of doing, there is nothing for it but the Fleet, a monstrously uncomfortable prison and one that it is far too easy to enter and far more difficult to leave."

"I have heard dreadful things of the Fleet prison," Tina said. "Is it really true they will take you there?"

"Indeed it is," Claude answered and for a moment his affected foppish airs seemed to leave him and instead he was only a frightened young man who was desperately in need of help.

"How much is it this time?" Lord Wynchingham asked.

Eagerly his cousin Claude drew a piece of paper from an inside pocket.

"It is only a bill for five hundred guineas, but I cannot hold them off any longer. I beg of you, Stern, save me and I give you my word of honour that I will not spend another penny if only you will settle this for me, just this once."

"That is exactly what you said last time," Lord Wynchingham pointed out in exasperated tones.

He took the paper and looked at it, then threw it down with an expression of disgust.

"Clothes again!" he commented. "It's always the same, you waste fortunes on clothes and to what end?"

"I admit it is my extravagance, my passion and my failing," Claude replied. "Some people like horses and some women."

He gave a glance under his eyelids at Lord Wynchingham as he spoke.

"But I happen to like clothes. Surely you can understand that we are all made in different moulds?"

"Well, thank the Lord, I am not made in the same one as you!" Lord Wynchingham exclaimed.

He moved to his desk, picked up his quill and wrote.

"Here is my note of hand," he said. "I have settled it for five hundred guineas. It's the last you will ever get."

"Thank, thank you, dear cousinly Stern. I am indeed in your debt. I will be more careful in future. That I swear to you."

"Whether you are careful or not will not concern me," Lord Wynchingham said. "As I have told you, this is the last time."

He passed the note of hand to Claude who hastily put it in the inside pocket of his coat and picked up his muff.

"*Merci mille fois*, my dear coz," he said in the same affected tones he had first used when he entered the room.

The look of despair had gone, he was back again as his foppish confident self, triumphant at having obtained what he had come for.

"Your servant, Miss Croome," he bowed to her and turned towards the door.

He had almost reached it when Lord Wynchingham said suddenly,

"Wait, you might be of use to us, Claude."

"What can I do?" his cousin enquired, obviously a little discomfited at the idea that payment might after all be taken back from him.

"Tina here is in need of suitable apparel if I present her, as I intend, to the Social world," Lord Wynchingham said. "As it is apparently the only thing you know anything about, perhaps you would be kind enough to suggest where she ought to buy her gowns, her ribbons, her bonnets and any other fal-lals a *debutante* requires."

Claude's eyes glinted with excitement.

"But, of course, no one is better able to help," he exclaimed. "Why, only yesterday Lady Jersey said to me, 'Claude, there is no one who has your taste where a woman's appearance is concerned' and her Ladyship asked me, nay commanded me, to attend her fitting for the gown she will wear next week at Carlton House."

"What did she choose?" Tina asked.

"Now let me describe it to you," Claude replied enthusiastically, only to be stopped by an angry gesture from Lord Wynchingham's hand.

"Don't chatter," he ordered. "Sit down at my desk and write. Put down the places that Tina should patronise."

"Surely you cannot intend that she should visit them by herself," Claude asked with raised eyebrows, "or did you perhaps, my dear coz, think of accompanying her?"

There was something spiteful underlying the question and Lord Wynchingham smiled grimly as he replied,

"Don't try and scent scandal, Claude. I can still stop that note of hand, remember. No, Tina, as befits my Ward, will be accompanied by her chaperone, our cousin, Anne Lovell, whom perhaps you recall?"

"But, of course, I remember Anne. She will make an excellent chaperone and, although she has lived in obscurity these last few years, people have not forgotten her. Why, indeed, the Duchess of Devonshire was saying only a few weeks ago how sad it was that she never met Anne anywhere these days."

"And you did not have the decency to give her Anne's address to make an effort to bring them together again, did you?"

"From what I recall, Anne has not been a guest in this house for some time," Claude retorted, "but perhaps she would have had nothing in common with the other *ladies* present."

He accentuated the word 'ladies' and the eyes of the two men met.

Tina could feel the tension in the air and woman-like strove to avoid it.

"Oh, please, Mr. Wynchingham," she pleaded, "write down the names of the best places for me to obtain some really ravishing gowns. I would not wish to disgrace my

Guardian when he has been so kind as to promise that I shall take my place among the *debutantes* who have come to London for the Season. Is it not an exciting thought?"

The antagonism between the two men was controlled, at least for the moment.

With a petulant shrug of his shoulders Claude turned his back on his cousin and settled himself at the desk.

"Now for gowns there is no one to equal Madame Rasché," he began. "You will have difficulty in persuading her to design anything for you at this late hour, but, if you mention my name, I promise you that she will not refuse. Your gowns shall outshine even those of Lady Elizabeth Forster."

"I am sure that Madame Rasché will show her appreciation to you in a practical manner for introducing a new client," Lord Wynchingham said disagreeably.

He was behind his cousin and Tina, standing at the desk, looked over Claude's shoulder with a little frown on her face.

It made Lord Wynchingham bite back some further caustic remarks he was about to make. Finally when, after a great deal of explanation, flourishes of the quill and many promises that, if Tina was disappointed he, Claude, would be devastated that his advice had been at fault, he departed, Lord Wynchingham was almost genial.

The door closed behind Claude and Tina, turned to Lord Wynchingham, a smile on her lips,

"Don't look so cross," she said, "He *has* been exceedingly useful."

"I loathe the fellow," Lord Wynchingham stormed. "He is not only a fop, but also vicious and untrustworthy. I swear that he lives on blackmail, ferreting out secrets from the gutters and making people pay for his silence."

"But he is your cousin," Tina queried.

"And my heir," Lord Wynchingham added bitterly.

"Your *heir*?"

She was somehow startled.

"If anything would persuade me to try and save something from the wreck I have made of my affairs, it would be the fact that, if I die, Claude inherits my title and anything that remains of the estates."

"Unless, of course, you marry and have a son," Tina interposed.

"A bit late to think of that," Lord Wynchingham replied.

"If we can find the one hundred thousand pounds that you owe Mr. Lampton," Tina said, "the best thing you can possibly do is to get married. You cannot allow someone like Claude to become the Earl of Wynchingham."

This was something that Lord Wynchingham had always thought himself, but now because she had flicked him on the raw, he said disagreeably,

"One Wedding at a time is, I think, quite sufficient. We have to get you married first."

"Yes, I know," Tina said with a little sigh, "and a very short time to do it in."

"Time," Lord Wynchingham muttered, "that is something we have stalking us. We must start with a party when I can introduce you to my friends. Then a dinner, I think, followed by a Reception."

He spoke seriously and suddenly he stopped.

"*Goddam it*! Everyone will think that I have gone completely crazed," he exclaimed. "A Reception here! That is not the sort of party I usually indulge in! Lord knows what sort of explanation I can give to my friends."

"Perhaps they will think that you are growing too old for youthful foolishness," Tina suggested with a hint of laughter in her voice.

He looked down at her for a moment angrily and then his own lips twitched.

"You little devil!" he exclaimed. "You are determined to turn the screw on me, aren't you? Two can play at that game. I will find you the ugliest, oldest and most cantankerous husband in the whole of London!"

She laughed back at him.

"Careful!" she admonished him. "It might be easier to find you an ancient, wrinkled old hag with half a million in her pocket and an ardent desire to wed a handsome husband!"

They were both shrieking with laughter as the door was flung open and the butler's stentorian voice announced,

"Her Grace the Dowager Duchess of Hertingford, my Lord."

CHAPTER THREE

For a moment there was the silence of sheer stupefaction as Lord Wynchingham and Tina turned to stare at the newcomer.

Her appearance was certainly something to make anyone gasp. While she was very small and old with a yellow wrinkled skin like parchment, the Dowager was dressed in the height of fashion.

A gown of brilliant strawberry-pink satin was caught up over a petticoat of silver lace and the bodice was embellished with silver ribbons, while down her chest fell a cascade of pearls, diamonds and rubies and a glittering profusion of necklaces that accentuated rather than detracted from her age.

Perched high on her white wig was a coquettish little straw bonnet, gaily bedecked with feathers and tied under her chin with ribbons. There were diamonds sparkling in her ears and diamonds dangling from her bony wrists.

In fact, on first sight, the Dowager Duchess was almost too fantastic to be real and then her voice, surprisingly low and deep, yet a little cracked with age, said sharply,

"Lost your tongues, eh? Your welcome, my dear grandson, overwhelms me."

Lord Wynchingham recovered his speech with an obvious effort.

"Your pardon, Grandmama," he said, stepping towards her, "but somehow you were the last person I expected to see at this particular moment."

"And why, may I ask?" his grandmother replied, extending her hand so that he could raise it to his lips. "You are well aware that I always arrive in London for the Season."

"I am indeed aware of that, ma'am," his Lordship replied, "but the last time we met you swore that you would never cross the threshold of this house unless I had preceded you by going out feet first towards the churchyard."

The Dowager Duchess chuckled.

"Did I say that? You must have incensed me more than usual and, if I did say it, it is all the more reason for you to be grateful to me for coming here today, after Mrs. Browning had told me of your predicament."

"She went to fetch Anne," Lord Wynchingham said.

"Yes, I know," his grandmother replied, "and it was fortunate for you that I happened to be visiting Anne when Mrs. Browning appeared. The poor girl is indisposed and as yellow as a guinea. It is impossible for her to act as chaperone for you or anyone else for the next month or so at least."

"Dammit, that is vastly inconvenient!" Lord Wynchingham exclaimed, vexation making his voice unnaturally loud.

The Dowager was not listening to him – she was advancing slowly across the room, her silken skirts rustling and her jewellery jingling as she moved towards Tina, who was standing on the hearthrug listening to this exchange of words with an anxious expression on her small face.

The Dowager proceeded with dignity, like a ship in full sail, until she was within a few feet of Tina, her eyes shrewd and bright despite her age, taking in every detail of the girl's appearance and then with a faint smile on her lips she turned to her grandson.

"Should you not present this child to me?" she asked. "Your manners, Stern, are worse than usual. I have spoken about them to you often enough in the past."

"Your pardon, Grandmama," Lord Wynchingham said again. "Allow me to present Miss Tina Croome, who has paid me an unexpected visit. She is the daughter of an old friend. Tina, this is my grandmother, who has bedevilled and berated me ever since I was in the cradle. I am sure that there is nothing I could do that would be right in her eyes."

The Dowager laughed.

"You underrate yourself, my boy. I have always said that you were devilish good looking, but that is the only compliment I am likely to pay you."

As she spoke, the Dowager held out her hand to Tina who sank into a low curtsey.

"You are pretty enough in all conscience," the Dowager said quietly, almost as if she was thinking aloud, "or you would be if you were fashionably dressed. Now let me think, you must be the daughter of my old friend, Nicholas Croome, the younger son, it is true, of a noble father. Yes, in a way, there is a look of Nicholas about you and you must be an heiress and all London will be flocking after you soon enough."

Tina opened her mouth to speak, but, as she did so, the Dowager sneezed.

"Tishoo! Where is my handkerchief? Where in hell is that dratted boy? I told him to stay beside me. Abdul! Abdul!"

Her voice rang out and, moving briskly in a very different way from the manner in which she had walked up the room, she crossed to the door and flung it open before her grandson could reach it.

"Abdul," she shouted. "Drat the child! I will take my stick to him when he does appear,"

There was a patter of feet and to Tina's astonishment, a small black boy, as fantastically dressed as his Mistress, came hurtling into the room to fling himself down on one knee in front of the Dowager and as he knew what she required, he held up with a beseeching gesture a little beaded reticule out of which peeped a white lace-edged handkerchief.

The Dowager snatched it from him.

"Tishoo," she sneezed again and then gave him a sharp tap on the top of his head.

"Keep beside me," she said sharply. "You are not to eat any more, you are too fat as it is."

While she was admonishing the small boy in his brilliant green turban, Tina turned to Lord Wynchingham.

"Explain to her who I am," she said in a low voice.

He nodded his head.

"I will, when I can get a word in edgeways," he replied.

Then his eyes narrowed and he said in a whisper,

"No, leave it as it is. Nicholas Croome is dead, but he must have been a relation."

"Yes, he was," Tina replied, "a very distant cousin. He never spoke to us, we were far too poor!"

"And now he will have to make amends!" Lord Wynchingham said. "My grandmother thinks that you are his daughter, let her think so!"

"How can I do that," Tina protested.

"Leave it to me," Lord Wynchingham said. "If you are an heiress, there will be no need to say anything more."

Tina could see his implication all too easily.

To introduce a penniless unknown girl to the *Beau Monde* was one thing, but to present an heiress was a very different matter.

"I cannot let – " she began, only to be silenced by Lord Wynchingham's upturned hand.

The Dowager had finished admonishing her page and she had also blown her aristocratic nose and glanced at her reflection in a tiny oval mirror encircled with jewels that she carried in her reticule.

Now she came back towards her grandson and Tina, continuing her conversation where she had left off.

"Mrs. Browning told me, child, that you had come to London to be presented and were in search of a chaperone. Well, Anne Lovell certainly cannot chaperone you, but I will."

"You, Grandma?"

The words seemed almost forced from between Lord Wynchingham's lips.

"Don't look so astonished, my dear boy!" she retorted. "Why else should I be here? To take Anne's place, of course. It will amuse me to see the young generation for a change. I am sick to death of Bath and of my own cronies with their aches and pains and their chatter about days that are past. There is still amusement to be found if one knows where to look for it, eh, my young blade?"

She gave Lord Wynchingham a poke with a bony finger and added with a chuckle,

"I hear you have been up to mischief. I saw that fancy piece of yours in her carriage last week. Costs you a pretty penny, I'll be bound."

Lord Wynchingham did not appear embarrassed.

"I am surprised, Grandma, you should even know about such things," he said with mock severity.

She laughed at him.

"There is not much I don't know," she answered. "I may be old, but I am not yet deaf, not too deaf at any rate, to hear of your peccadilloes and yet sometimes you manage to surprise me. Who would have thought that you would have been prepared to go bear-dancing with a *debutante*?"

"I am afraid, ma'am, I rather took him by surprise," Tina said gently.

The Dowager raised her eyebrows.

"So you have a voice, after all," she said tartly. "I was beginning to be afraid that you were just a pretty face. So you took him by surprise, did you? And what made you come to my grandson in the first place, I am curious to know."

"I am Tina's Guardian," Lord Wynchingham interposed hastily. "Her father left her in my charge, but she has been to school. She has in fact come straight from a young ladies' Seminary in the North of England. The posts are notoriously bad these days and I have not yet received the letter from her announcing her arrival. She must have come ahead of it."

"Guardian, eh?" the Dowager enquired. "Strange taste your father must have had, girl, to choose my grandson as your Guardian. But these rich men like to stick together. Perhaps he thought that your fortune might be safer in his Lordship's care than with someone less well endowed than himself. Could there be other reasons?"

She looked out of the corners of her eyes at her grandson who faced her stolidly.

"I think your assumption, Grandma, must be the right one. Anyhow, now that Tina is here what can we do for her?"

"You must give a ball, of course," his grandmother retorted sharply. "It is a long time since there was a *decent* party given in this house."

She laid heavy emphasis on the word 'decent' and then she chuckled.

"You will have to prune your companions on this occasion, won't you, boy?" she asked with glee.

Then turning to Tina she said,

"Have you any clothes, child?"

"No, ma'am," Tina replied. "As his Lordship has just told you, I have come straight from school."

"Well, you can afford the best and the best you shall have," the Dowager said. "I shall enjoy helping you to spend your father's money."

Tina gave Lord Wynchingham a despairing look, but he ignored her.

"As you have said, Grandma, Tina must have the best if she is to become the toast of St. James's."

The Dowager gave an indignant snort,

"The toast of St. James's indeed! I hope she will become nothing of the sort. All those vulgar men drink too much anyway. No, she must be properly launched on Society and meet, I hope, the best behaved and most eligible young men. Not your reprehensible cronies. I will not have any of them in the house, not one of them!"

"It almost sounds as though I shall have to move out myself," Lord Wynchingham said with a little twist to his lips.

"It might, indeed, be better from the point of view of the child's reputation," the Dowager retorted. "At the same time we shall need an escort, at any rate to start with. You may stay, if you behave yourself!"

"Thank you," Lord Wynchingham replied with mock humility.

"Now, to work," the Dowager continued with an enthusiasm which belied her years. "Get hold of that lazy secretary of yours, he never has enough to do. Tell him to compile for my approval lists of those to be invited to the ball and I will take the child with me to buy some gowns. She cannot be seen in what she is wearing now."

She gave Tina's white muslin a scornful glance.

"Fit only for a dairymaid!" she snorted.

"But, Grandmama, Tina has only just arrived after a long journey. She would, perhaps, like to rest."

"Rest? There's no time to rest," the indefatigable Dowager exclaimed. "The Season will be a short one this year. The Queen has said that she wishes to move to Windsor Castle as early as possible. Prepare your lists and leave us women to do our part."

She turned on her heel suddenly and clapped her hands, making them all jump, but Abdul understood that it was a signal and, running hastily to the door, pulled it open with some difficulty because he was so small and they could hear his feet clattering down the hall.

"He has gone to order my coach," the Dowager said. "Come child, whatever happens you must not be seen by anyone in that piece of cheese-muslin."

"I will fetch – my bonnet," Tina faltered and ran, almost as swiftly as Abdul had, from the room and up the stairs to where she had left her belongings in one of the bedrooms.

As soon as she was out of earshot, the Dowager turned to her grandson.

"Now tell me the truth this time," she said. "Why the sudden interest? Is your heart engaged?"

"No, no, of course not, Grandmama. I have never seen her until an hour or so ago," Lord Wynchingham replied. "Her father was a friend of mine and the girl is my Ward."

"It all sounds very normal," the Dowager said tartly, "and I don't believe for one moment that you are telling me the truth or at least not all of it. I have known you for many years, my dear boy. It is not like you to take an interest in any respectable girl, however pretty she may be."

"You make me sound like some kind of dissolute monster," Lord Wynchingham complained.

"Oh, I suspect you are well on the way to becoming one," his grandmother replied. "However, this chit of a girl brings me fresh hope."

She paused for a moment and then in a lower voice quizzed him,

"How much is she worth? I know that Nicholas was pretty warm in the pockets."

"I have no idea exactly what Nicholas Croome left," Lord Wynchingham said truthfully.

"And Tina is his only child?" the Dowager asked.

"As far as I know," Lord Wynchingham replied.

"I wonder whether North Shields, or whatever outlandish place he lived in, could tell a different tale," the Dowager chuckled wickedly. "Oh, well, on the face of it, Miss Croome should be a great success. She certainly has looks. Which of the young blades who digs so deeply at the green tables would be prepared to refuse such a pretty bride? Most of the girls with full coffers have faces that would make a sober man shudder."

"Grandmama, you have not lost your knack of putting things extremely bluntly," Lord Wynchingham smiled.

She answered him with a laugh of amusement,

"My frankness always did shock you, did it not, my lad?" she exclaimed. "You are ready to be dashing and dastardly yourself, but you like your women all flutters and foolishness. However, let's hope this wench has a little fire in her. The quiet ones of this world always bored me."

"I am only that hoping you will bring her out in the proper manner," Lord Wynchingham said. "I would not like her chances to be ruined because she was not well and properly chaperoned."

The Dowager gave an exclamation of rage, which, however, turned to one of amusement.

"You dare to doubt me! You know as well as I do nothing could give a girl more cachet than to be under my chaperonage. She will have a far better chance of making her mark hanging onto my skirts than she would have with kind and gentle Anne."

As she finished speaking, she saw Tina waiting in the doorway.

"Drat the child!" she exclaimed. "You have kept me waiting long enough. Come along, come along. We have got a lot to do."

She bustled across the room, shouting over her shoulder as she reached the door,

"Mind those lists are ready when I return. We shall require the best orchestra in London and I hope your chef knows how to prepare a proper supper. The young people may want to flirt, but the old ones want to eat."

Lord Wynchingham could hear her voice issuing instructions as she proceeded down the hall towards the front door, long after she and Tina were out of sight.

As finally the sounds died away, he sat down in his chair and put his hand to his forehead.

"I must be crazed," he said aloud.

He wondered if indeed there was any madness in his family.

For anyone to have taken on such a ridiculous, almost a monstrous, project made him feel as though he was ready for Bedlam. What could possibly come out of it all except further disaster?

Really, the best thing he could possibly do would be to blow out his brains, yet the thought of Claude taking over Wynch almost made him grind his teeth with impotent fury.

What could he sell? His horses? They would realise a few thousands. His pictures? But he knew that the moment he put anything up for sale, the duns would smell a rat and more bills would come flooding in at him with the demand for instant cash.

"Fool! Fool! *Fool*!"

He said the word derisively beneath his breath as he strode up and down the room, the sunshine from outside streaming through the window seeming only to mock his despondency.

In the meantime, Tina was almost in a Seventh Heaven of delight. She realised that what she was doing was wrong, knew that the whole thing was a mad impossible gamble, that there was only one chance in a million of it being successful.

And yet she could not resist the allurement of shimmering taffetas, of rich velvets, of fluttering ribbons and gauze that might have been spun by a fairy spider.

They swam before her eyes in a kaleidoscope of colour and after a while she lost all sense of cost and also of choice and just allowed Madame Rasché and the Dowager to fit her into whatever they wished.

As the coach turned into Bond Street, Tina, in a low frightened voice, had asked the Dowager,

"Where would you be taking me, ma'am, for my gowns?"

She had a sudden nightmare of being decked out in strawberry satin or perhaps even in the violent bilious green of Abdul's turban.

"And have you any preference?" the Dowager asked in a voice that Tina knew was meant to be crushing and to inform her that country wenches had no right to ask such questions.

"No indeed, ma'am," she said. "It was only that his Lordship's cousin, Mr. Claude Wynchingham, mentioned Madame Rasché."

"He did, did he?" the Dowager said uncompromisingly. "Claude is a worm and worms should be trodden underfoot, but, as it happens, the one thing he does know something about is clothes. He spends enough on his own, God knows. Madame Rasché is indeed the best *couturier* in London and that is where I am taking you. Now are you satisfied?"

"Thank you, ma'am, I am very grateful," Tina said.

"Don't soft soap me," the Dowager said. "You are not as dumb as you look. I knew that the moment I set eyes on you and I have yet to hear how you managed to get to London from the North, arriving at my grandson's house without a chaperone. What were the people who looked after you thinking about, I would like to know."

"Well, you see, ma'am, it was like this," Tina began, a little desperately wondering what lies she should tell and how convincing she could make it sound.

Fortunately, the Dowager's attention was distracted by someone else.

"Lord Hugh Warren," she said, leaning out of her coach to peer at a handsome curricle driving in the opposite direction. "Now, he would make a very good match. Ancient title, wide estates and not enough money to keep them up. I must remember to tell Stern to invite him to the ball."

Tina drew a deep breath."

"I assure you, ma'am," she said, "I should not be in the slightest interested in Lord Hugh or even in meeting him. I am determined that I will marry no one who is not a very rich man. I would not have them say that I bestowed myself upon a fortune-hunter."

It was a courageous effort and, although Tina managed to keep her voice steady, the colour came flooding to her cheeks.

To her astonishment the Dowager was not opposed to the idea.

"Perhaps you are right," she conceded almost graciously. "There is nothing more despicable than the man who has to toady to his wife while she holds the purse strings. A very rich man, indeed! Well, there are plenty. I am not saying that many of them will be to your liking. They have far too much sense of their own importance."

"Nevertheless, my husband must be very rich," Tina said firmly.

She sounded brave, but she knew, inside, that she was terrified. What would happen if this project failed, she wondered.

She was well aware that the ball would cost a great deal of money – then there were her dresses, but even while the expense of them loomed ominously in her mind, she had no idea until she reached Madame Rasché's how much she would require or how extravagant each article would seem.

Certainly as they drove back towards Berkeley Square both Tina and the Dowager were feeling tired and few words passed between them.

Otherwise, Tina thought later, she might have broken down and confessed the whole plot before those fabulously expensive gowns and all the accessories that were so much a part of them were delivered.

Lord Wynchingham was sitting in the library where they had left him. Now he was accompanied by a middle-aged man with a quill in his hand and with rather a sombre hangdog expression that made Tina know at once that he was the secretary the Dowager had spoken about.

"Good afternoon to you, Mr. Greychurch," the Dowager said in a somewhat disagreeable tone. "I hope that his Lordship has explained to you the need for haste?

The last time I asked anything of you I waited three weeks before I received a reply."

"I assure Your Grace, it was due to no fault of mine," Mr. Greychurch said humbly.

The Dowager pushed him aside and took up the long parchment he had been writing. She read one or two of the names aloud and then said,

"I will study this this evening to see if anyone is forgotten. In the meantime start preparing invitations. The ball should be the day after tomorrow. They must, of course, be sent by hand."

"The day after tomorrow!" Lord Wynchingham exclaimed. "Greychurch and I were thinking of next week."

"Then you both need your heads examined!" the Dowager retorted. "There is a Court ball next week. The child must be asked to that and to the other parties that are being given. We must get our invitations out at once. Hurry, Mr. Greychurch! Hurry! *Hurry*!"

She drove him from the room, a harassed expression on his face.

"That man will drive me crazy," she asserted before the door had closed behind him. "Why you keep him I cannot imagine."

"He was with my father," Lord Wynchingham replied. "He is good at handling the staff."

"In other words, you are lazy," the Dowager scolded. "It is the same with all men. Have you seen Tina?"

Lord Wynchingham had in fact not even glanced at Tina since she and the Dowager returned.

She beckoned and Tina, who had stood just inside the doorway, came forward.

For a moment Lord Wynchingham stared and then he gave an exclamation of astonishment.

"Good God!"

"There is a difference, is there not?" the Dowager asked.

There was indeed because, as she explained, she would not even drive back to Berkeley Square with Tina wearing that dress of cheese-muslin. Instead Madame Rasché had squeezed her into a dress of palest green gauze, on which an abnormal customs duty had been paid when it crossed the Channel, with a fichu of lawn round her shoulders and a knot of satin ribbons that could have only been woven in France.

Tina's golden hair was still unpowdered, but it supported a tiny, ridiculously expensive hat of chipped straw on which tiny ostrich feathers of the same green as her dress rioted like spring buds. The whole ensemble was absurdly simple and yet obviously most costly.

But Lord Wynchingham in his first astonishment at Tina's changed appearance, forgot that it would all have to be paid for.

"What do you think?" the Dowager demanded.

"I think she looks enchanting," Lord Wynchingham replied with obvious sincerity.

He walked towards Tina and raised her hand to his lips.

"London will be at your feet," he smiled.

"As I am already," a voice said from the doorway.

They turned to see a tall man, with square shoulders, a good figure and an elegant leg for a boot. It was difficult to believe that he was in fact nearing forty, as he crossed the room and bowed to the Dowager.

"I saw Your Grace entering the house," he said, "and tried to attract your attention. But you would have none of me, so I followed you. Welcome to London, it has been an empty and witless place without you."

"Flatterer! And I adore it," the Dowager said almost coquettishly. "Tina, let me present you, child, to someone who is obviously already an admirer. Sir Marcus Welton – Miss Tina Croome."

Tina curtseyed and smiled up at him prettily enough and yet somehow she had the uncomfortable feeling that his eyes, taking in every detail of her new dress, the whiteness of her shoulders and the provocative lowness of her fichu as it crossed over her breast, were too bold and too impertinent.

"Where have you been? Why have you not brought the sunshine with you before?" Sir Marcus asked.

She fancied that he held her fingers longer than necessary.

"I have just arrived in London, sir," she replied in a low voice.

"Then I am indeed fortunate that I am one of the first to call on you. Pray do not forget me. I promise I intend to see a great deal of you."

With an effort Tina took her hand from his.

He bowed, she thought in a most impressive manner, both to her and the Dowager and then, without a word to Lord Wynchingham, was gone from the room as suddenly as he had entered it.

"Marcus Welton," the Dowager said reflectively. "Well, you might do worse. He is rich, child, very very rich."

"An outsider and a bounder," Lord Wynchingham chimed in. "I have never invited him here, he has come with friends on various occasions. It's a blasted impertinence on his part, walking in as though he had bought the place."

"He did not come to see you, my dear boy," the Dowager said with laughter in her voice

"Damn him! we don't want him here making sheep's eyes at Tina," Lord Wynchingham exploded.

"That is for Tina to answer," the Dowager said, "and he is very very rich!"

There was something in the air that suddenly made the room seem intolerable.

"Your Grace will excuse me?" Tina said hastily, her voice shaking a little, "I would like to go to my room."

"But of course, child. You have had a long day. Run upstairs and rest. I will send you a message later to tell you at what time we shall dine."

"Thank you, ma'am."

Tina dropped a hasty curtsey without looking at Lord Wynchingham and went from the room.

He thought as he watched her go that he had had no idea what an exquisite figure she had. He liked the way she carried her head with that ridiculously provocative little hat perched on top of it.

His grandmother's voice broke in on his reverie.

"She will be a success, don't fret," she said.

"It is very important that she should be," he said, thinking of the bills Madame Rasché would be sending him, the bottles of wine that he had just ordered for the ball and the fact that the orchestra alone was going to cost one hundred guineas.

"You could always change your mind, of course," the Dowager pointed out.

"Change my mind?" Lord Wynchingham asked.

"About presenting the girl. There must be Croome relations who would see to it for you. I seem to remember a rather tiresome aunt living in Shropshire."

"No, no," Lord Wynchingham said hastily. "I have given my word, I will not go back on it."

"I don't think I would allow you to, really, even if you wished to do so," the Dowager said. "I have enjoyed buying gowns for someone who can show them off to such advantage. Many, many years ago I remember how such things looked on me – old age is very boring!"

"I have never heard you say that before, Grandmama," Lord Wynchingham exclaimed.

"And I shall not say it again," the Dowager answered. "It is useless regretting the past and the men who have sighed over me. I would not like to tell you how desperately in love some of them were. Now I can amuse myself only by laughing at other people, you, for instance, my dear Stern. You never fail to entertain me."

She walked away from him as she spoke and he heard her shouting to the wretched Abdul who doubtless, once again, had found his way into the kitchen.

"What the hell does she mean by that?" he asked himself aloud and, because there seemed no proper answer, he crossed the room towards a decanter of brandy that stood on a side table.

He had only just poured himself out a drink when he heard a movement and saw Tina come through the half-open door.

She had taken off her hat but was still wearing the nymph-like green dress with its fluttering satin ribbons.

She closed the door carefully behind her and then, almost on tiptoe, crossed the room to stand beside him.

"I had to speak to you," she said. "I don't want the Dowager to hear me come downstairs. I am worried, desperately worried."

"Why?" he asked.

"We spent a fortune this afternoon," she replied. "I could not stop her. She kept repeating that an heiress would be expected to wear the best ball gowns, afternoon creations, dresses for the morning, hats and sunshades, reticules, shoes and stockings and a hundred other things that I need not mention. Oh, what can I say? How can you ever pay for it?"

"I cannot," Lord Wynchingham said briefly.

"Then what are we to do?"

"There is nothing else we can do but go on with this farce, this comedy, this drama, whatever you like to call it."

"Oh, we were mad," Tina said holding her little fingers to her forehead. "It seemed a clever idea at the time and then your grandmother arrived and when I was alone with her I was frightened."

"That is nothing new," Lord Wynchingham said confidingly, almost like a schoolboy. "Everyone is frightened of Grandmama. She has terrified me ever since I was in the cradle."

"No, I don't mean like that," Tina said. "I believe that she is really very sweet if one does not listen to that sharp tongue of hers. I mean, I was terrified of what we had undertaken. Shall I run away? Shall I leave you to explain that the whole thing was a hoax?"

"You will do nothing of the sort," Lord Wynchingham said almost roughly. "Look here, we undertook this together, it was a partnership, if you like. You said that you would save me and I said I would do my best for you. If we rat now, what is there? Just an admission of failure with everyone laughing their heads off at us. We have to go through with it together, you and me."

He set down his glass as he spoke and put his hand on her shoulder.

"Damn it all," he said, "you are all right. *Everyone* will want to marry you. Look at that swine Marcus Welton bursting his way in here. Goddam his cheek, just because he had seen you crossing the pavement. This is only the beginning, don't you see, Tina? You are going to be a success."

For a moment his fingers tightened on her shoulder.

"Forget about me. Go along and enjoy yourself. If one of us gets out of this mess with flags flying it will be something at any rate."

"Nonsense," Tina said. "We will sink or swim together. I told the Dowager that I will marry only a very very rich man. I said – "

She hesitated for a moment and the colour came back into her face.

" – I said it was because I did not want my husband to be accused of fortune-hunting."

For a moment Lord Wynchingham stared at her, then threw back his head and burst out laughing.

"Damn it all, you are magnificent! I bet the old lady swallowed that hook, line and sinker. Don't want a fortune-hunter! That is splendid, that is, just the idea we want to put about. As your Guardian, I will make it clear that no one who is not really up to scratch need apply for the hand of my ward."

Tina clasped her hands together.

"What we are doing is wrong," she stated, "I am not pretending it is not, but is it really a very wicked thing to do?"

"No more wicked than you are," Lord Wynchingham said with a smile. "And if we survive without ending up in the Fleet, well, it will be due to our wits. We are entitled to everything we can get out of it."

"I cannot think what my father would have said," Tina remarked with a little sigh.

"I can't bear to think what my grandmother would say if she knew the truth," Lord Wynchingham answered.

They both laughed.

Then Tina said, glancing at the clock over the mantelpiece,

"I must go and lie down. I really am a trifle weary."

"Go and sleep," Lord Wynchingham urged her. "I would not mind a nap myself."

Tina hesitated a moment and then she put her hand out towards him.

"I would like to say 'thank you'," she said in a low voice, "but I don't know how."

"Forget it," he replied. "We both have a lot to thank each other for. You have helped me out of the depths of despair and you have given me hope, even though it is rather a forlorn one."

"We will succeed," she said suddenly, with a ring in her voice. "I *know* we will succeed."

"I wish I could believe that in all sincerity," he replied. "Anyhow we will have a damned good try. Thank you, Tina. I feel as though I have known you all my life."

"It's funny," she answered, "but I feel almost the same."

She looked up at him as she spoke and their eyes met.

Just for a moment something passed between them, something vital but quite impossible to explain.

Then Tina was running across the room, her skirts billowing out on either side.

She reached the door, turned and raised her hand in a salute.

Her hair was very golden against the dark mahogany, her eyes shining in the last rays of the evening sun as it sank behind the walled garden.

He heard her cross the hall and then there was only silence, a silence that was somehow unbearable as he reached towards his brandy glass.

CHAPTER FOUR

Lord Wynchingham leant against a marble pillar in his ballroom and started to calculated what the ball was costing him.

'Dammit,' he said to himself. 'I cannot see myself getting out much under one thousand guineas, and,' he added surlily, 'that is unlikely to include Tina's gown and all the other innumerable fahdilahs that the Dowager considered so essential.'

Lord Wynchingham turned as if to go towards the champagne bar that had been erected in the entresol outside the ballroom and then remembered that even one glass would cost him money. With tight lips he returned to his scrutiny of the dancers.

There was no doubt at all that Tina was enjoying herself and there was equally no gainsaying that she was, in actual fact, the belle of the ball.

Her dress of white gauze embroidered in diamonds had brought envious glances from all the women and her tiny radiant face and sparkling eyes ensured that there was almost a fight amongst the men as to who would be fortunate enough to partner her in the dances.

Lord Wynchingham watched her now moving rhythmically in a minuet with a handsome young man whom he did not recognise but whom he knew instinctively was not the catch that Tina and, indeed, himself were angling for.

He looked round and saw Lord Alfred Cartright, a rich young blood with a codfish expression on his face, watching Tina adoringly, but apparently making no effort to dance with her.

With a murmur of impatience Lord Wynchingham elbowed his way through the crowd until he reached Lord Alfred's side.

"Not dancing?" he asked in what he fondly imagined was a genial parental tone of voice and which was, in fact, somewhat like the bark of a sea lion.

"I am happy to watch her," Lord Alfred replied dreamily.

"Watching will not get you anywhere, my lad," Lord Wynchingham said. "You have to be bold and audacious to sweep a girl off her feet, certainly don't let nincompoops get in front of you and thrust you out of the way."

"I am no good at being aggressive," Lord Alfred said plaintively.

"Then you had better learn," Lord Wynchingham told him sharply. "My Ward is pretty enough, is she not? She would look well in the Cartright diamonds."

The young man's face actually flushed.

"That is just what I was thinking."

"Come along, then," Lord Wynchingham said roughly. "If you can't get her to dance, I will see what I can do."

He took Lord Alfred's arm and then realised that the dance was finished.

The dancers were crowding off the floor towards the supper room and the gardens, which were illuminated with tiny candles set amongst the trees and flowers.

"Where the devil has she gone to now?" Lord Wynchingham remarked angrily, half beneath his breath.

He might well ask the question.

Besides the fact that the whole of the house in Berkeley Square had been arranged as sitting out rooms with comfortable chairs and sofas, shaded lights and little alcoves where couples could whisper without being seen, the gardens in the square as well as the small private garden at the back of the house, were equally well arranged for those who wished to be romantic.

"Perhaps we had better wait until she comes back for the next dance," Lord Alfred suggested almost plaintively.

"No, we will go and find her," Lord Wynchingham said firmly with an uneasy feeling that Tina might have been lured to some secluded spot in the garden by her handsome young partner and might be in no hurry to return.

His fears were, in fact, unjustified. Tina, descending the stairs on the arm of the young man she had just danced with, was confronted by Claude Wynchingham, exquisitely dressed in a powder-blue satin coat with Valenciennes lace at the cuffs and his neck.

There was an agitated expression on his face and an obvious nervous intensity in the way he clutched at Tina's arm.

"I must speak with you," he whispered insistently.

"Of course," Tina answered, "but surely not now, as I have just promised this gentleman that he should take me down to supper."

"Now, this very instant!"

There was obviously something wrong, Tina could sense that, so she turned to her partner and said appealingly,

"Forgive me. My Guardian's cousin has something of importance to impart to me. I pray you will forgive me if for the moment I am unable to accompany you to the supper room."

"Perhaps I shall be more fortunate later on," the young man answered and, raising her hand to his lips, added, "I thought my luck was too good to last."

Tina laughed at him lightly and, slipping her arm through Claude's, said,

"Come along then, I will listen to what you have to say, but I cannot be long as I am booked for every dance, and there will be utter confusion among my partners if I am away from the ballroom for long."

Claude did not answer, but with a determined look on his face led her out through the front door and across the street into the garden with its myriad fairy lights flickering amongst the branches of the trees casting strange shadows on the grass beneath.

"How pretty!" Tina exclaimed, but he hardly seemed to hear.

Instead he drew her, unresisting, into the shadows on the far side of the Square where there were few people to be seen.

They found a seat piled high with silken cushions in a little arbour covered with honeysuckle.

"What is the matter?" Tina asked as she sat down.

Even in the very faint light of the candles she could see that Claude's face beneath its powder and paint was drawn, his eyes a little wild.

"Marry me!" he blurted out.

It was, somehow, the last thing she expected him to say.

For a moment she stared at him in amazement and then she laughed.

"Are you foxed?" she asked. "Was this the matter of great importance you wish to discuss with me?"

"I am not drunk, I am not joking," Claude answered. "I have just learned that you are an heiress and by marrying me you can save me from utter destruction."

"Why should I do a thing like that?" she replied.

He must indeed be insane, she thought, and wished that she had not come alone with him into the gardens.

Then she realised that he was trembling and felt a sudden compassion for someone so weak and so ineffectual.

"Why not tell me what is the matter?" Tina asked in a kind tone.

"I am ruined, utterly ruined," Claude moaned, putting his head down in his hands.

"You cannot be," Tina protested. "Why, Lord Wynchingham gave you five hundred guineas only three days ago. Surely you cannot have spent it as yet?"

"I have spent that and more," Claude muttered. "A friend gave me a hot tip for the races. He swore that he had the finest piece of horseflesh in all of Britain. He told me that I alone was in the secret that his horse would win at Newmarket and that the other jockeys had been paid to pull their mounts."

"You mean he crooked the race?" Tina asked.

Claude nodded.

"I gave him the note for five hundred guineas," he said. "I also raised a little extra on my cufflinks, my fob and one or two other small pieces of jewellery."

"And what happened?" Tina asked, knowing the answer.

"The horse lost," Claude replied. "And now the Jockey Club has called for an enquiry and my friend, although God knows, he is my enemy, tells me that all those with bets placed on his cursed horse are likely to be called as witnesses. I am *ruined*! Don't you see? Ruined, as well a bankrupt."

"They cannot make you responsible," Tina said in a practical manner.

"Indeed they can, if they can prove that I knew that such trickery was taking place," Claude answered, his voice rising to a crescendo,

Tina said nothing.

She knew little of these things, but she was well aware of the code of honour that was expected by gentlemen of other gentlemen and she supposed that if it could be proved that he was privy to the plot, then Claude would be blackballed from his Clubs and the amusements and pastimes of St. James's would be closed to him.

"I am indeed sorry for you," she said impulsively.

"Then marry me," Claude insisted. "If I had enough money, I would somehow quieten those who could say anything against me. We could even go abroad for our honeymoon and, when we returned, the whole thing might have blown over."

"Marrying me certainly would not solve your problems. It would be quite nonsensical."

Then, as she spoke, Tina remembered that she was supposed to be an heiress.

So in a different tone she added,

"Have you forgotten that your cousin is my Guardian?"

"You mean that he controls your fortune?" Claude said. "I had indeed forgotten that. Then what am I to do? Do you think Stern would listen to me?"

"Indeed, I think it very unlikely," Tina answered. "He is dipped himself at the moment."

"He has the money, if only he would give it to me," Claude said darkly, "the tight-fisted swine! He has always kept me on a shoestring."

"I don't think you are being fair," Tina replied, hotly.

Claude seemed about to retort angrily, but changed his mind.

"What am I to do? For God's sake help me," he whined.

"I will try to think of something, I promise you," Tina said, feeling that her words were in themselves a lie, for there was indeed nothing she could do.

"In addition to the debt that Stern gave me the note of five hundred guineas for," Claude burbled, "there is the bookie to be bought off, my jewellery to be redeemed, a number of grooms to be silenced, in case they might say I talked to them, I shall need at least one thousand pounds! How could it come out at less?"

"I will see what I can do," Tina promised again, as she rose to her feet.

She felt that she must be rid of him somehow and get away from his whining voice and his wild desperate eyes. She hated the way his fingers were clawing first at her arm and then at her dress like a drowning man clutching at a straw.

"You are only saying that because you are bored with listening to me," Claude said accusingly with a perception that comes to people when they are desperate. "Write me a cheque, give me some money, even a little would be better than nothing."

"I have none. I mean, I don't have any, your cousin has it all," Tina stammered.

"You are hard, cruel and heartless!" Claude stormed, suddenly becoming vicious like a cornered rat. "You and Stern, spending all this money on this senseless insane ball. Look at your gown. The price of that alone would keep me from going to the Fleet. Why should you come here, a chit of a girl from nowhere, and walk into what is really my property and my inheritance?"

He sounded crazed with resentment.

His hands were clenched together and although he made no movement, Tina was suddenly afraid that he might hit her.

She tried to move away, but he followed her.

"Curse you!" he growled. "Curse you for your hard heart and for your extravagance. I will get even with you somehow, you see if I don't!"

There was something horrible and evil about him and Tina lifted her dress preparatory to running with all her speed back to the lit doorway of the house, when a deep voice asked,

"Is anything wrong? Your voice, Wynchingham, is disturbing the nightingales."

Tina looked up in relief to see the handsome smiling face of Sir Marcus Welton.

"Oh, it's you!" she exclaimed unnecessarily.

"I have come in search of you," Sir Marcus said. "Our dance has already begun and yet the ballroom seemed empty because you were not there."

"I-I – was just coming," stammered Tina.

"I can see nothing here to detain you," Sir Marcus said, his voice like a whip as he looked scornfully at Claude, who still stood staring at Tina, his face pale and unpleasant, his teeth clenched together as if in an effort to prevent himself from saying more.

At Sir Marcus's words he seemed to pull himself together and then walked swiftly away from them over the grass towards the road.

Tina felt herself shiver.

"Has he frightened you?" Sir Marcus enquired.

"No, not exactly," Tina answered untruthfully. "He is just worried about his private affairs."

"For which he appeared to hold you responsible," Sir Marcus said.

"You were listening," Tina accused him.

"I always listen when there appears to be an altercation," Sir Marcus said suavely. "One learns a lot that way."

"Then you must realise that he is in terrible financial distress. Could you not help him perhaps?"

Sir Marcus laughed.

"Would that be a way of gaining your favour?" he asked, "to help that ridiculous unsavoury fellow, who has always been in trouble ever since I first made his acquaintance?"

"But this time the trouble really does seem to be serious," Tina replied.

"He will certainly believe it to be so," Sir Marcus answered. "No, not even for you, my dear, will I waste my good money on such a very unprepossessing cause. If you gave Claude Wynchingham a million guineas, it would slip through his fingers like water and he would be trying to borrow yet another fiver from you the following night."

"Is he really so hopeless?" Tina asked.

"Completely and absolutely. So do not worry your pretty head about him. They are, without exception, a dissolute lot, the Wynchinghams."

He was, Tina felt, trying to convey a special message to her, which she deliberately misunderstood.

"I am sorry for Claude," she said. "He must be a terrible trial to his cousin, my Guardian, Lord Wynchingham."

She looked up at Sir Marcus as she spoke so that he would understand what she wished to convey to him.

"I stand corrected," he said with a little smile.

"And now shall we dance?" Tina asked.

"I am afraid it is too late," he replied. "By the time we reach the ballroom the music will have finished. Let's sit here in the cool. At least you owe me a few more minutes of your company."

There was logic in his remark and Tina re-seated herself in the arbour that she had just left.

"You are very beautiful," Sir Marcus remarked as he sat down beside her.

"I am gratified that you should think so," Tina answered.

"I thought so the very first moment I set eyes on you," Sir Marcus said. "I watched you descend from the coach behind the Dowager Duchess and do you know what I said to myself?"

"No," Tina answered, "I have no idea."

She was thinking uneasily that she had been away from the ballroom a long time and Lord Wynchingham might be missing her and wondering what she was doing. She thought that she must be careful to return in time for the next dance.

The voice of Sir Marcus broke in on her thoughts.

"You are not listening," he said, not accusingly, but with a kind of patient persistence that, had she realised it, was far more dangerous.

Sir Marcus was a man who invariably got his own way because he was not impatient.

"I am sorry," she apologised. "I was wondering if the Dowager had been looking for me. Indeed she warned me not to come into the garden. It is apparently considered not entirely *comme il faut* for a *debutante*."

"I am far less troublesome than your last partner," Sir Marcus said, "but I was telling you what I thought when I first saw you."

"Yes, yes, of course," Tina said politely. "What did you think?"

She turned to find his face very close to hers and his dark eyes looking into hers with an intensity that made her draw in her breath a little sharply.

"I thought," Sir Marcus said slowly, and with emphasis on every word, "that you should be mine."

He made the words seem somehow prophetic and Tina felt as though a cold hand had been placed on her heart.

Sir Marcus was good-looking, exquisitely dressed and, from what she had heard, a very rich man and yet there was something about him that made her flesh creep and that made her long to run from him as she had wished to run from Claude.

For a moment she could find no words to answer him with and then his hand, strong, heavy and strangely cold, covered her fingers.

"I want you," he said quietly, "and what I want, I get!"

Quickly she pulled her hand free and jumped to her feet.

"I must go back to the ballroom, sir," she said not looking at him, the words tumbling between her lips. "The Dowager will be looking for me."

She did not wait for him to answer, but, lifting her full skirts, she turned and ran across the grass, speeding like a frightened faun under the trees.

She fancied, although she could not be sure, that she heard Sir Marcus laugh as she fled.

By the time she reached the doorway where the footmen, in their claret and gold livery, stood to greet the guests that were still arriving, her agitation had in part subsided.

She forced herself to walk slowly and steadily through the hall and up the stairs, yet she knew that her whole body was trembling.

It was ridiculous, it was absurd, and yet her heart was beating almost suffocatingly.

'What is the matter with me?' she asked herself. 'I shall never find what I am looking for – a very rich man whom I could love!'

And, although she chided herself for being so foolish, the trembling persisted.

She reached the top of the stairs to find Lord Wynchingham scowling at her.

She could have cried out in relief at seeing him, but the stormy expression on his face and the tightness of his lips, prevented her from saying anything.

"Where have you been?"

There was no disguising the fact that he was incensed and somehow, because he was angry, Tina recovered her own fortitude.

"In the gardens," she answered. "They were charming and most attractively lit. You should go and look at them."

"Your place is in the ballroom," Lord Wynchingham asserted. "I have here a partner for you. He is too shy to plead for the favour of a dance, so I must do it for him."

"But, of course, Lord Alfred," Tina said, smiling at his blushing companion. "Let me see, I am booked until dance twelve, but number thirteen is free, if that will please you?"

Lord Alfred Cartright bowed, murmuring something incomprehensible.

"I would be vastly obliged if you would procure for me a glass of lemonade," Tina suggested.

Lord Alfred bustled away obviously delighted to be of service.

Lord Wynchingham then turned on Tina savagely.

"Number thirteen, what are you playing at?" he demanded. "Cartright is a rich man. He would do you well."

"I don't want to appear over-eager," Tina answered.

"Don't be too elusive, either," Lord Wynchingham growled. "Don't forget that all this junketing goes on the bill."

"My father had a saying that one must use a sprat to catch a whale!"

"I should think it extremely unlikely we shall catch anything, if you ask me," Lord Wynchingham said disagreeably.

"We both know what is the alternative," Tina said, "so enjoy yourself."

"Come and dance with me."

"I am promised to someone who was more than a trifle annoyed an hour ago. I should think it very unlikely that he will arrive to claim me."

"Then you could have given the dance to Cartright," Lord Wynchingham said, his face darkening.

"I would so much rather dance it with you," Tina replied. "Come, you cannot work all the time, we must both of us have a few moments relaxation."

She said it in such a quaint way that he could not help laughing and without further protestation allowed her to lead him into the ballroom where the music had just started.

"I have not danced for months," Lord Wynchingham protested as they began.

"All the more reason why you should look as though you are enjoying yourself," Tina answered. "Remember, you are supposed to be proud of your rich and successful Ward."

"I have no doubt that my grandmother has exaggerated your fortune into millions," Lord Wynchingham said, "and if that does not prove an attraction nothing will."

"You are not very gallant," Tina said. "Your cousin has already made me an offer of marriage."

"Claude? I can hardly credit that he would have the impudence."

"Indeed he has. He is in trouble again."

"Then he can find his own way out of it," Lord Wynchingham said roughly. "I can give him no further help."

"Indeed, I can see no reason why you should," Tina answered. "At the same time he is desperate – perhaps – because – "

"Claude is dangerous to no one but himself," Lord Wynchingham said impatiently. "Even to talk of the fellow makes me feel sick. Who else has seemed interested in you?"

Tina was about to answer 'Sir Marcus Welton' when something stopped her. She did not know what. It was almost as though she was afraid to tell anyone what Sir Marcus had said and the way he had looked.

She told herself that it was because she was afraid that if Lord Wynchingham knew Sir Marcus might offer for her, he might press her into marriage. And yet she knew the reason was deeper than that as something held her back, something so fundamentally disturbing that she could not even speak of Sir Marcus.

"Everyone has been very kind," she said lightly. "I am certain of one thing, I do Madame Rasché credit."

"It will not make her reduce her bill a fourpenny piece," Lord Wynchingham said sharply.

"Forget money just for the moment," Tina begged. "I want to say something and you are making it exceedingly difficult for me."

"What is that?" he asked curiously.

"I want to say 'thank you'," she said, her eyes shining in the tapers in the crystal chandelier. "This is the most wonderful ball I have ever imagined, I feel like a Fairy Princess, and you are my Fairy Godmother."

"I think you have got me in the wrong sex," Lord Wynchingham said with a laugh. "At the same time I am glad that you are happy. For both of us it may be something to remember in the empty days ahead."

"They are not going to be empty," Tina replied. He felt her little fingers digging into his. "We are going to win, you and I. I am going to save you and find a place for me, both at the same time. We will not be defeated! We will not!"

"I am ready to believe anything when you say it like that," Lord Wynchingham said and almost in surprise realised that the dance had come to an end.

"Thank you," Tina said softly, as she sank into the traditional curtsey.

"Thank *you*," Lord Wynchingham answered as he raised her to her feet.

Just for a moment they stood, their hands entwined, and then Tina heard the Dowager calling her and she went hastily across the polished floor to where the Dowager, resplendent in a tiara of diamonds and emeralds, was seated in a high-backed chair.

"Come here, child," she said imperiously. "Are you enjoying yourself?"

"More than I can ever say, ma'am," Tina answered.

"You are being a success," the Dowager said generously. "A great success. Sir Marcus here suggests that he gives a party for you tomorrow night at Vauxhall. Will that please you?"

Tina raised her eyes and saw that he was standing behind the Dowager's chair, looking at her with that faint smile on his lips that made her feel cold and anxious.

"I think we have other plans for tomorrow night, ma'am, have we not?" she asked.

"No, I don't think so," the Dowager replied. "It would amuse me to see Vauxhall again. They tell me that they have made great improvements in the boxes lately."

"Yes, indeed," Sir Marcus answered.

He was not looking at the Dowager as he spoke.

"A glass of wine?" he suggested to Tina.

"No, thank you," she answered hastily. "I think Lord Alfred Cartright will be bringing me a glass of lemonade."

"Then let's go in search of him," Sir Marcus suggested.

He offered her his arm and, because she could think of no possible excuse not to accompany him, she put her fingers very gently on it and he drew her out of earshot of the Dowager.

"You look like a bird that has been caught in a cage," he said. "There is no need to be frightened."

"But captured birds *are* frightened," Tina protested.

"How do you know?" Sir Marcus asked. "They are no longer in danger from the sparrowhawks. They have warmth, security and comfort. Is not that something to be grateful for?"

"Perhaps they preferred freedom," Tina answered in a low voice.

"For what? To grow old to be at the mercy of all sorts of dangers? No, a cage can be preferable in many ways, especially if the door stands open."

Tina felt that she hated his arrogance.

"I cannot think where Lord Alfred can be," she said, looking round her.

"Why worry your pretty head?" Sir Marcus asked. "If you are in need of lemonade I will tell a servant to fetch you a glass."

"No, no, I am not really thirsty," Tina answered.

"Then stop running away," he commanded her.

She withdrew her hand from his arm and looked up at him.

"We have only just met, Sir Marcus. I am afraid that I am unused to the sophisticated manners of London. I take time to realise who are my friends. I cannot make up my mind so swiftly as apparently you can."

It was a brave effort, for she knew, even as she spoke, that he still had that hateful smile on his face and that dark smouldering expression in his eyes.

"Why waste unnecessary time?" he asked. "You and I both know what is the end of the story."

"I-I don't know what y-you mean. I – don't understand," she stammered.

"I think you do," he replied and this time he reached out, took her hand, placed it on his arm and held his other hand over it.

"You are very entrancing," he said in a voice that only she could hear. "I like women to flutter and try to escape, but not for too long. Life is too short for prolonged prevarication."

His fingers were covering hers, his voice, deep and insidious, seemed to sear its way into her brain.

She felt as if the prison walls were closing round her – and then, in front of her, there loomed up a pink perspiring face, a hand in a white creased glove holding a half-spilled glass of lemonade.

"I beg your pardon for having been such an unconscionable time," Lord Alfred Cartright said, "but I could not discover where you had gone."

Gratefully Tina took the glass of lemonade, overwhelming Lord Alfred with her thanks and chatting with him so amicably that he lost not only his heart but also his head and became completely incoherent in his answers.

Her partner for the next dance claimed her and soon she was dancing continuously, taking good care not to leave the ballroom again and gaining the approval of the older members of Society by the way in which, between dances, she went to the Dowager's chair, asking solicitously about her health and making a fuss of the old woman, so that it was impossible for anyone to have a private conversation with her.

Finally the evening drew to a close and the first fingers of dawn were beginning to come up over the roof-tops as the last guests moved from the marble hall across the pavement to where their carriages were waiting.

The last to leave was Lord Alfred Cartright.

Sir Marcus must have left earlier, although he had not said 'goodbye'. Tina had been conscious of him watching her from the side of the ballroom, then, when she had glanced to where he had been standing and found him gone, she felt that a load had fallen from her shoulders.

They were all in the hall when Lord Alfred stammered his thanks, kissed the Dowager's hand and went out through the line of flunkeys towards his coach.

"Thank God, that's the last of them," Lord Wynchingham exclaimed. "I thought the evening would never come to an end. My God, it's hot in the house."

He walked towards the door as he spoke and, because he was right in saying that it was hot in the house the Dowager and Tina followed him.

"Look how pretty the gardens in the Square are," Tina said to the Dowager.

"Several people remarked on it to me," Her Grace replied. "You remember the man said that he could turn it into a Fairyland, when we engaged him," Tina said.

"I hope it was worth the money you paid him," Lord Wynchingham said disagreeably.

"Don't carp, Stern," the Dowager said. "The child has enjoyed herself. Of course the place has seemed like a Fairyland to her. She is not as old and blasé as you are."

"In the morning when the candles are out it will not look so pleasant," Lord Wynchingham retorted.

"I am not going to listen to you," Tina said. "Come and look for yourself before the candles burn away."

She pulled at the Dowager's arm and the old lady allowed herself to be helped across the road and through the gate that led into the gardens.

"Arbours and soft seats!" she snorted. "I wonder what trouble they have caused tonight!"

"Or what happiness?" Tina suggested.

"You were a good child to stay in the ballroom," the Dowager said. "When I was young, I was always in trouble because of my headstrong ways. I swear on a night like this I would have had some handsome young fellow declaring for me, on his knees, pouring out passionate protestations of love. And by Heavens, I would have listened to him!"

There was a note of regret in the Dowager's voice that neither Tina nor Lord Wynchingham could fail to hear.

Then briskly the old lady added,

"Oh, what is the use of repining? I am too old for love, but I have had it in my time. My advice to you, girl, is not to play about too long. Snatch at youth and love while you can, the years pass all too quickly."

"The only offer Tina had tonight was from that worm of a cousin of mine," Lord Wynchingham sneered.

"From Claude!" the Dowager exclaimed. "What an impertinence! I hope you set him down?"

"What he wants was money, not love," Tina answered.

"Is that not what most people want?" Lord Wynchingham asked.

He was determined to be disagreeable, Tina could see that.

She looked up at the guttering candles and through the branches of the trees to where the stars were just beginning to fade from the sky and she said with a little catch in her breath,

"It is all so beautiful and I am happy. I think for the first time in my life, I am happy, and I cannot really believe it is true."

There was a sort of ecstasy in her voice that seemed to stifle the disagreeable words on the lips of Lord Wynchingham.

"It is all so beautiful," Tina went on. "You have both been so kind, so very kind and so wonderful to me. I don't know how to say 'thank you'."

"I think – " Lord Wynchingham started in a kinder voice than he had used before.

Then, as he spoke a sudden harsh report, which shattered the silence and the beauty of the garden, rang out almost deafeningly.

Lord Wynchingham staggered and put his hand to his chest,

"The Devil take it – I think – " he began in a different tone and collapsed at Tina's feet.

CHAPTER FIVE

For a moment both the Dowager and Tina stood as though they were turned to stone.

Then, with a little cry of consternation, Tina fell on her knees beside Lord Wynchingham.

She thought that he was dead and a feeling of numbness seemed to take possession of her so that she could feel nothing, but only watch with horrified eyes a flood of crimson blood spreading over the satin of his coat just below the shoulder.

Then, even as he stirred and opened his eyes, people seemed to appear from nowhere and the noise above their heads was a confusion of shouts and cries – the Dowager's voice giving almost incoherent orders, men running to every corner of the garden.

Lord Wynchingham stared up at her.

She could see his face quite clearly in the light of the illuminations on the branches of the trees above them.

"My God! I have been shot," he groaned.

"Keep still," Tina commanded almost automatically and added, "I thought you were dead."

"Dammit! I thought so myself," he answered.

He put his hand to his shoulder and then withdrew it to stare at his fingers red and dripping with blood.

"Don't move," Tina bade him.

She heard the Dowager roaring,

"Bring a gate, you fools. I have not been hunting all these years not to know that when a man falls he must be carried on a gate, a gate because he must be kept flat."

Lord Wynchingham gave a choke that was almost a laugh.

"My legs are all right, Grandmama," he said.

"Legs or broken collarbone, you need a gate," the Dowager snapped.

"I will walk," Lord Wynchingham replied and tried to struggle to his feet, but fell back with an ashen face, the blood now pouring in a stream over his coat.

"Don't be a fool, boy," the Dowager cried angrily.

At that moment two footmen came running from the house with a flat top of a trestle table.

Under the Dowager's imperious instructions, they managed to lift Lord Wynchingham onto it and Tina realised the fact that he permitted them to do so and made small protest was because he was too weak and in too much pain to argue.

They moved in a slow procession towards the house and, as they reached the front door, several footmen, who had been sent by the Dowager to look for the assailant, came panting up.

"There be no sign of anyone, Your Grace," one of them said. "No one about that we can see at this hour of the mornin'."

"*Dolts! Imbeciles!*" the Dowager roared angrily. "You don't suppose he stood there waiting for you to find him. Look down the side streets, see if anyone has a suspicious bump in his coat that could be a pistol."

She almost screamed her instructions, and then, with a gesture, contradicted them.

"Well, it's too late anyway, the felon will have reached Piccadilly or Tyburn, by now. Whoever he might be, he was obviously more fleet of foot than you louts."

The footmen looked abashed and humiliated by having let their prey escape, as the Dowager stalked into the house, the feathers in her hair fluttering in the dawn breeze and her hand grasping the ivory-headed stick she invariably walked with as steadily as a Guardsman.

Tina, on the other hand, while following the footmen with their heavy burden up the stairs, felt as though the end of the world had come when least expected.

What would happen now that Lord Wynchingham was wounded and, worse still, what would happen were he to die?

She could not help feeling, in a way, relieved that the footmen had not found the assailant, because she was already convinced in her own mind that she knew who it was – but how could she be sure?

Would Claude indeed go to such lengths? And yet his cousin's death was, he believed, the only thing that stood between him and a fortune.

As if the same idea had crossed the Dowager's mind, she turned to Tina as they reached the top of the stairs and said in a voice that she imagined was hardly more than a whisper,

"Where can Claude have got to?"

"I have no idea," Tina answered.

The voice from the table top startled them both,

"What has Claude got to do with it?"

"Don't trouble your head with questions, just now," the Dowager answered, "and at the same time don't be more bird-brained than usual."

Tina thought that she heard Lord Wynchingham chuckle, then the footmen carried him into his bedroom and she saw through the open door his valet hovering solicitously round him and heard the Dowager say,

"Cut off his Lordship's coat and shirt so that the wound is uncovered. Has anyone sent for the surgeon?"

"I think Mr. Greychurch is seeing to it, Your Grace," the valet answered.

The Dowager came out of the bedroom and closed the door firmly.

"His man will see to him," she said to Tina. "It will hurt taking his clothes off and he will want to swear and will have no desire for us females to be breathing over him. Come and sit down, child. There is nothing more we can do until the surgeon arrives."

"Do you think it is a very bad wound?" Tina asked tremulously.

"All wounds are bad," the Dowager answered, "and the devil who blew a hole in Stern aimed for his heart."

"Do you think he will live?" Tina persisted.

The Dowager looked at her.

"He is my grandson," she answered, "and as a family we do not give in easily."

From then on it seemed to Tina that there was an interminable time of waiting for the surgeon to arrive and, when he did come, grumbling and obviously not too pleased at being aroused from his bed, there was another century of waiting until they heard his verdict.

He came into the salon where the Dowager and Tina were sitting with blood over the none-too-clean cuffs of his shirt and with the bullet in his hand to show them that his probing had been effective.

"A ticklish job, Your Grace," he said. "His Lordship took it like a man, only cursed me to Hell because I was hurting him."

"Is he all right now?" the Dowager asked.

"He is as drunk as a Lord with the amount of brandy I had to pour down him to keep his mouth shut," the surgeon answered, his eyes twinkling in his red face. "Do you think you would be likely to recognise the bullet, Your Grace?"

"I would not," the Dowager answered, "but I have my own idea as to whose finger fired the pistol."

"Well, that is not my business," the surgeon replied. "I will look in again to see the patient later today. He will doubtless have a fever when he wakes. If he is hungry give him some broth, but nothing else."

He bowed perfunctorily to the Dowager and went from the room and they heard him stumbling down the stairs.

"May we look at him?" Tina asked.

The Dowager nodded and they crossed the wide landing to Lord Wynchingham's room.

The curtains had been drawn against the morning sunlight, but it was easy to see the pallor of Lord Wynchingham's face as he lay on the pillows, the bandaged shoulder just showing above the bedclothes.

His eyes were closed and to Tina he looked young and, somehow, vulnerable. There was a strong smell of brandy in the air and a nearly empty decanter stood on the bedside table.

The valet was moving in the shadows of the room and the Dowager asked, a note of apprehension in her sharp voice,

"Will his Lordship be all right, Jarvis?"

"I think so, Your Grace. But the bullet had gone deep. The surgeon gave his Lordship a powerful lot of pain in trying to find it. But he says it were a miracle that it were not worse. Look, Your Grace, this is what saved his Lordship."

The valet came towards the Dowager holding something in his hand. It was Lord Wynchingham's coat, stained with blood and slashed where they had cut it off him.

Down the front were six diamond buttons and Tina saw that one of them now was shattered and twisted almost out of all recognition.

"The one nearest his heart," the Dowager said grimly.

"Yes, Your Grace, the button must have deflected the bullet to his shoulder."

"Whoever fired at his Lordship must have been a good shot," the Dowager commented.

"Yes indeed, Your Grace, a killer with fire-irons!"

From the bed there came a sudden moan.

Tina turned quickly to see Lord Wynchingham moving his head from side to side and an incoherent murmur coming from his lips.

"The fever will be rising in him," the valet remarked.

"You know what to do?" the Dowager asked.

"I have nursed him often before," the valet replied. "I was with his Lordship when he was soldiering."

There was a confidence about the man that gave Tina hope that Lord Wynchingham was not as bad as he looked, but the ashen face and incoherent murmurs were frightening.

He had seemed so strong, so confident, indeed almost terrifying in his autocracy when they had been quarrelling earlier in the evening.

Now he appeared little more than a boy – a boy who had been smitten down.

"There is nothing more we can do," the Dowager said firmly, "so let's to bed."

Tina thought that it would be impossible for her to sleep after all that had happened, but when at last the sun was risen high in the sky and she slipped between the cool sheets in her bedroom, only a few minutes after her head touched the pillow she was fast asleep.

*

It was afternoon before she awoke to find a maid by her bedside with a tray of food and, after she had eaten, she rose hastily to go in search of the Dowager.

She had already learnt that his Lordship had passed a very restless night. But the physicians were not unduly worried, there had been quite a posse of them calling while she had slept, doubtless, she thought, sent for by the surgeon.

She put on one of her new dresses and, worried as she was, she could not help knowing that she looked very different from the countrified schoolgirl who had arrived in this house such a short time ago.

She decided before leaving her room that she had to see for herself how Lord Wynchingham was.

Then, as she stepped out onto the landing, she heard a loud chatter of voices in the hall below.

Curiously she went to the banisters and stared over.

To her surprise she saw, not as she half-expected, a throng of friends enquiring as to the health of their host of the night before, but a collection of tradesmen, holding in their hands bunches of bills, arguing loudly and rapaciously with Mr. Greychurch who stood at the foot of the stairs.

"I tell you," Tina heard the secretary say, "his Lordship is not well enough to see anyone. He has had an accident."

"He has a bullet in him," one of the tradesmen shouted, "and that I know for certain. If he be a-goin' to die, we want our money. Aye, that we do."

Their clamour sounded like the growls of savage animals and Tina felt herself shiver.

"You will be paid when his Lordship is better," Mr. Greychurch said firmly. "Nothing will be gained by making a disturbance now or indeed by badgering him when he is too ill to do anything about your demands."

"I have been owed for nigh on two years," one man shouted,

"And I for a twelve-month," another yelled.

"Everything will be attended to in due course and in a proper mariner," Mr. Greychurch persisted. "If you will leave your accounts with me, I will see that they are brought to his Lordship's notice as soon as he is well enough to inspect them."

"And what if 'e dies?" one man asked roughly. Tina could see from his apron that he was a butcher. "Do I get paid or don't I?"

"You will get paid," Mr. Greychurch repeated firmly. "But you have forced your way in here and, if I relate to his Lordship what has happened, I should not be surprised if he takes his custom elsewhere."

"I am not sure if we would not be better off if he did," a small ferrety-looking man said nastily.

There was a murmur of agreement at this suggestion, but Mr. Greychurch went on suavely,

"Listen, gentlemen, nothing is to be gained by upsetting his Lordship when he is ill and in a fever. You must accept my promise, and I give you my word on it, that I will do all that is possible to press your claims as soon as his Lordship is well enough to hear of them. Will you be content with that?"

"We've not much choice," the burly man who might have been a baker said resignedly.

"No, indeed," Mr. Greychurch agreed, "you have no choice but to leave here quietly. Please place your bills on the hall table and, as I have said, his Lordship will deal with them at the first possible opportunity."

Sheepishly, their protests having died in them, they did as Mr. Greychurch suggested. Only when they were outside the front door could Tina hear them arguing with each other as they moved away down the Square obviously disgruntled and dissatisfied at the fruitlessness of their call.

The door was closed and she saw Mr. Greychurch give a deep sigh, then stagger to a chair and sit down as if the effort had been almost too much for him.

"I will bring you a glass of wine, Mr. Greychurch," the butler said in a sympathetic tone. "It takes it out of you a thing like that, don't it?"

"It does indeed," Mr. Greychurch answered in his quiet cultured voice.

Tina drew back from the balustrade.

She was well aware that if she appeared at this moment it would not help in any way and would only make Mr Greychurch uncomfortable.

She felt her heart beat a little faster.

Lord Wynchingham's creditors had not looked a kind or pleasant mob and, although there had been actually not too many of them, there were, she was convinced, many more to make trouble and show their determination to be paid in full.

Tina put her fingers to her head.

How had she been so mad as to allow herself to do anything so dangerous or indeed so reprehensible as this?

When she found out the position Lord Wynchingham was in, the least she could have done was to return to Yorkshire or start seeking right away a position as a Governess or a companion.

She felt her dress rustle as she moved and thought guiltily how much it had cost, the price of it might at least have gone towards paying one of the long bills that the men who had stormed the house waved so threateningly in Mr. Greychurch's face.

She felt ashamed of herself and of her own actions and then, almost as though she hugged the secret to her heart, she remembered the ball last night.

At least she had known the thrill and excitement of being the most feted and acclaimed woman present and there were still a few days left of luxury, excitement and the drama of being in High Society.

She knew only too well what a mad gamble the whole thing was and yet, until this moment, it had seemed only an adventure, an almost childish attempt to escape from the misery of poverty and from a situation that was unpleasant and uncomfortable.

Now she saw that things were in fact very different.

Lord Wynchingham was in danger not only of being put in the Fleet, but also perhaps in physical danger from the men who when they knew that he could not pay them, would take their revenge in some barbaric manner that, although it could give them no money, would give them some satisfaction.

It had been brave of Mr. Greychurch to defy them, Tina thought and she wondered if, in the same circumstances, she herself would have been so brave.

Because she was so perturbed and, without waiting to find the Dowager, she knocked on the door of Lord Wynchingham's room.

When the valet opened it, she asked,

"How is his Lordship?"

"The fever be high," the man answered in a whisper, "but it is not increasin' as I feared it might."

"Let me look at him," Tina asked.

She felt that she must see for herself and almost before the valet could move from her path, she was in the room and had crossed to the bedside.

~93~

A cold cloth was on Lord Wynchingham's forehead, but his face, flushed and burning, was wet with sweat.

For a moment she thought that he was asleep, but he opened his eyes and saw her,

"Cleo, no, not Cleo. Tina," he said almost wildly. "I remember now – pretty girl – making nuisance of yourself with that fellow – send him away."

"He doesn't know what he be sayin', miss," the valet said at Tina's elbow.

"Money – money – money – what am I to do?" Lord Wynchingham enquired. "Cleo – no, no, Tina has a solution – better than suicide – clever girl, Tina."

"He doesn't know what he be sayin'," the valet repeated.

Tina put out her hand and laid it on Lord Wynchingham's.

The skin was burning hot.

"Have you sponged him down with vinegar?" she asked the valet.

"No, miss, never heard of it."

"It will bring the fever down," she told him. "And don't let the cloth on his head get warm. Keep applying it. Is there any ice to be had?"

The valet shook his head.

"Not in London this time of year," he answered. "Now if we were at Wynch, that would be a different thing, it keeps all the year round in the ice house, it does. He looked up at Tina and added, almost beneath his breath, that's an idea, miss."

"What is?" she asked.

The valet moved away from the bedside to the far corner of the room. Tina saw that he had something to say and followed him.

~94~

"Why don't we get his Lordship down to Wynch, miss?" he asked. "Never could stand the heat in London and I understands there were a bit of trouble downstairs."

"Yes, I saw them," Tina answered.

"It is not only them," the valet went on. "What if the person who blew a hole in his Lordship has another go? He'll have learnt by now he were not successful in bringin' down his bird."

"Do you think he will try again?" Tina asked him.

"Why shouldn't he? He wanted his Lordship dead and he ain't dead."

"I never thought of that," Tina said with a sudden quaver in her voice.

"I've been thinkin' of it, all right," the valet replied. "Let's get his Lordship away, miss. He loves Wynch. It ain't more than an hour's journey. He'll travel all right tomorrow."

"Are you sure of that?" Tina enquired.

"We'll have to ask one of them doctors, I suppose," the valet conceded grudgingly. "But I knows it's fresh air what his Lordship needs and what's more, he always feels well at Wynch."

"I will speak to Her Grace," Tina promised.

A voice from the bed made them both start.

"Money – money," it muttered. "Why is it always money? – Damn you, Lampton – you have had everything – what more do you want? – My God! I have been shot!"

The valet hurried across to the bedside.

"There, there, my Lord. 'Tis all right," Tina heard him say in tones of a nurse soothing a fractious child. "Don't you worry about nothin', my Lord. You'll be as right as rain tomorrow. Just shut your eyes and go to sleep."

His voice must have been almost hypnotic for Lord Wynchingham did not speak again and after a few moments Tina tiptoed from the room.

She found the Dowager seated in the library writing letters. She looked up as Tina entered and put down her quill.

"No need to ask if you slept well, child," she said. "A few hours suffice me, but the young can always sleep the clock round."

"Your pardon, ma'am. I had no idea I was so fatigued."

"Have you heard how my grandson is?" the Dowager enquired.

"Yes, ma'am, I was told as soon as I awakened. I was just passing his bedroom on the way down here and as the door was open, I looked in. He seemed to be talking about going to Wynch. It sounded as though he would very much like to be there."

"Wynch?" the Dowager exclaimed. "Well, that is certainly an idea, but I doubt if the doctors would let him travel."

"Perhaps, ma'am, if you suggested it, they would agree," Tina said. "I don't know exactly where Wynch is, but it is in the country, and it would surely do him more good than being here where it is so hot and airless."

The Dowager looked at her speculatively, as though she thought that there was some reason why Tina wished to visit Wynch, but aloud she said,

"It would certainly be an idea to go there. After all, with your Guardian indisposed, you can hardly appear at balls and routs, for a few days at any rate. Let me see, today is Thursday. We could go there tomorrow and you and I could return on Tuesday or Wednesday of next week."

"That would be delightful, ma'am," Tina enthused.

"In the meantime it will do your admirers no harm to cool their heels a little."

"My admirers?" Tina questioned.

The Dowager waved her hand towards the side table and Tina saw, for the first time, that on it were two huge baskets of flowers.

The first was of orchids, deep purple and somehow over-sophisticated and ornate with their long tongues and yellow stamens. There was a card on the handle of the basket and even before she opened it, Tina knew who had sent her such a magnificent offering.

"Sir Marcus Welton!" she said aloud.

"You have certainly made a conquest there," the Dowager said. "I am told he is extremely wealthy."

"I do not like him," Tina said. "There is something about him, I don't know what it is – "

The Dowager shrugged her thin shoulders and her long cascading necklaces, their jewels jangling against each other, sparkled in the sunlight streaming through the windows

"I have always thought," she continued, "that money and attraction seldom go hand in hand. Few women get everything they desire from life. Why not take a poor husband and forget you have to keep him?"

"No, no," Tina said hastily. "The man I marry must be rich."

"Then you will have to go a long way to find anyone as rich as Sir Marcus," the Dowager replied. "There are stories about him, I admit, that are not particularly savoury, but few men are blameless and Sir Marcus is unlikely to have reached the age he has without having people gossip about him."

"I don't mind what is said about him," Tina said. "I don't really mind what he has done. It is just something about him. Some people feel the same about snakes and rats."

"Well, there is no hurry!" the Dowager remarked and Tina bit back the response that there was indeed every necessity for haste.

She turned to the other basket.

This was filled with pale yellow roses, which smelt delightful and were somehow reminiscent of a country garden. Again Tina guessed the donor before she opened the card.

"Lord Alfred Cartright," she read aloud.

"I am told by one of the servants that he rode into the country in search of them this very morning," the Dowager told her. "Quite a romantic turn or it may be that he knew that they were cheaper outside the City!"

"Don't spoil the story, ma'am," Tina begged, laughing a little. "I like to believe the more romantic version. Poor Lord Alfred."

"He has never been a success with women," the Dowager said. "His mother was very shy and incredibly gauche, but I was fond of her. You might do worse, child."

"He has a wet and flabby hand," Tina pointed out.

The Dowager gave a hoarse laugh.

"It always makes me think of Parsons and fishmongers," she confessed. "Not that I have ever met a fishmonger, but I am sure that their hands are wet and slightly slimy."

Tina was laughing when she saw that the card from Sir Marcus, which had fallen on the floor after she had read it, had something written on the other side.

She bent down to pick it up.

The bold, rather aggressive writing she felt was characteristic of him as she read,

"To Tina, who will be mine."

She felt herself flush at the arrogance of his words.

She gave an exclamation and tore the card to pieces, an action that was not missed by the Dowager watching her.

"He is very determined," she said.

"How do you know?" Tina asked.

"He brought the flowers himself," the Dowager replied. "He told me simply and without any amplification to arrange your marriage as soon as possible."

Tina stamped her foot.

"How *dare* he?" she fumed.

Even as she spoke she felt that a dark cloud had hidden the sunshine and was encompassing her.

Yet it was what she wanted. A rich man as a husband and yet now that the opportunity presented itself, she was prevaricating and finding fault.

"Who is he? What do you know about Sir Marcus?" she asked, almost as if she was playing for time.

"Not too much," the Dowager said. "He is not of noble birth, of course. But he is a gentleman, his father was a Squire in the North, who inherited great estates and married a woman with a big endowment. Sir Marcus was their only child. He has been clever. He has increased the money he inherited by various means – a great deal of it by gambling."

"In which case he is likely to lose it as quickly as he gained it," Tina said, thinking of Lord Wynchingham.

"Oh, no," the Dowager answered, "he is not so corkbrained as that. He plays with young simpletons, countrymen who have come to London, wide-eyed, but with warm pockets. He plays, I am told, very late in the evening, when most men have dined well. Sir Marcus himself looks sparingly on the bottle."

"He is obviously odious!" Tina exclaimed.

"But rich," the Dowager added, watching her.

"Does money matter so much?" Tina asked defiantly.

"Apparently to you it does," the Dowager retorted and Tina was silenced.

They stayed quietly at home that day, refusing to entertain the many callers who came to make enquiries about Lord Wynchingham.

When the doctors arrived in the evening, they announced that the fever was down and agreed with the Dowager that convalescence had much better be in the pure Hertfordshire air at Wynch, rather than in the stifling atmosphere of Berkeley Square.

Tina found herself possessed by a sudden urgency to get away. She might have slept well after the ball, but the following night she found herself tossing sleepless, reliving over and over again the moment when Lord Wynchingham put his hand up to his shoulder and then fell at her feet.

Suppose he had in truth been dead, what would she have said? How could she explain that their whole relationship was one of fraud and pretence?

'I am not an heiress, we were trying to find a rich man as my husband so that I could save him from his debtors.'

What a story! And now she could imagine, far better than she had been able to do before, what scandal and gossip it would cause in social circles, what an embarrassment it would prove for the Dowager and how it would seriously damage Lord Wynchingham's reputation.

She was surprised, looking at the cards and notes that lay in a pile on the hall table, how many people really cared enough about him to call or write in sympathy and friendliness.

~100~

She had the idea that even he had no notion that there were so many who were interested in him, not only because they were getting something out of him, but because he was a neighbour, someone they knew, part of the social circle, perhaps in some ways an ornament of it.

He had a distinguished record of service in the Army and he was a friend of the young Prince of Wales and he had the reputation of being open-handed and a sportsman.

Tina learnt all these things from the notes scribbled on the cards and from the letters, many of which the Dowager opened and passed to her to read.

"Take all these down to Wynch," she ordered Mr. Greychurch. "It will amuse his Lordship to read them when he is well enough."

"I hope that will be soon, Your Grace," Mr. Greychurch replied.

*

And so the notes and cards travelled with them in the coach that set off from Berkeley Square at noon the following day.

There were three coaches, each drawn by four perfectly matched horses.

Lord Wynchingham went in the first. They had improvised a kind of bed that stretched across the seats so that he could travel recumbent on his pillows with only his valet beside him.

The Dowager and Tina went in another, Abdul perched up on the box between the coachman and the footman.

The servants travelled behind with the heavy load of luggage.

They moved slowly at first through the traffic that led to Tyburn, but soon they were out in the open countryside.

There was blossom on the trees, the spring grass was green in the meadows.

Tina had brought all her new gowns with her, but she was embarrassed when just before they left another consignment of boxes arrived from Bond Street, containing country gowns and chip-straw bonnets, which the Dowager had informed her had been ordered especially for her trip.

"You don't want to look like a town zany," she said. "We had chosen all your gowns with a view to balls and parties. We had not imagined that you would also need more simple things."

"But, ma'am, even these will be very expensive," Tina remonstrated with a little catch in her breath.

"Madame Rasché is never cheap, but what does it matter?" the Dowager asked. "Money is no object and you are only young once."

Money was far from being 'no object', Tina thought.

She could see all too clearly the angry expressions on the faces of Lord Wynchingham's creditors.

She could hear Lord Wynchingham himself muttering in his fever, 'money, money, money.'

'Had ever two people put themselves into such a predicament?' she wondered. 'Would she also be sent to the Fleet Prison if all was discovered?'

Then she remembered that she could always save herself and, if necessary, Lord Wynchingham.

She closed her eyes against the insidious picture of Sir Marcus as, even when he was not there, he seemed to thrust himself upon her.

Almost as though she knew what she was thinking, the Dowager said with a little chuckle,

"Sir Marcus will be incensed when he finds that the bird has flown."

"How soon do you think he will discover that we have left?" Tina asked.

"By tonight, I imagine," the Dowager replied. "He is not the sort of man to let the grass grow under his feet. As soon as he thinks circumstances permit he will be round asking you to accompany him to some party or other."

"But I need not accept," Tina answered.

"You cannot as we are at Wynch," the Dowager replied. "But that will hardly circumvent him."

"Do you mean that he will follow us?"

"I am sure he will have every intention of doing so."

"Well, I have no wish to see him," Tina said pettishly. "It is too soon for me to be forced into making decisions one way or another."

"But of course," the Dowager answered. "When we return to London, there will be plenty of time for you to find someone else. However, I have to be frank with you, there are not so many eligible men in London as there were. The extravagance of the Prince of Wales set has made holes in many of their pockets, while a number of those who might be interested have Mamas who would not countenance their son marrying a comparatively unknown young woman, however rich she might be."

Startled, Tina regarded her wide-eyed.

"I had not thought of that."

"My dear, you may be a catch, but mothers of sons will always look higher still. Most of them, however, have an ancestral estate that requires funds to put it in order or a title that has become a trifle dusty because it has been so long on the shelf, so there is always hope."

She spoke sarcastically and Tina could not help laughing.

"You miss nothing, do you, ma'am?"

"Not much," the Dowager agreed. "I may be old, but my eyes are still sharp and I have always thought that Society is composed of sheep and sheep are stupid creatures! The longer I live, the fewer reasons I find to change my opinion."

Tina found herself laughing again and again at the Dowager as they travelled onwards towards Hertfordshire. The old woman's sharp wit, her cynicism and her extraordinary knowledge of human nature made her a fascinating companion.

Tina was disappointed afterwards that she had missed quite a lot of the countryside, only realising how long they had been travelling when they passed through a pair of magnificent ornamental gates and the Dowager exclaimed,

"We are here!"

"Already?" Tina asked and leant forward to receive a blinding impression of the miracle of spring.

The lilacs and rhododendrons were in full bloom, their pale colours mingling with the pink and white blossom of the cherry trees that seemed to make the long drive to the house a Fairyland of beauty.

Then suddenly the house came into sight. Its worn red stone, weather-beaten through the centuries, was set like a jewel among the grey balustraded terraces and green lawns that sloped down to the Parkland where the deer lay somnolent in the shade and to a silver lake where white swans glided beneath arched bridges.

"It's so beautiful," Tina sighed in an awed tone.

"It has been in the family since Queen Elizabeth lived at Hatfield House," the Dowager answered. "It has passed from father to son and there has always been a Wynchingham at Wynch."

"I had no idea that anything could be so lovely," Tina said almost beneath her breath and remembered that Lord Wynchingham had said that all this must be lost to him if he could not pay his debts.

'How could he have risked it?' she asked herself.

'How could he have taken the chance that any man might take away this inheritance, not only from him but also from the family, from his children, from their children and from all the generations that were to come?'

"My mother was a cousin of the Wynchinghams," the Dowager said, "and so I have their blood in my veins and I am proud of it. That is why, before I die, I hope to see my grandson settled here with a wife and with an heir to succeed him."

Tina longed to beg her to stop and to say no more, because she could not bear it.

If only the Dowager knew, she thought, that there were only a few weeks left before this lovely house and estate might pass over to another owner.

Every moment seemed to reveal something more beautiful, the carved statues on the terraces, the diamond-paned windows iridescent in the sunlight and the azaleas in the formal garden.

Now, at last, the carriages were drawing up at the front door and the servants in claret and gold uniform were running down to open the coach door and carry Lord Wynchingham up the steps and into the home of his ancestors.

"Let us pray that he has stood the journey well," the Dowager said and there was a softness in her voice that made Tina realise, with a sudden stab in her heart, that the old lady loved her grandson.

"I am sure that his Lordship will be all right after a night's rest," Tina said reassuringly and added, "No one could fail to get better here, it is so beautiful and so peaceful."

She stepped out of the carriage as she spoke and felt as though she too was coming home to a house such as she had sometimes dreamed about, imagining in her sleep that a place like this was her background, rather than the small dilapidated house that she had lived in with her father.

She had always been profoundly affected by beauty and she thought, as she entered the hall at Wynch, that it was not only as she imagined it would be with its glowing polished furniture and great gilt-framed portraits, but there was an atmosphere of peace and happiness as if everyone who lived here had left their mark, not in violence and tyranny but in love and affection.

Lord Wynchingham was taken upstairs and his valet reported later that, although he was very tired, the country doctor who had been waiting to attend him found him to be in a better condition that he had expected.

There was a glass of wine waiting for the Dowager in the drawing room, a long low room looking out over the garden and ornamented with exquisite pieces of furniture that, Tina learned, had all been designed especially for the house in the reign of King Charles II.

There were cupids everywhere, on the stand of the lacquered cabinet, their arms outstretched to hold the Royal crown on the high-backed carved chairs and on the pelmets they flew over carrying not only crowns but entwined hearts.

"The Lord Wynchingham who came to Wynch after the Restoration," the Dowager explained, "fell in love with the most exquisite creature, one of the few women, I believe, who ever resisted the King, and he brought her here and tried to make the whole house a bower for her loveliness. They were extremely happy. They had eight children and both lived to be quite old and died within a few years of each other. They were buried together in the Private Chapel. I will show it to you tomorrow."

"What a lovely story!" Tina said eagerly. "That is what marriage should be like, is it not? Two people loving each other until they die."

"Exactly," the Dowager said drily, "but I believe that she was quite penniless. She went to Court with only one dress and captivated everyone including the King himself."

Tina turned towards the window.

There was no mistaking the insinuation in the Dowager's voice and she knew only too well that she was reading her a lesson, thinking that in her insistence on money rather than love there was something wrong in her composition.

She stared blindly across the gardens.

'But I too want to love,' she whispered in her heart. 'I too want cupids to surround me because I am happy.'

CHAPTER SIX

Soon after their arrival the Dowager went upstairs to rest and Tina, left on her own, explored part of the house.

It was, she thought, as she went from room to room, exactly as she had expected it would be from her first glimpse of Wynch.

Each room was more enchanting than the last.

Low ceilings, some with beautiful Tudor plasterwork, some supported by great ship's beams, mullioned windows with iridescent glass, huge stone mantelpieces carved with strange devices, others in mellow Tudor brick large enough to sit inside so as to be close to the warming flames.

Tina was knowledgeable enough to know that the furniture was unique in that it was a potpourri of every generation who had bought the best for the house they loved. Queen Anne walnut jostled Charles II gilt tables.

There were fine examples of Cromwellian oak and beautifully inlaid pieces of marquetry that had crossed the Channel from Holland when some Wynchingham had gone adventuring.

'It is lovely, lovely,' Tina kept saying to herself and every time she said it there was a further pang when she thought that it must pass from the family who had collected such treasures into the keeping of strangers.

She felt a sudden envy of this man who had won so much more than money from the owner of Wynch and yet she knew that in reality she ought to hate Lord Wynchingham who had been so foolish and spendthrift as to risk his home and his heritage on a game of chance.

Next to the salon was a library filled with books reaching from floor to ceiling and whose windows looked out over the Herb Garden. The room had a studious air and yet at the same time Tina had the feeling that it was seldom used.

To her books were always a delight and she passed from shelf to shelf seeing many volumes that she wanted to read, wondering how many she would be able to hold in her hands before she must leave for London.

In this room the mantelpiece was of grey stone bearing the Tudor rose and she knew that it must have been erected when the house was first built. She touched it reverently with her fingers and looked inside the great open fireplace where there was room for two people to sit opposite each other, being warmed by the fire, and perhaps reading by the light of the flames.

She sat on a worn wooden seat and looked upwards. She fancied that she could see a glimmer of light and wondered if the climbing boys who had cleaned the chimney were afraid to go upwards into the darkness.

Hearing the door open in the room behind her, she came from her hiding place a little guiltily, wondering if whoever was entering would think it strange to find her there.

A tall grey-haired man was standing by the door who she realised was the butler.

"Your pardon, miss," he said respectfully, "but Her Grace is asking for you."

"I will go to her at once," Tina said quickly. "I was admiring this wonderful old fireplace."

"It is indeed very ancient, miss," the butler replied. "This is one of the oldest rooms in the house. One of the wings was burnt down about a hundred years ago and replaced, but this room has remained untouched, they tell me, since Wynch first came into being."

"It is all so lovely," Tina said moving towards the door, "and the carved staircase, it is the most beautiful one I have ever seen."

"It was made by a Mr. Grinling Gibbons about a hundred years ago," the butler said with almost a tinge of contempt in his voice for someone so modern.

Tina looked at him.

"You love this house, do you not?" she asked.

"I have lived here all my life," the butler replied. "I started as pantry boy with his Lordship's grandfather and I have had no other home since then."

"I can understand you loving it," Tina commented.

She moved away from him across the hall and up the wondrously carved staircase and, as she went, she thought suddenly that it was not Mr. Lampton she hated, but Lord Wynchingham.

'When he is better, I will tell him what I think of his action,' she told herself and then realised that it would do no good.

She turned and looked back into the hall.

The sunlight was coming in through the windows, casting a rainbow pattern of colour on the polished boards. It seemed to her that the Wynchingham ancestors looked down at her almost with pleading eyes.

'You can save it,' they seemed to say. 'You can save it.'

She turned to run away from them, but remembered that she did not know where to go.

And then a housekeeper, in rustling black silk with a chatelaine of keys at her waist, appeared from nowhere.

"Her Grace is expecting you, miss," she said politely.

She led the way down a wide corridor and opened one of the doors.

The Dowager was sitting up in an enormous four-poster bed looking more fantastic than ever.

Her hair was covered with a cap of lace and muslin into which she had thrust several diamond brooches.

She had undressed and was wearing over her nightgown a dressing jacket edged with ermine but her pearls and jewelled necklaces still hung around her neck and her thin wrists were almost weighed down by the bracelets that encircled them.

Abdul was sitting on a stool at the end of the bed and the Dowager was lecturing him sharply for some misdemeanour as Tina came into the room.

"Ah, there you are, child!" she said. "They have been an unconscionable time finding you."

"I am sorry, ma'am, I was exploring."

"Interested in the house, are you, child?" the Dowager asked. "Well, I am not surprised. It is an exciting place. I remember doing just the same when I first came to Wynch as a girl, not much older than you."

"I am sure that Lord Wynchingham loves it very much," Tina said a little hesitantly.

"He does not," the Dowager said sharply. "Do the young love anything but themselves? Wynch is a part of my grandson and he has not realised yet how much a part. As he grows older, he will begin to appreciate it, just as men learn to appreciate their wives if they are the right sort."

Tina made no reply. She was thinking that Lord Wynchingham had little time now to appreciate all he had lost.

"I sent for you," the Dowager continued, "because I understand that the Head Gardener's wife is ill. I always go to see her as soon as I arrive at Wynch, a tradition that I have kept up for years. But today I am too tired and she is too ill to come to me. I thought it would interest her to see you. Take her this note and say that I will visit her on the morrow."

"Yes, of course I will," Tina answered. "Where does she live?"

"You will find the Gardener's House at the end of the Kitchen Garden," the Dowager answered. "Turn right as you pass out of the front door, go through the stables and beyond you will find the gardens."

Tina was glad to have something positive to do.

She took the note and hurried down the stairs out into the courtyard. The sun was hot on her bare head, and yet there was a faint breeze coming from the lake, fragrant with the scent of lilac.

She walked through part of the garden and reached the stables.

The grooms were busy rubbing down the horses that had brought them from London. She could hear them whistling through their teeth as they worked and she thought that tomorrow she would visit the horses and perhaps give them a carrot or apple as she had been wont to do when she lived with her father.

They had little money, but the stables were his pride and even if he did at times have to groom the horses himself, he never let them become unkempt.

Her feet rang out over the cobbles that covered the stable yard and then she passed through a doorway over which there was a fine clock and found herself facing the entrance to what the Dowager had called the Kitchen Garden.

It was surrounded by high Tudor walls of red stone and, when she passed through the doorway, she found everything neat and in good order.

There were vegetables in rows, French beans growing up their high posts, peas ripening against the spindly sticks that had to support them later and the asparagus standing up like sturdy fingers pointing towards the Heavens.

The tidy paths were edged with small box hedges and led her to the far end of the garden where in the distance she could see the roof of a cottage.

When she reached the cottage, she was told that the gardener's wife, Mrs. Piper, was asleep and the doctor had given orders that she was not to be disturbed.

The child who told her that, a little girl of about ten years old, was very positive that her mother was not to be awakened, so Tina gave her the Dowager's note, told her to say who had called and turned to retrace her steps.

Then she thought that it would be fun to explore further and went on past the cottage and down through a narrow rather dusty lane, the hedgerows high on each side, which bordered the Park on one side and grass fields on the other.

She thought that if she walked far enough she must come to a small village but after a while, as the lane seemed just to twist and wind, she thought perhaps that she should go back.

It was then, in one of the green fields, that she saw a gypsy encampment.

There were a number of painted caravans in gay colours drawn up in a circle round fire on which some savoury stew was being cooked in a pot.

Tina wondered with a smile how many of Lord Wynchingham's chickens, rabbits and perhaps pheasants, had found their way into that pot one way or another and, as she stood looking, she was aware of dark swarthy faces watching her from behind the tiny curtains of the caravans.

A gypsy man with long dark hair, falling nearly to his shoulders, came from behind one of them and stood looking at her.

She had the uncomfortable feeling that she was intruding and turned hastily to retrace her steps along the lane towards the Gardener's House.

On her way she passed two gypsy women, one was old with her hair neatly plaited and drawn up on top of her head. The other was young and her hair hung over her shoulders like a dark cloud. Her chin was pointed, her eyes curious and excited.

She reminded Tina of some woodland animal and she saw that they both carried big baskets filled with clothes pegs and their feet, moving lightly over the stony road, were bare.

"Good afternoon," she said, her voice warm and friendly.

The gypsies stopped.

"Will you buy some clothes pegs, lady?" the older woman asked.

She had rather a fine face, Tina thought. There was something distinctly Oriental about her high cheekbones and dark sloe-like eyes.

Tina remembered her father saying that the gypsies came originally from India and that their journeyings had brought them across Persia to Egypt, and from Egypt to Europe and finally, in the reign of King Henry VIII, to England.

"I am afraid I have no use for clothes pegs," Tina answered.

"Let me tell your fortune, lady," the gypsy pleaded.

Tina laughed and shook her head.

"I have no money with me," she replied. "Perhaps another day. I have to cross your palm with silver to hear the future, have I not?"

She spoke gaily and almost with surprise realised that, although she had lived in the country all her life, this was the first time that she had ever really spoken to a gypsy.

"That's right, lady," the gypsy answered, "but 'cos you be young and pretty, I'll give you this bit of soothsayin' for nothin'."

She paused for a moment and her eyes narrowed, almost as though she was seeing Tina in a different perspective and then she said in a low deep voice,

"There be danger around you. Danger! Beware of a dark man. He bodes ill and in his shadow there is blood."

Her eyes opened and she smiled.

"Remember what I've told you, lady, and come and see us again."

"And don't forget to bring your silver with you," the younger gypsy interpolated, speaking for the first time.

"I will not," Tina answered, "and I will remember what you have said."

She went on her way feeling amused by the brief encounter.

It was small wonder that country people were frightened by gypsies. They managed to create an air of mystery with their superior knowledge that Tina knew could frighten the cottagers, both young and old, when they began to talk about fortune or misfortune.

Danger from a dark man!

What rubbish it was, and yet, she thought, Sir Marcus was dark. Perhaps they would consider it dangerous for her to marry him. She would undoubtedly be desperately unhappy. Yet what alternative was there?

At the back of her mind all through the day there had been a sense of urgency, of time running out.

She felt that she ought not to be away from London. She ought to be going to parties, to balls, to routs with the

Dowager and giving herself every possible chance to find the rich husband who, she had assured Lord Wynchingham, was both his and her only chance of salvation.

Sir Marcus was not the only man in the world.

There was, of course, Lord Alfred Cartright. She had the feeling that even were she to accept Lord Alfred's attentions it would take weeks, perhaps months, to bring him to the point of a proposal.

Could she afford to wait so long? She remembered the expressions on the faces of Lord Wynchingham's creditors and knew the answer to her question.

It was so hot in the walled Kitchen Garden she was glad to hurry through it and, avoiding the stables, she walked instead round the other side of the house.

Here was peace and a curious impression of timelessness.

The Herb Garden would have been planted when the house was built.

She could almost see where each generation had added a vista or a different type of flowerbed, planted shrubs or trees or erected ornamental fountains that had been carried across the seas from Italy.

Yet everything seemed to blend together to be part of the whole and she knew, as she came at last to the view of the lake with the swans dipping their yellow beaks beneath the silver water, that she had lost her heart to a house.

Lord Wynchingham was not well enough to see either the Dowager or herself that evening, his valet told them.

He was tired and the doctor had given him a potion to make him sleep.

"A sensible thing to do," the Dowager approved. "These country practitioners have far more sense than the fashionable quacks one finds in London. Old Dr. Williams may be nearly eighty but he has more wisdom in his little finger than all these fah-dilah creatures who charge a guinea a visit and know less about the human body than I do."

"I hope the fever has passed?" Tina said tentatively.

"His Lordship's skin is quite cool," Jarvis answered.

"How long do you think it will be before he is well again?" Tina enquired.

The valet permitted a faint ghost-like smile to twist his lips.

"I know his Lordship, miss. He will not let his bed hold him one second longer than is absolutely necessary."

The valet bowed and prepared to leave.

"Now, he is not to get up too soon," the Dowager said sharply.

Then, Your Grace, we will have to clamp him down with chains!" the valet replied.

The Dowager laughed and, when the valet had gone, she said to Tina,

"That man adores Stern. I cannot think why. My grandson keeps him up half the night and takes him rattling all over the place in one of those fast phaetons of his, which almost shakes the teeth out of the poor wretch. At times I have despaired of Stern, but as long as Jarvis continues to worship him, I have always felt that there must be something in him worth saving!"

The Dowager laughed again and was still chuckling as she went upstairs to change for dinner.

She and Tina dined sedately in the huge dining room at a table that could comfortably have seated twenty other guests.

Afterwards they sat for a little while in the salon and then the Dowager announced that she was tired and would retire to her bedroom.

"Do you think I could borrow a book from the library?" Tina asked tentatively as they reached the hall.

"Yes, of course," the Dowager answered. "I daresay you will find them thick with dust. I do not believe my grandson has opened a book since he was at Oxford."

"I love reading," Tina said sincerely.

"Then hurry, I cannot wait here all night."

Tina longed to say that she could find her own way upstairs, but she thought perhaps that the Dowager felt a responsibility towards her, so she hurried into the library holding on high one of the silver candlesticks that the butler had left for her and the Dowager to light the way to their bedrooms.

The shutters had been closed since she was last in the room and with the light of only one candle it was difficult to choose what she wanted.

She vaguely remembered on the left hand side of the fireplace she had seen a bound edition of a book that her father had once read aloud to her.

She snatched it out of the bookcase and hurried out of the room, afraid to keep the Dowager waiting longer.

"Come along, come along, child," the Dowager said impatiently.

The candles were still lit in the silver sconces that ornamented the walls and the Dowager held her candle as though it was impossible to see without it.

The corridors upstairs were also well lit and when she reached her bedroom and had said 'goodnight' to the Dowager outside her room, she found two great candelabra on either side of the mirror were lit and another candle burned at the side of her bed.

'They are very extravagant in this house,' she said to herself, remembering how careful she and her father had always been to blow out any candle before they left a room.

~118~

She undressed slowly, thinking over the events of the day and of the night before.

She felt as though she had packed so much into the last few days that she had lived half a lifetime and she was, in consequence, immeasurably older than she had been when she travelled down to London on the stagecoach from school.

She looked at herself in the silver-framed mirror.

Who would recognise the schoolgirl in the reflection that peered back at her? The Dowager's own maid had done her hair before dinner.

Her dress, simple in design, had cost fifty guineas. There was a string of pearls round her small neck, which the Dowager had insisted on her wearing for the ball and, when she tried to return it, had told her to keep it.

How incredible it all seemed, at the same time so extravagant, the great house, this retinue of servants ready for their arrival.

From some remarks the Dowager had made at dinner, Tina had learned that the house was always ready in case its Master chose to return unexpectedly and so there was no need to send a message.

The beds were kept aired, the rooms open and flowers arranged by the gardeners. There was always food in the kitchen for a dozen or more guests.

Tina had no idea that there were people who lived in such an extravagant manner. She remembered how she and her father had eked out the tiny pension they lived on, penny by penny, always afraid that by the end of the month they would have spent too much and find themselves in debt.

Would Lord Wynchingham ever understand, until he experienced it, what poverty was like? She could not help feeling sorry for what lay ahead of him, unless, of course –

Her thoughts shied away from the words that kept repeating themselves over and over again in her brain.

She would read and forget it for the moment, she thought.

She picked up the book that she had borrowed from the library then, when she opened it, she realised that it was not the book she intended to choose, but one that was written in Latin.

She gave an exclamation of annoyance and threw it down on the dressing table.

She climbed into bed and blew out the candle on the dressing table, leaving one burning beside her. She did not feel sleepy and did not want to be alone in the dark.

She watched the shadows on the ceiling and tried to think of other things rather than of herself – but always her thoughts came back to the same thing, Lord Wynchingham's plight and her own, Sir Marcus Welton and the creditors standing at the bottom of the stairs brandishing their bills.

She heard a clock strike in the distance, then another hour passed and it struck again. Impatiently she got out of bed. Only reading could distract her mind from her thoughts and perhaps send her to sleep.

She slipped her feet into soft slippers and put on a wrapper of muslin and lace that the Dowager had insisted on buying for her at Madame Rasché's. Her fair hair hung over her shoulders and she brushed it back impatiently from her forehead and, picking up the candlestick beside her bed, she softly opened her bedroom door.

The landing outside was in darkness. Someone had extinguished the tapers there and also down the stairs into the hall.

There was a warm fragrant smell of beeswax and spring flowers and there was a strange drowsy silence that comes to old houses at night and makes them seem as if they were sleeping like a human being.

Tina went slowly down the stairs.

She crossed the hall, her slippered feet making little sound on the Oriental rugs that covered the polished boards.

She opened the door to the library and realised, with a sudden leap of her heart, that there was a light in the room.

At the far end, standing by the mantelpiece, was a man with his back to her. His candle was on the mantelshelf so, for a second, he was only a silhouette and she thought for one moment that it was Lord Wynchingham.

Then, as he turned his head, she saw that it was his cousin.

Some instinct must have warned him that someone was there for she had made no sound.

"God in Heaven!" he exclaimed. "What are *you* doing here?"

There was no mistaking the astonishment in his voice.

"I was just about to ask you the same thing," Tina answered, her first moment of fear leaving her now that she recognised Claude. "I thought you were a thief."

"Perhaps I am," Claude answered almost defiantly, "but you, why are you here?"

"We came down today because the doctors thought that it would be best for Lord Wynchingham to be in the country," Tina told him. "Did you not you know that he had been shot?"

He watched Claude's face as she spoke, raising the candle in her hand a little higher and going towards him.

"Yes, yes, I heard of the accident," Claude replied hastily.

"You did not hear about it," Tina said accusingly. "You knew, did you not? You did it and ran away and this is where you ran to because you thought that it would be safe because no one would look for you here."

She spoke grimly and her voice seemed to ring out the accusation.

She thought that Claude was trying to defy her, but his eyes would not meet hers.

"You are being nonsensical," he blustered. "Why should I shoot Stern? Anyway from what you tell me he is alive."

"You hoped that he was dead, didn't you?" Tina said. "He would have been if you had not hit the button on his coat. How could you do anything so outrageous?"

"I didn't do it," Claude almost snapped at her. "I am admitting nothing and you cannot prove that I shot at him."

"No, I cannot prove it," Tina said, "but you did it and I know why. You thought that you would get his money if he was dead. You thought that you would inherit Wynch. I suppose, having failed to kill its rightful owner, you are now trying to steal what you can while he is still too ill to prevent you?"

She spoke with such vehemence and scorn that Claude quailed before her.

"I am not a petty thief," he pleaded indignantly, "whatever else I may be."

"You are a murderer!" Tina retorted. "Only you didn't succeed. If you are not stealing, what are you doing here, creeping into the house at dead of night?"

She glanced towards the window as she spoke and saw that one of the shutters was pushed back and the window behind it was open.

"If you want to know the truth," Claude said with an attempt at dignity, "I am looking for the treasure."

"Treasure, what treasure!" Tina asked.

"The family treasure," he answered. "That is about the only thing that can save me now. If I find it, I shall take it. I shall not say a word to Stern either. Finders are keepers and if he cannot find it, why shouldn't I?"

"I don't know what you are talking about," Tina responded.

"Haven't they told you?" Claude asked petulantly. "It's usually the first story anyone is told on coming into this house. The Wynchingham treasure was hidden by the family before they galloped away to fight for King Charles at Worcester. But they were all killed with the exception of a child of ten whose mother escaped with him to France and, when he returned to England, he came with Charles at the time of the Restoration. He took back Wynch and his estates, but he did not know where the treasure had been hidden and there was no one alive to tell him, so all through the ages Wynchinghams have gone on searching for the treasure. Stern and I used to look for it when we were children. When he grew up, I think he ceased to believe in it. I know it is here somewhere and I am going to find it! It is the only thing that can save me!"

"How do I know all that is true?" Tina asked. "How do I know you are not here to make another attempt on your cousin's life? I have a good mind to call the servants and tell them that it was you who fired the shot which wounded their Master and to tell them to put you out of here as quickly as they can."

"If you do that," Claude said harshly, "I shall tell them I had an assignation to meet you here after everyone had gone to bed. That will not do your reputation much good!"

~123~

He was like a cornered rat, Tina thought suddenly and, because she despised him so utterly she was not angry, she merely laughed.

"You are quite safe," she said, "I am not going to call the servants because I would be ashamed to let them see how a Wynchingham could stoop so low. The Dowager knows you fired the shot because when I said to her in the coach, 'what are you going to do about finding the assailant who tried to kill Lord Wynchingham?' she replied quite simply, 'I think it's a good thing he got away'."

Tina paused to let her words sink in.

"Her Grace does not want a scandal in the family," she continued, "and I for one will certainly not add to their embarrassment."

Claude, realising that he was safe, stopped being defiant and looked at Tina reflectively.

"You are really very pretty, you know," he said. "Why don't you marry me and save us all a lot of embarrassment?"

Tina laughed.

"I would not marry you if you were the last man in the world," she said, "so don't bother to ask me again. And as to your treasure hunting, if it is really true, I think you had best get out of here before anyone else finds you. You know how Lord Wynchingham's valet is always on the alert in case anything or anyone should hurt his Master and, if he hears movements, he is certain to rouse the house and then where will you be?"

"Very well, I will go," Claude said sulkily, "although I will tell you this. I have come here before and I shall come again. I have to find that treasure. It is somewhere in this part of the house, we all know that. Where the devil could the fools have hidden it?"

"I expect the Cromwellian troops have found it long ago," Tina answered.

"No, they didn't. That is the one thing we do know," Claude replied. "In General Fairfax's diaries it is written, 'we searched Wynch this day for the reputed treasure of the Wynchinghams, but there was nothing to be found, although my men made most diligent search'."

"Well, I just hope that Lord Wynchingham finds it before you do," Tina said.

"If he does, I will make him give me my fair share," Claude snarled.

Tina suddenly lost her patience with him,

"Go away and leave your cousin alone! Get out of here! You make me sick! And if I find you troubling Lord Wynchingham again, I will hand you over to the Justices. Remember, I was in the garden when you shot at him and I will swear I saw and recognised you."

"You little tiger cat," Claude growled at her. "You don't know what it is like to be as desperate as I am. I have got to have money, I have got to and someone has to provide it for me. But you are obviously clinging on to your own money and Stern's as well."

The innuendo in his voice made it all too obvious the way his thoughts were leading.

Tina pointed to the window,

"*Get out!*" she stormed.

"All right," Claude said, "I will go, but you have not seen the last of me!"

Tina did not deign to answer him.

She watched him climb through the open window and drop down onto the terrace outside and then she slammed the window to, fastened the catch and watched him slip away through the shadows of the garden.

She thought that he must have a horse somewhere as he would have ridden down the night before after he had shot Lord Wynchingham and perhaps he had slept for part of the day in one of the many summerhouses in the garden or maybe at the local inn where they knew him and could be trusted to say nothing.

He had waited for the night knowing that there would be an opportunity when the house was shut and quiet, to slip in and look for the treasure.

'Was there really such a treasure?' Tina wondered.

It sounded like one of the endless legends of old houses – ghosts or hidden treasure were connected with nearly all of them and she thought that, after all these years, Claude had a poor chance of finding anything.

Just for a moment she dreamt of how wonderful it would be if the treasure was really here and she and Lord Wynchingham could discover it.

Then all their troubles would be at an end, he could pay off his debts and she need not marry Sir Marcus.

Then she told herself severely that things only happened like that in Fairytales, in real life one faced marriage with someone detestable or being employed as a Governess at a pitiable salary that would hardly pay for the tax expended on candles in this house.

She gave the window catch another push to be certain that it was firm and then realised that it was defective, which was the reason Claude was able to get in.

She wondered how she could bring it to the housekeeper's attention without seeming nosy or interfering.

She closed the shutters and crossed the room to where she had put her candle down on a small table. The candle Claude had lit was burning on the mantelpiece.

She went towards it to blow it out, then looked at the mantelpiece itself for a moment and her hand went out to touch the wood, to feel with sensitive fingers for a tiny catch or spring.

Then she laughed at herself. Generations of Wynchinghams had gone over this very spot. What was the use of expecting to find anything where they had failed?

She blew out the candle on the mantelpiece and picked up her own. It was too late now to worry about a book.

She crossed the hall and went slowly up the stairs.

It was pleasant to think that she had vanquished Claude and turned him out of the house, but all the same she could still see the expression on his face and hear the threat on his lips when he had said menacingly,

'*You have not seen the last of me*'.

CHAPTER SEVEN

Tina woke next morning with a sense of foreboding, as if a heavy cloud lay over her.

It was belied by the brilliant sunshine streaming in through the window.

She arose and looked out over the Park with the chestnut trees with their pink and white blossoms like candles pointing towards the blue sky, the bushes heavy with blossom and the rhododendrons reflected in the lake.

'Why,' she wondered, 'must everything that is lovely and made for happiness be overshadowed?'

It seemed to her as though Sir Marcus stood behind her with that confident expression on his face that she could not seem to forget.

She dressed hastily and went downstairs to learn that the Dowager had passed a bad night and was not to be disturbed before noon.

The butler also informed her that his Lordship was slightly better and hoped to receive visitors later in the morning.

Tina passed through the hall and out into the garden where she walked for a while beside the lake, watching the swans and wishing that she had brought some bread from her breakfast tray to feed them.

She must have walked about the garden for over an hour before a kind of restlessness, which was unusual to her, drove her back to the house.

She knew it was because, whatever else she tried to think of, her thoughts always returned to the same subject, to the future and the desperate ever encroaching problem of what choice she must make to save both herself and Lord Wynchingham.

She entered the house by a side door and, as she found her way back to the hall, she passed the open door of the sitting room and heard voices inside.

She stopped, wondering who could be calling at such an early hour and then she heard a man say,

"It will suit you well, Rapson, just the sort of place you have been looking for, isn't it?"

"It will, indeed, Mr. Lampton," the man answered. "And how soon do you anticipate I can take possession?"

There was a silence and then the first man, whom Tina now identified as Mr. Lampton, replied,

"Lord Wynchingham has under three weeks left in which to meet his debt to me, but, as I have already explained to you, it will be impossible for him to find the money. We share the same Solicitors and I have a very shrewd idea of his situation at the moment. Therefore as soon as he defaults, Wynch shall be yours, provided, of course, a bill of sale can be completed by then."

"It shall be ready," came the answer. "I can assure you, sir, that this is exactly the place I was looking for. In fact I might almost say the sort of place I have dreamed about."

Because the anger rising within Tina made her unusually courageous, she walked boldly through the door to face the two men who were standing at the far end of the room looking out onto the garden.

t was a room that she had not entered before, but she realised that it was an antechamber to the salon – the sort of room, she thought, that would be used for guests if the butler or the Major Domo, who had received them, was not quite certain where they should wait until they were received.

"Good morning, gentlemen," Tina said with a touch of ice in her voice.

Both men turned hastily.

She saw that Mr. Lampton was exactly as she had expected him to be, tall and middle-aged with the hard, dried-up calculating expression of the habitual gambler.

The other man, in contrast, was short, fat and, Tina guessed at a first glance, a self-made man from the North, the type of wealthy landowner who longed to come South and get into Society, believing he would cut more of a figure away from his old associates than living among those who knew too well about his humble beginnings.

Both gentlemen bowed and Tina dropped a small almost impertinent, curtsey.

"Can I be of any assistance?" she asked. "I expect you have already heard that Lord Wynchingham is indisposed and is not receiving visitors and his grandmother, the Dowager Duchess, has not yet risen."

"We must make our apologies for calling so early," Mr. Lampton said smoothly, "but my friend, Mr. Rapson, has to make a journey North this afternoon and was very anxious to enquire about Lord Wynchingham's health *en route*."

"I am sure that his Lordship will be most obliged for such consideration," Tina said sarcastically. "May I offer you some refreshment."

"The butler had already been kind enough to offer us the hospitality of the house," Mr. Lampton replied. "We both felt a glass of wine would be most welcome as we have been riding for over three hours."

"Indeed," said Tina. "Have you come from London? If so, what was the latest gossip? Or was it indeed too early for you to glean it?"

She saw the curiosity and speculation in Mr. Lampton's eyes.

He was finding it, she thought, very difficult to place her and she guessed that he had not heard of her appearance in Society or the fact that the Dowager had given the ball for her.

Banking on this, she asked,

"But I am mistaken, you have not come from London – you have been away, I think. I am almost certain that I heard someone mention your absence."

"I have indeed," he replied. "As it happens I have been staying in the North with my friend here, Mr. Rapson. He wished to see me on certain matters of business, so, although it was the middle of the Season, when I think London is at its best, I travelled to York, a long journey, but I must admit well worth the effort."

"Thank you!" Mr. Rapson smiled. "I am glad to have made you comfortable, but, as I explained to you, I have had reasons for wishing to live in the South these past five years."

"Yes, you told me," Mr Lampton said hastily, obviously feeling that Mr. Rapson had been too revealing in what he had to say.

"Then if you have been away," Tina said sweetly, "you have, of course, missed all the excitement that has been taking place at Wynchingham House."

"Excitement?" Mr. Lampton asked, his voice sharpening.

"Yes," Tina answered. "Of course it may not seem exciting to you, but my Guardian, Lord Wynchingham, has been introducing me to London and his grandmother, the Dowager Duchess of Hertingford, has been chaperoning me. They gave me the most wonderful ball. Indeed a great many people claimed that it was the best party they had ever known."

"A ball at Wynchingham House?" Mr. Lampton exclaimed in surprise.

"It was most elegantly done," Tina answered. "We sat down forty, or was it fifty to dinner, I really cannot remember. My eyes were so bewildered by the gold plate that decorated the table, the magnificent dishes that succeeded each other and, of course, the wines. They did not interest me particularly, but the gentlemen were in rhapsodies over them."

"That must have cost a pretty penny!" Mr. Lampton exclaimed almost beneath his breath.

Tina gave a little laugh.

"It was only the beginning of the evening. We had the finest orchestra in all London and the favours for the cotillions were quite fabulous."

By now she was drawing on her imagination.

She could see the look of incredulity growing on Mr. Lampton's face and continued,

"Everything was decorated, the gardens in the Square, the gardens at the back of the house and my gown. Oh, I wish I could describe my gown to you!"

"You say Lord Wynchingham gave you this ball?"

"He is my Guardian," Tina answered. "My father committed me to his care before he died."

She gave a little sigh and cast down her eyes.

"My poor father was so afraid that I should be tricked or pursued by men who could not be trusted, such as fortune-hunters, so he begged his dear friend, Lord Wynchingham, whom he had served in the Army with, to take care of me."

She raised her eyes to see the expression on Mr. Lampton's face and it almost made her laugh aloud.

"You are an heiress," he said bluntly and heavily.

Tina cast down her eyes again.

"I have always been told that one should never boast about one's possessions, sir," she answered repressively.

"That is quite right," Mr. Rapson interposed eagerly. "I have always said to my daughter and my son too, for that matter, 'never boast about what you possess, it doesn't make people admire you, it only makes them envious'."

"Ah, sir, you understand," Tina replied. "Your children are lucky to have such a wise father to guide and protect them. It is difficult when one is alone without father or mother, but I have been fortunate, very fortunate, in being able to depend on my Guardian."

"Look here," Mr. Lampton said almost roughly, "are you quite certain that Lord Wynchingham is not well enough to receive me? I would like to speak to him."

"I am afraid that is impossible," Tina answered. "He has had a fever and his physician has forbidden any visitors. Ah, here are the refreshments, which I hope, gentlemen, you will enjoy and not feel that your journey has been too wasted."

She watched with satisfaction Mr. Lampton drink a glass of wine glumly and without enjoyment.

Mr. Rapson, on the other hand, chatted away happily, admiring the furniture in the room, the picture over the mantelpiece and rhapsodising again and again about the view from the window.

"Just the sort of mansion I have always wanted," he finished.

With a little smile on her face Tina saw Mr. Lampton give him a sharp dig with his elbow that reduced him quickly to silence.

"Let's be on our way," Mr. Lampton said. "Please give my compliments to Lord Wynchingham and to Her Grace. Pray tell them how disappointed I am not to have been able to pay my respects in person."

"I will indeed give both of them your message," Tina said sedately. "The Dowager Duchess and I will be returning to London very shortly, I think. We have so many invitations to balls, routs, masques and parties that it would be a pity to stay away too long. Besides, as you gentlemen will understand, I have dozens of gowns waiting for me to fit and jewellery too. I wish that you could see the necklace my Guardian has promised me for my birthday. I declare, as I have already told him, it is fit for a Queen!"

She saw Mr. Lampton's lips tighten almost in a fury, watched him go headlong down the steps, mount his horse and ride off without a backward look.

On the other hand Mr. Rapson kept turning his head over his shoulder first to gaze at Tina and then to stare at the house with an almost awed expression on his plump face.

Tina watched them move out of sight and then with a smile on her lips gave a little sigh.

She might have scared off Mr. Lampton for the moment, but at the same time in less than three weeks he would know the true state of affairs.

The shadow was there crushing her, enveloping her until she fled from her own thoughts up the stairs and along the corridor that led to Lord Wynchingham's bedroom.

She knocked at the door, which, after a moment, was opened by Jarvis.

"Can I see his Lordship now?" Tina asked.

"Please to wait a moment, miss," he answered, half-closing the door.

Tina heard the murmur of voices and then Lord Wynchingham's voice, surprisingly strong,

"Come in, Tina. I was just going to send for you."

She entered and saw him propped up on the pillows.

His face was very pale as though it had been drained of blood, but the fever had gone from his eyes and the hand he held out to her was steady.

"Come and sit down," he said. "Tell me what has been happening. I feel as though I have just risen from the grave."

"You might have been in it," Tina said.

"Yes, yes, I know that," he answered and raising his voice said to his valet, "That will be all, Jarvis, for the moment. I will ring when I want you."

"Very well, my Lord," the valet answered and added with the familiarity of an old and tried servant, "Don't you be doin' too much, now. You're not all that strong either in your body or your head."

Lord Wynchingham laughed as the door closed behind Jarvis.

"He is right, you know," he said to Tina. "All yesterday I felt as mad as a March hare. I had the most absurd dreams, mostly about you."

"Have you any idea who would have shot you?" Tina asked.

He looked at her and his lips twitched.

"You know as well as I do who shot me. But what can we do about it? We cannot have a scandal in the family."

"I never thought he would be mad enough to try and do that sort of thing. And what do you think? I found him here last night."

"Claude – here last night?" Lord Wynchingham said. "What impertinence! Come here to find out if I was dead or not, I suppose."

"No, indeed," Tina answered. "He was very astonished to see me. He was seeking the treasure in the library."

"Oh, Lord! The man's more of a dolt than I believed him to be," Lord Wynchingham exclaimed. "He has been obsessed by that treasure ever since he was a child. He used to force me to go on looking for it long after I was bored with the search and longing to be doing something else. He has been over this house from attic to cellar, and considering Oliver Cromwell's troops and every succeeding generation of Wynchinghams have done the same thing, the chances against our finding fourpence are about ten million to one."

"Claude believes in it," Tina pointed out.

"Claude believes that money is always going to drop on him from Heaven," Lord Wynchingham answered. "If the silly clot only knew it, by shooting me he is not going to be a penny the richer."

"We must not tell him that," Tina answered. "He will talk and then your creditors in London will be after you."

"What do you know about my creditors in London?" Lord Wynchingham asked.

Tina told him how they had come to Berkeley Square as soon as the news was out that he had been shot.

"Damn their impertinence!" Lord Wynchingham exclaimed. "They are just like vultures, not even waiting till a chap's decently in his coffin before they start snatching at his possessions."

"Mr. Greychurch got rid of them," Tina went on.

"Three cheers for old Greychurch. He is not such a dried up collection of bones as he looks," Lord Wynchingham smiled.

"But what are we going to do?" Tina asked, her voice suddenly pathetic. "All those men waiting to pounce on you! And then there is Mr. Lampton already selling the house over your head."

"Lampton's doing *what?*" Lord Wynchingham almost shouted. "What are you talking about?"

Tina, relating what had happened just before she came upstairs, saw him flush with anger and strive to prop himself higher up on his pillows.

"Curse him! How dare he assume I am beaten before I am actually out for the count!" He let out a stream of oaths that made Tina put her fingers to her ears. *Blast his soul in Hell*," he finished. "I'll not live to see him handing over Wynch to some outsider without a by-my-leave or thank you."

"It is what he intends to do," Tina answered, "unless we can stop him – we have to stop him!"

"In other words we have to pay him," Lord Wynchingham said. "What are you going to do about it? Why are you down here? Damn it, you are not going to find millionaires dropping down the chimney or lurking in the Park. Get back to London!"

Tina laughed.

"As a matter of fact we were rather worried about you," she said.

"I was worried about myself if it comes to that," Lord Wynchingham answered. "I know full well that if I die now I not only hand Wynch and everything I possess over to that swine, Lampton, but I leave you in the cart. In my dreams I saw people snatching your gowns away from you. Yes, I remember now. The man who was trying to pull off the one you wore at the ball had a face rather like Lampton's."

"It was only a dream, but we both know it might come true."

"Then save us, Tina! for God's sake save us both!" Lord Wynchingham exclaimed.

He lay back against his pillows suddenly exhausted.

"I never really believe in this bird-brained scheme of yours," he murmured, "but now it seems the only solution. What else can we do except find you a wealthy husband?"

"There is nothing else," Tina replied quietly.

She rose from beside the bed and walked across the room.

She stood at the open casement looking out into the sunshine.

From this room there was a different view from any other she had seen before.

Here the gardens sloped gradually upwards to a long grass walk bordered with trees and shrubs, at the far end of which, quite a long way from the house, there was an exquisite little Grecian Temple standing silhouetted against a crescent of poplar trees. It was so lovely and so ethereal that for a moment Tina forgot her own troubles.

"How lovely the Temple is!" she cried.

"It was erected to Aphrodite, the Goddess of Love, by one of my ancestors," Lord Wynchingham told her and then added, in a kind of frenzy, "Love! What is the point of talking about such nonsense. What we want is money? Money for me! Money for you and for Wynch! Money to throw in the face of that smirking devil Lampton."

For a moment Tina let him rage, hardly hearing the anger in his voice, her eyes on the little Temple of Love. Standing there white and pure in the sunlight, unrelated to the troubles, struggles and miseries of mankind, it seemed like something out of a storybook.

Then deliberately she turned away from the window and went back towards the bed.

"All right," she said. "We have to concentrate on money. There is nothing else we can do."

"Did no one offer for you at the ball?" Lord Wynchingham enquired.

"I suppose that you would call it an offer," Tina replied.

"From whom?" he asked eagerly.

"Sir Marcus Welton," she told him and felt her voice quiver as she said the name.

"Welton indeed! Well, he is rich enough, though I cannot say he is a chap I have ever taken to particularly."

"Is he really rich?" Tina asked, hoping almost against hope that the answer would be 'no'.

"I believe he has untold millions," Lord Wynchingham said lightly. "He has always thrown money about as though it was water. They say the Prince of Wales borrows from him incessantly."

"There is something about him, I don't quite know what, that frightens me," Tina said almost beneath her breath.

"He is rich," Lord Wynchingham said quickly. "That is what matters, isn't it? Although he is not a man you will be able to lead by the nose. You might marry him and he would refuse to cough up."

"I would not marry anyone until they had fulfilled the conditions that I shall make, before they put the ring on my finger," Tina said.

Lord Wynchingham looked at her admiringly.

"You have more courage than half the men I know," he said. "When I first saw you, I thought you were pretty, but too pretty for reality, if you know what I mean, the sort of girl who would swoon away if things were difficult or if there was the slightest smell of danger."

"You forget I am a soldier's daughter/"

"Dammit, I believe your father would be proud of you."

He saw the colour come into her face and a sudden glow into her eyes.

"We have not won through yet," she said quickly. "All the same I have the uncomfortable feeling that Sir Marcus will be calling to see you."

There was a hint of despair in her voice and an expression in the darkness of her eyes that made Lord Wynchingham say quickly,

" You hate him, don't you?"

"He repels me," Tina answered. "I don't know why."

"Then we shall have to find someone else," Lord Wynchingham said quickly.

"But is there time?"

"Not if you continue to sit here chattering to me about Wynch," he replied. "Dig my grandmother out of her bed and make her take you back to London."

Tina shook her head.

"We cannot go today. We have arranged to stay until Tuesday at any rate. We thought by then that you might be well enough to travel with us."

The hours are passing," Lord Wynchingham said. "Think of it, twenty-four hours today, twenty-four hours tomorrow, all time wasted when you might be ingratiating yourself with someone rich and attractive."

"I don't believe that the two things go together," Tina said.

"Fustian!" Lord Wynchingham retorted. "There must be heaps of men."

"There is Lord Alfred Cartright," Tina said tentatively.

"Lord Alfred!" Lord Wynchingham exclaimed. "I suppose I forgot to tell you, in fact I know I did because I only heard it just a few minutes before I was shot. Lord Alfred is not as rich as we had thought. His estates are pledged and I believe that he is looking for a rich wife."

Tina giggled.

"You mean he was doing a little fortune-hunting when he was paying attention to me? "

"Exactly," Lord Wynchingham said. "What a disillusionment if you had accepted him and then he found that he had a pretty but penniless wife on his hands, when he expected an heiress."

Tina suddenly put her hands up to her face.

"Oh, it is all so sordid, so horrible!" she cried. "I feel as though I am an animal in the cattle market. I feel soiled and degraded."

As she spoke she felt the tears rush to her eyes.

She would have risen from her chair and gone from the room had not Lord Wynchingham reached out swiftly as she rose and caught hold of her wrist.

"Let me go," she cried, almost incoherently.

"No," he replied. "Listen to me, Tina. Now listen carefully."

Her head was turned away from him and she fought to control her tears. He held her firmly by the wrist and gave her arm a little jerk.

"Listen, Tina," he repeated. "If it upsets you so much, we will call the whole thing off. I will face up to things as you know I ought to have done at the very first. I will sell everything that is saleable and hand Wynch over to Lampton. I might be able to salvage enough to give you a small amount of money. It won't be much, you know, when I have paid the creditors, but somehow I will manage. It was a crazy idea from the very first and, let's be honest, you talked me into it."

"Yes, I talked you into it," Tina agreed.

"And I will talk you out of it," Lord Wynchingham said kindly. "Don't cry, Tina. I am not worth it. You will manage somehow if I can find you a few hundreds. And anyway my grandmother likes you, she won't let you starve."

"What will happen to you?" Tina asked.

"I will go abroad," Lord Wynchingham replied. "There are lots of fools like me drifting about on the Continent, picking up a living somehow. I might even join the French Army. I believe the King is short of good soldiers and he might even welcome me."

Tina had to laugh through her tears.

"You are talking rubbish," she said. "Can you picture yourself strutting about in French uniform or on sentry duty at Versailles?"

"Don't worry about me," Lord Wynchingham said. "I will find something, even if I have to become the *cher ami* of some ageing Duchesse."

"We are only pretending such things are possible," Tina said a little uneasily, turning her face to him for the first time so that he could see the tears glistening on her dark lashes. "We have chosen the only sensible, in fact the only practicable course, and we are not going to fail Wynch or each other now."

"But you are having to do something you hate. You are making the greatest sacrifice. I promise you this, Tina, if I could do something for you, I would. I don't know any rich women and if I did they would not marry me."

"I am afraid your reputation has made you suspect," Tina said. "It's the only advantage I have found so far of being a nobody from nowhere, one can make all sorts of statements and no one is knowledgeable enough to contradict one."

"What do you mean by that?" he asked.

She told him then how she had made Mr. Lampton believe that she was a great heiress and how he had left the house in dismay.

"Blast him! He doesn't want the money!" Lord Wynchingham said. "I have always known that what he really wants is to humiliate me, to see me disgraced and cast out of Society. It would be his revenge and I believe that he has been cogitating over it for a long time."

"Do you think he cheated you?" Tina asked.

Lord Wynchingham shook his head.

"Mr. Lampton is too careful for that. He waited until I was really foxed and then he needled me into diving deeper and deeper into the pit he had dug for me. My God! I am a fool! I don't deserve any sympathy and I know it only too well."

"We all make mistakes," Tina murmured.

"Mistakes!" he almost shouted at her. "I have been lying here, looking round the room at all my possessions and realising for the first time what they mean to me. I have been looking out of the window at the trees, remembering how I climbed them as a child, listening to the cluck of the pheasants, knowing that they are all part of my memories of Wynch, of my childhood and of the days when I was so happy here before I went to London. How could I have wanted any other sort of life?"

He looked at Tina despairingly and added,

"Sometimes I think that there must be a streak of insanity in the family and that I have inherited it."

There was so much feeling in his voice that Tina feared his temperature might rise again.

"Don't worry about it now," she said soothingly, "it will not seem so frighteningly overpowering when you are up again. It is when one is ill and feeling low that one has no courage to face anything."

Lord Wynchingham suddenly closed his eyes,

"I am sorry, Tina, I am being such a brute to you and you are so understanding – "

His hold slackened on her wrist and after a moment his hand dropped on the bed.

She stood very still, looking down at him and in a few seconds she realised that he had fallen asleep, the heavy deep sleep of utter exhaustion.

He looked very young with his head tousled, his eyes closed and she wondered how she had ever been afraid of him. He was young and vulnerable and foolish. Was he a man who had made a hideous mistake? Or perhaps only a boy who had been bemused by the grandeur and perhaps the evil of London?

He was breathing rhythmically and she moved very softly from the bed and across the room to stand for a moment at the window, looking up the long green avenue towards the Temple.

She wondered if generations of Wynchinghams had looked at it and thought of the Goddess to whom it had been erected.

The whole house seemed redolent of love – cupids in the salon, the Temple in the garden, the great four-posters in every room whose curtains could be drawn to hide the happiness of lovers from the prying eyes of the world.

Tina gave herself a little shake.

She herself must not confuse the issue with thoughts of anything but money.

Money, money, money!

The words began once again to repeat themselves over and over in her mind as she turned from the window and tiptoed across the room to the door.

She opened it softly and found Jarvis standing outside, touchingly faithful in his devotion to his Master's needs.

"His Lordship is asleep," Tina told him.

"He's been talkin' for far too long," Jarvis replied.

"I know," Tina answered, "but I don't think that it can have done him any harm, at least I hope not."

"He has come to enough harm already, if you asks me." Jarvis said almost surlily. "I have warned his Lordship over and over again about Mr. Claude.

"'He'll have you, my Lord,' I said, 'you mark my words', but all his Lordship has ever done is laugh at me."

"Does everybody think it was Mr. Claude who did it?" Tina enquired.

"Who else stands to gain anythin' by his Lordship's death?" the valet asked with irrefutable logic. "But I will tell you somethin', miss, there isn't any of them that works at Wynch as would stay here with Mr. Claude. He's a bad one, that's what he is."

"I am afraid I agree with you, Jarvis," Tina answered.

She walked away down the corridor.

She had only just reached the top of the stairs when she heard the sound of voices in the hall below and, looking over the banisters, saw a man come in through the front door.

He handed his hat and riding whip to one of the footmen and stood, divesting himself slowly of his gloves.

Tina's heart gave a frightened leap.

There was no mistaking the square shoulders and the aggressive carriage of the man's head.

She did not need the confirmation of who the new visitor was when she heard the butler say suavely,

"Will you come this way, Sir Marcus. I will find out if Her Grace will receive you."

Just for a moment Tina felt like panicking.

She had a wild desire to run away and hide in her bedroom, to lock the door and refuse to meet him.

Then even as she pulled herself together and fought to control the beating of her heart, she heard a rustle of silk behind her and turned to see the Dowager coming from her bedroom outrageously dressed as usual in an orange silk gown over a gold lamé petticoat, her wig a masterpiece of the coiffeur's art, her face painted above a veritable cascade of glittering jewels.

"Ah, Tina, my child!" the Dowager exclaimed smiling. "I was hoping to see you. I hear my grandson is better. There is nothing of any consequence to keep us longer at Wynch. I declare I always have the megrims in the country and the pollen from the flowers has kept me sneezing my head off half the morning."

"It's lovely outside, ma'am," Tina protested.

"Boring, child, boring! You and I need amusements, gaiety, invitations and, of course, men! I have already decided that we will return to London tomorrow. My grandson can follow us as soon as he is out of the physician's hands."

The Dowager paused and glanced towards the stairs and the butler approaching.

"What is it, Saintley?" she asked.

Tina had the impression, as she spoke, that the Dowager knew all along what Saintley had come to say and was indeed amused and intrigued by the fact that it was Sir Marcus, and that she and Tina were not doomed to be alone for luncheon.

"Sir Marcus Welton has called," the butler replied. "He hopes that Your Grace will receive him."

"I shall be delighted to do so," she answered. She looked Tina up and down, "You look dishevelled, child. Your hair is blown by the wind and, I declare, your skirts are slightly creased. Go and change, put on an elegant gown, then come and show these blades from London we need not look countrified even if we must seek peace and quiet away from the *Beau Monde*."

Tina said nothing.

The Dowager turned towards the stairs and then she looked back with a sudden kindly expression on her face.

"Run along, child," she said, "and don't look so miserable. Whatever you may feel about him, he is only a man, and a man can always be forced to his knees which indeed is the right place for him!"

"I will go and change."

She heard the Dowager chuckle as she swept downstairs and wondered what was amusing the old lady.

She herself felt very like crying – crying for something that she knew was utterly and completely out of reach.

CHAPTER EIGHT

Tina stood at the window of her bedroom in Berkeley Square and watched an old man turning the handle of a hurdy-gurdy while a monkey in a red coat danced on the pavement and held out a minute cup towards those passing by.

It was a dull cloudy day and she felt that the weather matched her mood.

She tried to remember her first feelings of excitement when he had come to Berkeley Square, journeying from the North by herself and feeling, with the bravery of youth, quite unabashed at the hazards and difficulties of the journey and yet now, only a short time later, she was depressed and frightened not only of the future but of herself.

It had been an unpleasant journey from Wynch to Berkeley Square because the Dowager was in one of her moods, berating Abdul, finding fault with the servants, complaining about the coach and altogether behaving as only a spoilt and autocratic old lady could.

Tina had had the feeling that in Wynch she was leaving everything that mattered and was going towards an unknown destination and even an unknown set of circumstances that she anticipated with dread.

She tried to tell herself that she was being ridiculous.

After all Sir Marcus was not the only man in the world and in London she would have a chance of meeting a selection of eligible husbands and one of them, she tried to comfort herself, was certain to offer for her.

She knew that all this was wishful thinking.

The point was that time was running out and she knew that the very latest when she dared to make a decision was at the end of the week.

That would leave exactly two weeks in which to announce her betrothal and arrange her marriage. It was an almost impossible task, for people liked to take their time when anything so important and so fundamental as a Wedding was concerned.

Already Tina was racking her brains as to what excuse she could make for speed. Perhaps, she told herself, she could pretend her father had only recently died and she was, therefore in mourning, but then she realised that that would seem absurd in the face of the balls she was attending and the routs she was eagerly accepting invitations for.

Surely, surely, it need not be Sir Marcus?

And yet who else was there? Who could be persuaded to come up to scratch at such short notice?

She told herself that she had not been given time to think. A few days in London and one ball, and yet even in that short time she had captivated a rich and eligible suitor.

"Don't look so miserable," Lord Wynchingham had admonished her when she had gone to his room to say 'goodbye'. "No man has ever wanted to wed a dismal sobersides. Smile, girl, and the bucks will come flocking round you."

He spoke roughly with a kind of brusqueness that to her consternation made the tears prick her eyes.

"It is very easy for you to criticise," she retorted hotly as they were alone in the room. "But I have to marry the man who asks me. I cannot pick and choose."

"That has been the way of the world since Adam," Lord Wynchingham replied almost petulantly. "There is no use feeling sore at a convention that cannot be altered."

"I am sorry," Tina said, suddenly contrite, "but I dislike Sir Marcus. He has bamboozled the Dowager with his flattery and the smooth side of his tongue, but I am sure that there is another side to him. Nevertheless we are to dine with him tonight at Vauxhall Gardens."

"Why the hell can I not accompany you?" Lord Wynchingham exclaimed, moving restlessly and wincing as the movement hurt his bandaged shoulder.

"I wish you could," Tina sighed.

She moved from his bedside across the room to look up the long grass vista to the little Temple.

Somehow the sight of it soothed her, it was so imperturbable, standing there white against the green background interspersed with sudden patches of gold from the laburnum trees whose golden blossoms hung from the delicate branches like necklaces.

"I will be up in another forty-eight hours," Lord Wynchingham said behind her. "These damned doctors are not going to keep me lying here one moment longer than I can help."

"It is nonsensical to be in too much of a hurry," Tina told him.

But she felt her heart lighten a little at the thought that if Lord Wynchingham was there Sir Marcus would not seem quite so overwhelming.

"What did he say to you?" Lord Wynchingham asked.

There was no need for either of them to ask who he was referring to.

"All the usual collection of compliments and blandishments," Tina answered. "One can never believe anything he says, because his eyes belie his mouth. It is indeed his eyes that make him so frightening. They are bold – possessive – and – oh, I cannot explain."

"*Blast him in Hades*!" Lord Wynchingham said. "I cannot think why the only man who is attracted by you has to be someone I have always disliked, an outsider I have never wanted in my house."

"It's not fair to say that he is the only man," Tina said in a piqued tone. "After all, there was no time at the ball to get to know many people and then having to come down here obviously prevented those who might have called on me from doing so."

"All right! All right!" Lord Wynchingham replied testily. "I was not casting aspersions on your attractions, only bewailing the fact that it had to be Marcus Welton. He has never really been up to snuff."

"And yet he is rich," Tina whispered almost beneath her breath.

She heard Lord Wynchingham give a groan and, forgetting her own troubles, she ran to his bedside.

"Is your wound hurting you?" she asked. "Is there anything I can do?"

He looked up at her and she fancied that there was an appeal in his eyes.

"There are worse things than pain," he said darkly. "I am ashamed that having got you into this I cannot stand by you at this moment. If you have to go to Vauxhall with him, at least I should be there to see he is not up to any of his damnable tricks."

"What sort of tricks?" Tina asked anxiously.

"I don't suppose he is worse than many other fellows or any worse than I am if it comes to that," Lord Wynchingham replied. "Dark corners in the gardens or the backs of the boxes always seem to create the right atmosphere when you are with a pretty girl. I don't suppose that I have to explain to you what I mean."

'That is just what he should do,' Tina thought, realising in her innocence and ignorance the surprises she had encountered in her first week in Society when she had been utterly at a loss to know what to expect.

But Lord Wynchingham's worried expression prevented her from probing further.

She said quietly,

"Don't worry yourself. I am assured that it will not be as bad as you anticipate and, as you say, you will be with us in a day or so."

She spoke lightly and thought that the frown on his Lordship's face faded a little.

Yet now that she and the Dowager were back at Berkeley Square, she knew that she missed him more than she could express in words even to herself.

She told herself it was because she wanted someone to talk to, someone who knew the truth, someone with whom she need not keep up this absurd pretence of being an heiress.

Not once but a dozen times a day the Dowager referred to her money.

"Have you any idea how much you have, dear? It would be nice to give the fortune-hunters and the match-making Mamas something tangible to whet their curiosity with."

It was such remarks as these that made Tina long over and over again to blurt out the truth and reply,

'I am poor and penniless. If I don't find myself a husband, I shall be forced to seek employment."

She could almost see the expression of astonishment, incredulity and finally horror on the Dowager's face.

And if the great world was also let into the secret of her perfidy, Tina knew all too well that the baskets of flowers in the hall, the invitations piled high on the marble tables and the continual callers at Berkeley Square would cease automatically.

It was extraordinary that, although they had only been in the house for an hour or so, the word had been passed round St. James's and the knocker was busy rolling out a rat-tat that could be heard all over the Square.

"This is an invitation from the Duchess of Devonshire," the Dowager said with satisfaction as she opened a crested envelope.

"Her ball is one you most certainly must not miss! Not that I really approve of the way that Georgina is gambling night after night, while that crafty Lady Elizabeth Foster makes eyes at the Duke. Still, no one who is anyone would miss a party at Devonshire House and you must have a new gown for the occasion."

"Oh, no, ma'am, surely I have enough gowns," Tina protested, knowing only too well that she would be overruled and yet another bill would be added to the mounting pile of debts.

She hoped all the afternoon that it would rain really hard and they would not be able to go to Vauxhall, but, although the sky was overcast, it was still fine and she knew that behind her, lying on the bed, was one of her exquisite new gowns waiting for her to don it and go downstairs to dazzle Sir Marcus Welton.

She had an insane desire to put on the dress she had arrived in and to leave her hair unpowdered and to make herself look as unattractive as possible.

Then she remembered that it was when she had first arrived that Sir Marcus had noticed her!

With a sudden perception that even a few days in Society had brought her, she guessed that Sir Marcus really fancied young and innocent girls, who would fall for his blandishments and would not be so hard to seduce as older or more experienced young women.

Even as she thought of this, Tina had a sudden throb of anxiety.

Suppose after all she had misunderstood him. Perhaps marriage was the last thing he was going to offer, but instead his interest was in hunting her down and making her his possession in fact if not in name.

For a moment she felt panic-stricken at the thought and then remembered that even Sir Marcus would not dare to play such a trick on a protégé of the Dowager or on the Ward of Lord Wynchingham.

No, he would offer marriage and unless some miracle happened to save her she would have to accept him.

Listlessly and without interest she allowed the maids to dress her.

The Dowager's own Abigail came to put the finishing touches to her hair and when at last, half-sulkily, she looked into the mirror, she had to admit that the result was overwhelmingly successful, even though she almost resented the fact.

"*Qu'elle est ravissante!*" the Dowager's maid exclaimed and the other maids pulling out the silken skirts of her gown echoed the remark in the broad accents of the Counties they came from.

"Thank you all," Tina said sweetly, picking up her reticule, which matched her gown and walked downstairs to the Red Salon where she knew that the Dowager would be waiting.

Despite her mood of depression, she could not help feeling in some ways enchanted by being turned from the dull and untidy schoolgirl into the exquisite creature in lace and satins with powdered hair and sparkling jewels which she could see reflected in the gilt mirrors in the hall.

Two footmen opened the doors for Tina as she swept into the room to find quite a congregation of people waiting for her. They were all friends of Sir Marcus, for he had asked the Dowager if they might meet at Berkeley Square before proceeding to Vauxhall.

The women were all exquisitely dressed, but hardly outshone the men in their colourful satin coats and lace cravats.

The Dowager herself outdid everyone in a gown of yellow brocade. A piece of the same material had made a coat for Abdul, who stood stolidly beside her holding her reticule and supporting a turban in which a yellow aigrette was held in place by a topaz and diamond brooch.

"Your pardon, ma'am, if I am late," Tina said feeling suddenly shy as all the guests turned their eyes upon her.

"One is always prepared to await the arrival of Persephone," Sir Marcus said and Tina thought that he looked not unlike the Prince of Hades himself coming from the underworld as he bent over her hand to kiss it and his dark plum-coloured velvet coat seemed to cast a sombre note among the brighter creations of his friends.

Yet his buttons sparkled with huge diamonds and there was a magnificent stone in his cravat and another in a signet ring on his little finger.

'Rich! rich! rich!' the words seemed to be whispered in the air all around her and Tina pulled her fingers from his as if the touch of his lips against her bare skin was almost too repulsive to be borne. As always he seemed quite unperturbed by her lack of encouragement.

Instead, his eyes rested on her in a manner that she could only describe to herself as triumphant.

"There are eight coaches," Sir Marcus announced. "Now how shall we journey?"

Tina held her breath waiting for him to suggest that she should accompany him, but Sir Marcus was far too cunning to be so obvious.

Instead he gave his arm to the Dowager.

"No one will outshine Your Grace tonight," he said suavely, "and may I say how proud I am to be your escort?"

"You may say it," the Dowager replied, "and I shall try to believe it. A woman is never too old to listen to pleasant things even though she knows that the gentleman who says them is a jackanape who has some ulterior motive behind his honeyed tones."

Her shrewd old eyes looked up at Sir Marcus, but instead of being put out he laughed down at her.

"We understand each other," he said and with her hand resting on his arm escorted her towards the door.

Tina found herself partnered by a rather serious-faced young man, who told her that his father had just bought him a Commission in the Army.

"You will enjoy it?" she asked him.

He shook his head.

"It will bore me to tears," he replied. "There is not likely to be any fighting, the only thing that really interests me is war."

"How can you be certain that peace will last?" Tina enquired.

"I am praying it will not," he replied, "but war, even a small one, is too much to hope for. Our Diplomats are getting far too experienced these days. They talk instead of 'doing battle'."

"I prefer it that way," Tina answered, thinking of how her father had suffered from his wounds in America and how nearly Lord Wynchingham had been killed.

She came to the conclusion that the Officer and the other couple in the coach were bores long before they reached Vauxhall Gardens.

But after they arrived she made no effort to listen to anyone's conversation.

The garden, the bands playing softly, the great rotunda, the boxes filled with elegant and distinguished guests all took her breath away. She sat almost open-mouthed, listening to the entertainment.

A soprano sang like a nightingale.

There were conjurors. tumblers and many other amusements for the delectation of those who paid to see and hear them.

There were all kinds of delicious food, but Tina was too interested in everything to realise what she was eating and all too soon dinner was over and Sir Marcus proposed that they should walk a little and look at the sights before proceeding homewards.

Afterwards Tina was never quite certain how it all happened. Suddenly she found herself in a flowery arbour, lit only with fairy lights, alone with Sir Marcus.

She had been so interested in what was going on around her and what she was seeing that she could not imagine how she had managed to become detached from the Dowager and the rest of the party.

Tina looked around her apprehensively, saying in a voice that had a sudden touch of fear in it,

"We must have lost your friends. Let's retrace our steps and see if we can find them."

"I expect they will contrive to manage quite well without us," Sir Marcus replied in an amused tone.

"I am sure they cannot be far," Tina said quickly.

"In which case we need not worry about them," Sir Marcus answered as he put his arm through hers and drew her to a seat in an arbour cunningly made from a thick hedge of roses and honeysuckle.

The seat was comfortable and, although she wanted to protest, Tina felt that it would be undignified to do so.

She sat down gingerly, her back very straight, her heart beating a little quickly because she was afraid.

"I will not eat you," Sir Marcus said quietly.

"No, of course not."

Tina forced herself to laugh, but found it impossible to meet his eyes. His face was too close to hers and he was looking at her intently.

"You are very lovely and very young," he said, his voice suddenly deep.

As Tina sought for a reply, he added,

"But not too young to misunderstand me. I want you. Why should we play all the conventional game of retreat and advance, advance and retreat?"

"I do not think, sir, I quite understand what you are trying to say," Tina said, looking across the garden and praying that someone would come by whom she knew and recognised.

"I think you do. When are you going to marry me?"

Tina's heart gave a sudden lurch.

"It's too soon to talk about marriage," she said primly. "We have only just become acquainted."

"I am a man of quick decision," Sir Marcus answered. "I knew when I first saw you gliding across the pavement in Berkeley Square that you were a girl I wanted to know, a girl whom I intended to know very very well."

"But that was only a few days ago," Tina reminded him.

"Long enough to know what I want and what I intend to have," he answered. "The Dowager favours my suit, she has told me so. I will deal with your Guardian as soon as he is well enough to listen to me. Why then must we jump through the hoops?"

"I think," said Tina quickly, "that we should go and find the others. The Dowager will think it strange that I have disappeared alone with you."

She rose to her feet, but found herself held prisoner as his hand clamped down on her slender wrist.

"The Dowager will understand," he persisted. "Listen to me for a moment instead of worrying about other things. You are young, you are frightened and you want to be wooed. Very well, I will woo you, but it's a waste of time. We might just as well get married and let me do my courting afterwards."

At the back of her mind Tina knew that this was what she had been asking for – a man who was prepared to scrap the preliminaries and to marry in under a fortnight so that she could save both herself and Lord Wynchingham.

Yet somehow she could not force herself to accept what should have seemed a providential offer just when she most needed it.

Like an animal in a trap she tried feverishly to find some method of escape and some way to play for time.

"I-I don't know – what to say," she managed to stammer at last.

"Why not leave it to me to make the decisions?" Sir Marcus asked.

She felt his arm go round her waist and now, to her horror, she felt him draw her close to him.

There was no one about only the distant sound of music to tell her that she was not entirely alone and isolated with this man whose presence seemed so overpowering.

She strove to escape the inevitable, but her hands went out ineffectually against the soft velvet of his evening coat.

Now his arm encircled her completely and with his free hand he lifted her tiny pointed chin upwards.

"No! *No!*" she whispered, hardly able to breathe the words because she seemed to be stifled by the fierceness of her revulsion.

Then his lips were on hers, thick, hot, greedy lips, as she had known they would be, almost from the first moment she had seen him.

She felt herself struggle as ineffectively as a kitten might struggle in a bucket of water that it was being drowned in.

She wanted to cry out at the horror and bestiality of it, but her voice died in her throat.

She could only submit abjectly and with a feeling of utter humiliation to the pressure of his mouth and the strength of his hands.

Then she made a violent effort to free herself, but knew that her weakness was so complete that she could only feel as though she was being swept down into the dark depths of a sea and there was no escape.

Down, down, down – and his mouth was sucking her soul from between her lips and into his keeping.

He was afire with desire for her.

She could feel him overwhelming her and she was trying to save herself – trying – trying –

'*God help me*!'

Somewhere far away a child was praying and she did not realise that it was herself.

She felt his fingers fumbling with the laces at her breast and then, suddenly, with a strength she did not know she possessed, she fought him off, kicking and scratching and taking him by surprise, so that for a moment his grip on her relaxed.

"No! No! *No*!"

She tried to scream the word aloud and knew that the only sound she made was that of her breath coming in a frightened gasp from between her bruised lips.

She heard her gown tear as she ran down the dark path, through a crowd of merry-makers and on, madly, wildly, not knowing where she went, only anxious to be free of some fiend who had frightened her as she had never been frightened before.

She was sobbing and almost exhausted when finally she came to a halt.

She had no idea where she was. She only knew that she could no longer hear the music and she seemed to be alone in some dark maze of yew hedges.

She leant for a moment against a tree, striving to still the tempestuous heaving of her small breasts beneath the tight bodice the maids had laced her into.

Tina was so insensitive to anything but her own terror that when someone spoke to her she started with a sudden jerk because she had not heard him approach.

"Can I be of any assistance, madam?" a man's voice asked.

She turned apprehensively to find a young man standing beside her.

He was neatly but not over-fashionably dressed and she guessed that he was not a gentleman but some respectable clerk or shopkeeper out for a night's enjoyment.

With an effort Tina pulled herself together.

"I am – a-afraid, sir," she managed to say, "I have – lost my way."

"It's a very easy thing to do in these gardens," he replied. "Can I be of assistance in finding your party or your carriage?"

"I am – indisposed," Tina answered. "Would it be possible, sir, for me to hire a carriage – to take me home? I do not wish to spoil my – f-friends' enjoyment by asking them to – accompany me."

The young man frowned.

"It is possible," he said, "but it is not particularly desirable for a lady of quality to travel alone. There are footpads about at night and many other dangers."

"Nevertheless, I am prepared – to risk them," Tina insisted.

"Then allow me to escort you," the young man said politely.

Tina looked at him searchingly.

There was something about him that she felt she could trust and, even if not, she would rather, at the moment, be with him than with Sir Marcus.

"I would not wish, sir, to put you to – any inconvenience."

"It would be a pleasure, ma'am," he replied.

They moved from the darkness of the yew hedges into a lit way that led to an outer gate, a different one from the one they had arrived at.

He found a carriage and helped her into it and waited for her to give him her address. She told him where to go and saw an expression of surprise on his face before he climbed in beside her.

Tina made herself very small in the corner of the carriage.

She was wondering whether she had been over-rash and certainly over-credulous in accepting a perfect stranger as companion.

Suppose he were a thief or, much more likely, a seducer out to take his fun wherever he might find it.

And then, as he settled himself back on the seat beside her, Tina knew that her fears were unfounded.

The man who had befriended her might not be a gentleman by birth, but he was certainly one by nature.

They drove back to the West End and Tina learnt that she had not been mistaken in her first assumption – the young man was a clerk in the Admiralty. He had not been in London long, having lived in the country all his life and having attained his post through an uncle who had influence.

"I am not enamoured of this City," he told Tina. "There is much that is bad and evil about it. A man can take care of himself, but you, ma'am, must be more careful. I would not wish to see any sister of mine alone in Vauxhall Gardens at night."

"You have been – very kind to me," Tina answered. "How can I – thank you?"

"I can only hope that I shall have the pleasure of being of service on another occasion," her deliverer answered.

She learnt that his name was Robert Watson and he had just attained his twenty-first birthday.

She gave him her hand to kiss when they reached Berkeley Square and would have liked to offer to pay for the hire of the coach, fearing that he could not afford it.

But she knew intuitively that it would hurt his pride and she thought that he would gain stature in his own eyes for having travelled with what he believed to be a member of the aristocracy.

"Thank you again, sir," she said, curtseying, as two footmen hurried to open the door of the coach and she saw Mr. Watson glance in a somewhat awed manner at their livery and the brightly lit hall behind them.

He drove off in the carriage, but she was certain that he would not have gone a hundred yards before he stopped the coach, paid his dues and walked the rest of the way home.

'I understand the ways of the poor better than those of the rich,' she told herself.

Tina went into the house only to find the butler looking at her with a surprised expression.

"You are alone, ma'am?" he enquired.

"Oh, oh, yes, I am," Tina answered, suddenly remembering how strange her appearance must be. "I did not feel well and did not wish to incommode Her Grace by telling her that I wanted to return. Please convey my apologies when Her Grace returns."

The butler bowed and Tina went upstairs to her bedroom, but she did not undress, feeling that the evening was not yet over and that she was likely to receive both reproaches and accusations before she could finally go to sleep.

She was not wrong.

Half an hour later there was a peremptory message from the Dowager asking her to descend immediately and that she and Sir Marcus were awaiting her in the Red Salon.

Tina went slowly downstairs.

She felt rather like a schoolgirl being summoned to the Headmistress's study. She knew that she had behaved badly in deserting the party without an explanation – at the same time she felt that there was nothing else she could have done in the circumstances.

She had a sudden longing for someone to protect her and she wished that Lord Wynchingham were there.

He at least would have understood and almost whimsically she thought that Mr. Robert Watson had deserted her too soon.

A footman opened the door to the Red Salon and she walked in, feeling very small and insignificant – a child rather than a grown-up young lady dressed in the height of fashion.

Sir Marcus was standing in front of the fireplace and the Dowager was sitting on the sofa.

She gave a little cry as Tina appeared.

"Gracious, child. I swear that I never expected to see you alive and in the flesh. We imagined you had been abducted and carried away by cutthroats or footpads. How could you have left us so apprehensive and so upset with anxiety about you?"

This was not so much a reproval as concern and instantly Tina ran forward, her heart touched by the genuine warmth in the Dowager's voice.

"Oh, ma'am," she said bending her head to kiss the Dowager's old parchment-like fingers.

"Forgive me, I beg of you. I did not mean to upset you – in any way. It was just that I got lost and – a kind gentleman brought me home."

"I have never heard of such a thing!" Sir Marcus spoke almost in a voice of thunder. "Trusting yourself to a stranger, to a man you have never met before. You must be demented. Her Grace has been nearly distraught with anxiety and I myself have searched Vauxhall Gardens from one end to the other."

"Please – forgive me," Tina said in a low voice speaking not to Sir Marcus but to the Dowager.

"There is nothing to forgive, child," she said. "You doubtless had your reasons."

She turned to Sir Marcus.

"Goodnight, Sir Marcus," she addressed him, holding out her hand imperiously. "It has been a pleasant evening and we are grateful for your hospitality. Both Tina and I are now fatigued and would to bed."

"I-I would like – " Sir Marcus began only to be silenced by the Dowager's upraised hand.

"Not another word, sir," she commanded. "We will talk about it tomorrow when everyone is less overwrought. The child is fagged out, you can tell it by her face and I am not as young as I used to be."

There was nothing that Sir Marcus could do but bow and go from the room.

Tina's head was turned away from him and his eyes lingered a moment on the whiteness of her shoulders before he opened the door and let himself out into the hall.

The moment the door was closed behind him, the Dowager dropped her protective pose and asked sharply,

"Now, what happened, child?"

Tina drew a deep breath.

"Sir Marcus proposed marriage," she answered.

"And that was enough to put you in such a fret that you had to run away and have everyone in the gardens looking for you? It brought me to such a flurry that I felt as though my heart might stop beating."

"Oh, please, ma'am, forgive me," Tina begged. "It was not the fact of – his proposal that upset me, it was – "

"It was what?" the Dowager enquired.

"He kissed me," Tina answered. "I resisted him, he is so big and I-I could not escape until I fought – and scratched at him."

The Dowager sat down on the sofa.

"Really, what a fuss about a kiss!" she exclaimed. "Have you never been kissed before?"

"No, indeed ma'am, it is – the first time," Tina answered.

"And it put you in a panic. Well, you will have to get used to such things for how else can you be married except by kissing the gentleman who asks for your hand?"

Tina began to feel very small and rather foolish.

Now that it was over, now that she was back home in the company of the Dowager, she wondered why it had indeed seemed so horrible, so utterly and completely repulsive.

Had she been kissed by a leper or a crossing-sweeper she could not have minded more. And yet Sir Marcus was handsome, a man who was rich and who wished her to become his wife.

She bent her head.

"It was very – stupid of me," she admitted.

"Very stupid, I should say," the Dowager retorted. "But what is wrong with Sir Marcus? I declare young women have been angling for him ever since he came to London. Many may not like him, but what does that signify? It may be that they are jealous or he is too clever and, of course, he has made conquests that they resent. I assure you, my dear, if you are looking for a rich husband, you could do far worse than accept Sir Marcus. He has assured me of his devotion and his desire is only to make you happy and smother you with gifts and benevolence. In fact I should think that there is hardly a thing you could ask for that he would not be prepared to give you."

Tina drew in her breath and with a graceful little movement knelt down at the Dowager's side.

"I can see that I have been – very stupid," she said in a low voice.

"Not exactly stupid but uncivilised, a little gauche," the Dowager replied. "In the country girls run away and in London they learn to handle men. What is more, they permit no familiarity other than that they wish to accept. They flirt and yet keep a man at arm's length. You are ignorant, my child, and, I suppose, too innocent of the world that you have been plunged into so quickly."

"I am sorry," Tina muttered. "I see I have been very stupid."

"A little inconsiderate," the Dowager said. "You had me all of a twitter with worry and I have never seen Sir Marcus more concerned."

She paused and then added with a hint of laughter in her voice,

"Do him good, as it happens. There are far too many women, I dare say, anxious for his kisses and ready to accept anything else he cares to offer them. A little resistance will not do him any harm."

She stopped and looked kindly at Tina's bent head.

"But you don't want to be too elusive, my child," she said. "Not unless you intend to refuse him once and for all. Sir Marcus is not a man to dangle too long beneath a maiden's window. He is the type that likes to storm the portcullis and get on with it!"

"Must I make up my mind so quickly?" Tina asked, knowing the answer even as she asked the question.

"Oh, no," the Dowager replied, "there is plenty of time. Keep him dangling for a month or so. You do not, of course, wish to be married before the winter at the very soonest."

The Dowager's words were like a death knell to Tina's hopes.

"You are right," she said quietly with a note of despair in her voice. "I have been extremely foolish. Tomorrow I will write a note and apologise – to Sir Marcus. Do you think he will call again?"

"I should think it unlikely! You have antagonised him completely!" the Dowager said sarcastically, but with a note of laughter in her voice. "All the same never drive a man too far! A little resistance encourages him, makes him all the keener, but tonight I thought that you were dangerously close to the parting of the ways. No man likes to be made to look a fool in front of his guests. It was quite obvious when he returned without you what had happened."

"Do you think – they guessed?"

"They would be fools if they did not. Now, child, let's go to bed now you have learnt your lesson. Tomorrow I will try and instruct you on how to keep a man interested, amused and entertained without allowing him to take liberties."

"That is something I very much wish to learn," Tina said in all truth.

"Of course, it comes with experience," the Dowager responded crushingly.

She swept up the stairs in front of Tina, her head with its twinkling diamonds held high, and Tina followed humbly behind feeling, although the Dowager had not said so, that she was slightly in disgrace.

Alone in her own room she locked the door and flung herself face down on the bed.

She could feel the trap closing in on her.

It was getting nearer and nearer and there was nothing she could do about it. It was a tide that she could feel encroaching upon her and there was no escape from it.

There were no tears in her eyes, she only lay with her face pressed into the pillow trying to reason with herself why her whole body shrank from Sir Marcus and why his kisses were such indefinable horror that even now she dared not think about them.

'There must be other men in the world,' she whispered to herself and, even as she said the words, another question came into her mind.

Would she like them any better? Could she bear any man, other than Sir Marcus, to touch her, lift her chin towards him and then fasten his lips to hers?

She could feel again the hot possessive urgency of his mouth and as she writhed against the memory of it, she answered her own question, knowing that it was not only Sir Marcus she shrank from but all men, every man except one.

And then blindingly, like a light flashing before her eyes, like a sudden roar of music in her ears, she knew the truth.

She had been fighting against it not only tonight but almost, it seemed to her, for a century of time.

There was one man she would kiss willingly enough, whose touch she welcomed and whose arms she craved for, one man to whom she would give herself willingly in any way that he wished, the man she loved with her whole heart.

CHAPTER NINE

"Look out for 'is Nibs, 'e be as mad as the devil about summat."

The door of Tina's room was ajar and she heard quite clearly what one footman passing another on the landing said.

For a moment she sat very still and then one hand crept to her breast as she quelled the tumult that had suddenly arisen in her heart.

She was at her secrétaire striving to write a letter of thanks to Sir Marcus Welton for his hospitality the night before.

The Dowager had commanded her to do so, but she was finding it almost impossible to express her gratitude and apologise for the anxiety she had caused them without insinuating that she resented his behaviour and the attentions that he had forced upon her.

But now, in a moment, everything was forgotten.

She sprang to her feet, crossed the room to the door and yet, even as she did so, her feet were checked.

What could she say to Lord Wynchingham? How indeed could she meet him with the newfound knowledge of what he meant to her flooding over her like a spring tide?

She turned away and crossed to the dressing table looking at her reflection, both glad that she appeared so attractive and afraid that she showed her gladness at his arrival too obviously in her sparkling eyes and the sudden tremor of her lips.

She loved him!

She had lain awake all night whispering his name over and over again, telling herself that this was the last touch to an episode of complete and utter madness.

She knew that it was not only wrong but utterly impossible that she should love, of all people, the man she was trying to help, the man who of all others in the whole world could not possibly ever think of her as his wife.

And yet what did words matter to a heart that leapt at the thought of him, breath that came quicker between parted lips and a body that trembled at the sudden thrill of hearing someone speak of him?

"I must go down and greet him," Tina said aloud to her reflection in the mirror and tried to compose her face to one of sedate pleasure instead of wild, almost ecstatic delight.

It was no use, such circumspection was impossible. Forgetting all her good resolutions she ran towards the door and passed through it to hurry helter-skelter down the stairs.

She knew where he would be.

In the marble hall she turned instinctively towards the library. It was there they had first met, there that she had first seen him coming across a room towards her.

She must have known at that moment, she thought, and yet, blind that she was, she had believed that, in helping her towards her purpose in finding her a rich husband, he was fulfilling everything she desired for herself.

She went to the door of the library and pulled it open.

She found him just as she had expected, sitting in the big winged armchair by the fireplace. He was looking pale and very exhausted.

There was a glass of brandy in his hand as if he had fortified himself with the fiery spirit against collapse.

She ran to him on feet that hardly seemed to touch the ground.

"Why are you here?" she cried. "You should have stayed at Wynch! The doctors must have been demented to have let you come all this way when you are still so weak."

The words tumbled breathlessly from her lips and then Lord Wynchingham smiled and her heart turned over in her breast.

"I wanted to see you," he said.

"Oh."

Tina had been expecting him to say many things, but not that.

It took her unawares, it brought down her defences and the pretence that she had promised herself to enact faithfully and sensibly.

She felt herself throb, a sudden thrill such as she had never experienced before rushed through her body like a flame.

Because she could find nothing to say, she could only stand before him, her eyes fixed on his face, her lips quivering. Because her emotions were so intense her whole body vibrated like a musical instrument at the Master's touch.

He set down his glass of brandy on the table beside him and held out his hand.

"What have you been doing?" he asked. "I thought of you last night and decided that my chaperonage was essential. I don't trust the Dowager to keep a strict enough eye on you."

She slipped her cool fingers into his and, because her legs felt as though they could no longer support her, she slipped down beside him in a billow of silken skirts to look up at him for a moment adoringly and then turn her head away lest he should see the secret in her eyes.

"You seem to have lost your tongue," he commented. "Is it such a shock to see me? I assure you that my bones rattled together like a skeleton over those rough roads. It's a disgrace that they should not be mended more often."

"You ought not to have come," Tina managed to gasp at last. "You are not well enough."

"I refuse to waste my life lying about in bed, especially as things are at the moment. You have been behaving yourself?"

"I don't know what to answer to that," Tina said in a low voice. "Her Grace will tell you I behaved badly, so will Sir Marcus Welton. But I could not help it."

"What did you do?" Lord Wynchingham asked and now his voice was harsh and he took his hand from hers and picked up his brandy glass again.

"I ran away from Sir Marcus in – Vauxhall Gardens," Tina confessed. "He – he – he frightened me. I came home alone with a stranger, a kind young man who is a clerk at the Admiralty. He brought me back safely. The Dowager was annoyed and – so was Sir Marcus."

"Damn his impertinence! What has it to do with him?" Lord Wynchingham asked aggressively.

There was a moment's pause.

"He has asked me to marry him," Tina answered.

She dared not look at Lord Wynchingham as she spoke and she knew that her voice was somehow despairing.

He drained the brandy in his glass and set it down with a bang on the side table.

"What have you answered?" he demanded.

"I have not said anything as yet," Tina answered.

"And what do you intend to say?"

It seemed to her that he almost shouted the question at her.

She dropped her head lower and felt the tears prick at the back of her eyes.

"What *can* I say?" she asked.

"Tina, look at me."

His voice was urgent but far gentler than the way he had spoken before.

At his command she turned her face towards him and he saw her eyes swimming with tears, her little mouth trembling.

He bent forward.

"Listen, Tina," he said. "You must not, you shall not do anything that is against your inclination. We will find some other method – "

"But what?" she interrupted.

"I don't know, There must be some way out of this, something that would not hurt you. We are partners remember, you and I. There is no reason why you should undertake anything which is more than you can bear."

Her eyes were held by his.

She stared at him and for a moment she felt as though they both looked into each other's souls.

The words died on his lips and he leant forward still further.

"Tina – " he said hoarsely.

The door at the far end of the room opened,

There was an apologetic cough and Mr. Greychurch stood there looking at them.

Lord Wynchingham jerked himself back in his chair.

"Yes, what is it?" he said sharply.

"May I speak with your Lordship? It is of the utmost urgency."

"It cannot be as urgent as all that," Lord Wynchingham said disagreeably. "Well, go on as you are here. Tell me what it is you want."

Mr. Greychurch looked apologetically at Tina.

"Would you like me to go?" Tina asked.

"Well, perhaps – " Mr. Greychurch began hesitantly and then added quickly, "No indeed, Miss Croome. Please stay, you might be of assistance."

"What is it? What is it?" Lord Wynchingham trumpeted. "I do wish, Greychurch, you would come to the point and not dither about. It makes me nervous. What catastrophe can possibly have occurred to shake you out of your habitual calm?"

Mr. Greychurch crossed the room and stood respectfully at a little distance from Lord Wynchingham.

"I am afraid, my Lord, things are very serious – "

"What things?" Lord Wynchingham interrupted. "What could be more serious than usual? Money I suppose. You never speak to me about anything else."

"I ask your pardon, my Lord," Mr. Greychurch said unhappily. "It appears to fall to my lot always to carry disagreeable tidings to your Lordship."

"And what you are going to say now is undoubtedly disagreeable. But go ahead, I must try to bear it."

"It is Hunt and Dunstable, the wine merchants, my Lord," Mr. Greychurch said. "You remember they supplied the champagne for the ball?"

"Yes, of course," Lord Wynchingham answered. "Why should they not? They have been my wine merchants long enough."

"It's just the trouble, my Lord. I did not tell you at the time, it was all such a rush and your Lordship so busy, they only agreed to provide the champagne and, of course, the other wines, on condition that some part of their bill, which had been owing over three years, was met."

"Three years and how much does that amount to with, of course, the addition of our last order for the ball?"

"Nearly two thousand pounds, my Lord."

There was a few moment's silence and then, as no one spoke, Mr. Greychurch went on,

"It is a vast sum of money for a small firm to carry and, although Mr. Hunt regrets exceedingly the necessity, he feels some substantial payment must be made immediately."

"And if he doesn't get his money, what then?" Lord Wynchingham asked.

"I am afraid, my Lord, you will not like this, but Mr. Hunt, it appears, has already been in touch with your other creditors."

"All right, Greychurch. There is no need to say anything more," Lord Wynchingham interrupted.

"What can they do?" Tina asked breathlessly.

She knew the answer before Lord Wynchingham spoke.

"They can send me to the Fleet, my dear, a damned uncomfortable place, but I daresay that I shall find quite a number of my friends there who also have been unable to meet their debts."

"But such a thing cannot happen!" Tina exclaimed. "It is ridiculous and absurd!"

She was speaking more for Mr. Greychurch than for herself. It seemed to her this nightmare had been in the back of her mind and Lord Wynchingham's too long for there to be any novelty about it.

"There's one thing," Mr. Greychurch said, "if Miss Croome felt inclined to help us with a temporary loan."

"What do you mean?" Tina asked.

"He means," Lord Wynchingham said drily, "that out of your immense fortune, my dear, you might be able to spare a few thousands for your Guardian who is in an exceeding difficult situation at this particular moment."

Tina put her fingers to her mouth and looked at him despairingly.

If only she could help, she thought. If only there was something she could do. She felt humiliated that Mr. Greychurch should think her so unwilling to be of help when the situation was so desperate.

"Unfortunately," Lord Wynchingham said slowly, "my Ward's money is tied up by the most stringent regulations until she should come of age and several years must pass before she is twenty-one. And so, Greychurch, Miss Croome cannot be of assistance to us."

"I hope Miss Croome will accept my apologies for even thinking of anything so unconventional," Mr. Greychurch said hurriedly. "There just seemed no other way of coping with the situation."

"I assure you that there is a way," Lord Wynchingham said. "Inform Mr. Hunt and my other creditors that their bills will be met in full in exactly fourteen days from now."

"Fourteen days, my Lord!" exclaimed Mr. Greychurch in astonishment. "But how? It is not for me to question your Lordship, but, having handled your affairs for some years, I cannot see – "

"That is enough, Greychurch," Lord Wynchingham said slowly. "You have my permission to retire and inform Mr. Hunt and any other damned bloodsuckers waiting outside exactly what I have told you."

"Very good, my Lord," Mr. Greychurch bowed and went quietly from the room.

Lord Wynchingham leant back against his chair, his face suddenly drained of colour, his eyes closed.

"This is all too much for you," Tina suggested. "You must go to bed and you must see the doctor."

She knew how bad he must be by the fact that he made no protest and did not argue with her.

She pulled hurriedly at the bell and when the footman came to answer her summons she ordered them to carry their Master upstairs.

She sent another footman post-haste for the doctor and then ran ahead up the stairs in search of the Dowager.

Her Grace was sitting up in bed, magnificently coiffured, already decked in her jewels.

"Good morning, child," she said brightly as Tina entered. And then, when she saw her face, she added quickly, "What is it? What is amiss?"

"His Lordship has arrived," Tina answered, "but he is ill and weak. It was madness to travel in his condition. I have had him carried to his bed and sent for the doctor."

"He was told to stay at Wynch until the end of the week," the Dowager said sharply. "Stupid boy! I wonder what made him so anxious to come to London and disobey my instructions."

"I think he is worried," Tina answered without thinking.

"Worried?" the Dowager queried.

Tina remembered too late that the Dowager had no idea of her grandson's financial circumstances. With an effort she tried to erase the impression she had created.

"I think, as a matter of fact," she said forcing a smile to her lips, "Lord Wynchingham was lonely there and missed us. He thought that he ought to be here to act as chaperone, but really, I think he was jealous of us having all the fun and going to all the parties without him."

"Well, this certainly will not improve the speed of his recovery," the Dowager said. "Give orders for the doctor to come and see me as soon as he has examined his Lordship. I want to find out exactly how bad the poor boy is."

"Yes, of course," Tina answered.

She turned towards the door only to be arrested by the Dowager's next question.

"You have written to Sir Marcus, child?"

"Yes, Your Grace, I had nearly finished the letter when I was interrupted with the news of his Lordship's arrival."

"Then finish the note quickly and send it round by a groom. We don't want to leave him too long with the bad impression you created last night. Men, like kettles, go off the boil. You want to keep him up to scratch. He is the best offer you have had so far."

"Yes, of course," Tina replied dully.

The Dowager was being sensible, she knew that, but she had no idea how absolutely to the point her words were or how imperative and vital it was that Sir Marcus should not, as she had put it, 'go off the boil.'

There was no escape now.

Tina was well aware that there was no longer time for her to prevaricate, to run away or pretend even to herself that someone might rescue her.

She must accept Sir Marcus and the sooner all the arrangements for the Wedding were complete the better.

She went from the Dowager's room and down the stairs to give her instructions to the butler.

She was standing in the hall when there was a rap on the knocker. She turned her head automatically rather than from any real curiosity, as the footman opened the door.

"Is Miss Croome at home," she heard someone say and knew before he stepped into the hall who was there.

She walked towards him, forcing a smile to her lips, trying to pretend even to herself that she did not feel a shrinking which made every step an effort.

"Miss Croome – Tina!"

Sir Marcus swept his hat from his head and bowed over her hand.

He was attired in claret-coloured satin with an embroidered waistcoat, while a sapphire as big as a pigeon's egg sparkled from the centre of his cravat.

"I had hoped that you might spare me a few minutes of your time," he said straightening himself.

He seemed to tower over Tina so that she felt as usual overpowered by him.

"Of course," she answered. "We will go into the morning room."

A footman opened the door of the small salon decorated in pale blue and with elegant inlaid furniture, which Tina had learnt from the Dowager had been in the family's possession for over a hundred years.

"Will you not seat yourself, Sir Marcus," Tina invited politely, indicating a chair by the hearth and seating herself on the sofa.

To her consternation Sir Marcus sat down beside her.

"You are looking very lovely this morning," he said in the voice she most hated.

She made herself face him, a smile on her lips that seemed to stiffen her whole face.

"You are always so kind," she murmured.

"I was wondering," he began, "if you had thought of me last night?"

"Last night?" she enquired in surprise.

"After I left you, or rather after you left me," he explained. "Did you think about my offer for your hand in marriage?"

"Oh," Tina murmured.

She thought that he might have come to speak to her on the subject, but somehow she had not expected him to be so blunt or to come to the point so quickly.

"Yes, indeed," she answered.

"I would not wish to hurry you, of course, but apart from my great desire to know whether or not you will be my wife, I have plans to make plans which, I am sure you understand, are dependent on whether or not you will make me an extremely happy man."

"What plans?" Tina asked, not because she wanted to know but merely because she was striving in any way she could to play for time before she had to give him a direct answer.

"I was with the Prince of Wales this morning," Sir Marcus replied. "Actually I was in attendance on His Royal Highness while he was dressing. He said that he was already bored with the London Season and he suggested that I should accompany him and, of course, Mrs. Fitzherbert with whom, as you know, he is tremendously enamoured, to a place called Brighthelmston, a small fishing village His Royal Highness has discovered on the South Coast. It might be amusing to rusticate for a short while, but I would not wish to leave London unless, of course, you would accompany me. That would be simple enough if you agreed to become my wife."

Tina looked down at her hands clasped together in her lap.

'It ought to be simple to say 'yes',' she thought.

And yet somehow she felt as if every nerve in her body was holding her back, whispering in her ear that she must wait.

Once the decision had been made, it was irrevocable.

Wait! Wait!

His words seemed to tempt her, but she knew that the temptation came not from an instinct of self-preservation or some presentiment that her sacrifice was unnecessary, but from her own inner dread of committing herself into this man's hands – a man she knew she hated.

"I dreamt of you last night," Sir Marcus said when she did not speak. "I dreamt that I was holding you in my arms as I had done in Vauxhall Gardens and I kissed you. You kissed me back and your kisses were very intoxicating, my little Tina, even in my dreams!"

There was something almost hypnotic in his voice and yet, as he leant nearer, she could feel her loathing of him well up inside her making her shrink from the very proximity of him.

She longed, as she had never longed for anything in her whole life, to be able to answer him and run from the room.

For one fleeting second she imagined herself running upstairs to Lord Wynchingham, leaning over his bed, putting her face against his, whispering to him she could not, no, she could not say 'yes' to Sir Marcus because in truth she loved another!

But in that second Tina knew, because of her love, what her answer must be.

Only she could save Lord Wynchingham! Only she could ensure that his creditors would not tear him to pieces and that he would not be dragged humiliatingly to the Fleet Prison!

And she knew, because she loved him desperately, that she would be given the strength to do what she had to do. Before she had been fighting for herself, now she was fighting for someone she loved not only more than herself but more than life.

She pressed her fingers together until the knuckles showed white and then in a voice controlled and even she said,

"I am deeply grateful, Sir Marcus, for the honour you have accorded me and first, before I say anything more, I must apologise – for my behaviour last night. You took me by surprise and you must forgive me in that I inconvenienced both you and Her Grace by running away in such a tiresome manner."

"You are not to say another word," Sir Marcus replied. "I promise you that I will forgive far worse things. It was my fault that I frightened you. You fluttered in my arms like a little bird caught in a trap and it excited me. I shall have to teach you, my dear, what love means to a man and also – to a woman."

There was a meaning beneath his words that made the colour rise in Tina's cheeks.

She managed to say quietly,

"I will strive to behave in a more circumspect manner in future."

"You will marry me before we go to Brighthelmston?" Sir Marcus questioned.

She glanced at him and saw in that moment the sudden fire behind his eyes.

She knew then that, while he was holding himself in control, he was passionately excited by her almost beyond restraint.

She was almost persuaded in her own mind that the story about the Prince of Wales journeying to Brighthelmston was just a pretence to hurry her decision. Sir Marcus was impatient, eager and possessive almost to the point of abnormality.

Her whole body screamed out at the horror of having to surrender to this man and whose very touch made her flesh creep.

Yet there was no alternative! Whichever way she looked a great wall surrounded her and she could only say in a voice that suddenly quivered,

"Before I give my answer Sir Marcus, I have – I hope you will forgive me putting it in this manner – a condition to make."

"A condition?" he asked. "Well I feel sure that it's not a very difficult one. I want you, Tina. Unless your condition is too hard for me to comply with, I will readily acquiesce in anything you desire."

"Thank you, Sir Marcus," Tina said primly. "But I think it would be best, before you give me your promise, that you should hear what it is."

"Very well," Sir Marcus answered.

There was a smile on his lips, the smile of the conqueror, and Tina knew that it was only a question of moments before his great hands reached out and drew her to him and before his lips, hot and hungry, were seeking hers again.

For a moment she felt that she must faint, but with a superhuman effort she forced the words to her lips.

"The condition is this, Sir Marcus," she said and, because she was agitated, she rose to her feet. "It is that, if I promise to marry you, you will give me, unconditionally, one hundred thousand pounds before I leave for the Church and before we have been pronounced man and wife."

She had said it.

She dared not look at him. It seemed as if her words rang round the room, repeating themselves over and over again. "

One hundred thousand pounds!

Sir Marcus rose slowly to his feet, his expression was serious but his eyes were bright with curiosity.

Before he could speak Tina said quickly,

"I cannot – that is part of the condition – I cannot and will not answer questions."

He did not reply for a second or so.

She thought that after all he was not going to agree and he would withdraw his offer.

She was torn between her desire to be free of him and her fear that, if he withdrew at this late hour, she would be unable to save Lord Wynchingham.

She waited holding her breath, realising the enormity of her request and the outrageousness of it. What other woman would dare to ask so much?

But then what other woman would risk losing a magnificent alliance unless in actual fact the money was more important than the man she demanded it from?

Still Sir Marcus did not speak, but suddenly Tina felt his arms go round her, felt herself drawn closely against him.

"You little devil," he murmured. "You are teasing me, aren't you? You are playing the game of difficult to get and testing my devotion. Well, if you force me to pay one hundred thousand pounds for your favours, I shall not quibble! I have a feeling that they will be cheap at the price."

She knew by the sound of his voice that his desire for her was mounting as he spoke. She would have hidden her face against his shoulder, but once again his hand was beneath her chin, turning her face up to his.

She saw the fire in his eyes before his lips were on hers searing their way, she felt, into her body and drawing her very spirit from her.

She made no effort to resist him, only let his passion rage over her.

He kissed her wildly, fiercely, bruising her mouth, then her eyes, her cheeks and finally, the soft whiteness of her neck.

She felt as though Hell could hold no greater torture and that no humiliation could be deeper or more degrading.

Then suddenly, when she felt that she could sink no deeper into the depths, she was free.

Sir Marcus walked away from her across to the window.

"You go to my head, Tina," he said in a voice that was thick and almost unrecognisable as his own. "But I have not to wait long for you to be mine, then I will teach you to return my kisses and to want me as much as I want you."

He gave a little laugh.

"You certainly know how to attract a man! I have always, all my life, liked a horse that was unbroken and a woman who was not too willing."

Tina did not move.

She stood as he had left her, almost as though she was turned to stone.

She felt in some way that his remarks insulted her, yet she did not really care.

All that mattered was that in her heart she held her love secret and untouched.

Sir Marcus's kisses had disgusted her.

But she told herself that they were only superficial.

What really mattered was untouchable, he could take her body, torture and defile it, but he could not touch her heart. He would possess her in name but not in anything that really mattered.

She closed her eyes against the sight of him and heard him laugh again.

"I thought that I was past being transfixed by cupid's arrow," he said, "but here I am as lovelorn as any country bumpkin with his first wench.

He crossed the room to stand beside her again.

"You shall have your money and I will ask no questions, not now at any rate, but I also will make a condition. We will be married within the week. Is that agreed?"

For a moment Tina hesitated and then she knew that, if she acquiesced in Sir Marcus's demand, it would make it easier for Lord Wynchingham.

He would be able to pay Mr. Lampton and then some of his possessions would be sold immediately to meet the demands of the creditors.

There were pictures and silver at Wynch that would fetch thousands of pounds, enough at any rate to stave off Mr Hunt and the more importunate duns.

Lord Wynchingham had promised them payment in a fortnight, well, they would have it.

The moment Mr. Lampton received his debt of honour there would be no reason for Lord Wynchingham to conceal the fact that he could meet the more pressing claims by disposing of a few family treasures.

Tina drew in a deep breath.

"I agree," she murmured faintly.

Sir Marcus came towards her and would have kissed her again, but she eluded him.

"I must go and tell Her Grace," she said and ran from the room before he could catch her.

She heard him call her name as she hurried upstairs, but she did not look back.

Only when she reached the top landing did she rub her mouth fiercely with the back of her hand, striving to wipe away not only the touch of his lips but his wealth, his position, his power and his desire of her.

Dear God. How she hated him!

She heard the door at the far end of the landing open and saw the doctor coming from Lord Wynchingham's bedroom. He was an elderly man, looking grey and walking slowly.

For one moment Tina felt with a kind of sick horror that he was about to carry bad news to the Dowager.

Then he saw Tina and bowed politely. She had met him after Lord Wynchingham was wounded before they went down to Wynch.

"What of his Lordship's condition?" Tina asked, her voice unsteady.

"Nothing to cause any deep concern," the doctor replied. "The wound is healing excellently, but it was unwise of his Lordship to travel to London so soon. However Lord Wynchingham is young and in good condition and it will not do him any harm."

Tina felt relief sweep over her like a flood tide.

"He will be quite – all right?" she asked almost incoherently.

"Completely. I give you my word that his Lordship will soon be about again. In fact I'll stake my reputation on it."

He realised from the sudden radiance in her eyes what she had feared and added,

"You will forgive an old man's presumption, Miss Croome, I hope you will both be very happy."

His words took Tina by surprise.

She had no words to reply with and, by the time she had thought of what to say, he had left her, moving slowly towards the Dowager's bedroom.

Tina stood looking after him.

If only she was in truth, as the doctor had suspected, engaged not to Sir Marcus but to Lord Wynchingham, how different her feelings would be!

She felt the tears gather in her eyes. It was one thing to make great sacrifices for the man one loved and quite another to remember that one had to carry on without him, to look forward to years of a long life with a man she hated rather than with the man she loved.

Almost without realising where her feet were taking her, she walked towards Lord Wynchingham's bedroom.

When she reached it, Jarvis came out carrying a tray, turned and went down the corridor towards the back stairs.

Tina slipped through the door that he had left ajar.

The blinds were half-lowered and she could see Lord Wynchingham's head dark against the pillows.

She guessed that the doctor had given him something to relieve his pain and to ensure that he rested after his journey.

The room was very quiet save for a bumblebee buzzing against the windowpanes.

She crept towards the bed, Lord Wynchingham was sleeping peacefully. The bandage peeped just above the bedclothes. His other hand lay limp and half open on the white sheets.

She stared down at him, her love in her eyes, her whole body yearning for him and a deep ache that was a physical pain in her heart because she knew that in one week's time he would pass from her life for ever.

She would never see him again, she thought, and she could not bear for him to be aware of her love.

It would make it harder, much harder, if she was to meet him with other women.

It was agony to know that his life would go on as it had done before, while hers stopped short.

She could not, dare not, think about Sir Marcus!

The bee was still buzzing angrily against the windowpanes.

Lord Wynchingham stirred restlessly and his lips moved as though he would say something.

Tina looked down at him and then, because of the tears that filled her eyes and flowed down her cheeks, she could see him no more.

She bent her head, pressed for one instant her lips against his hand and ran from the room groping blindly for the lintel.

She fled to her own room, to sob her heart out, desperately, wildly and blindly in a tempest that shook her whole body until she felt as if she could bear no more.

CHAPTER TEN

The days were passing with almost terrifying rapidity.

Tina felt that she had no time to think, no time even to feel.

She seemed to move in a state bordering on hypnosis as she went from fitting to fitting, standing for an hour while a ball gown was pinned on her and then for another hour while a redingote was taken to pieces and rearranged because the Dowager found some slight fault in the fitting at the waist.

There were day gowns and feathered bonnets, negligées so thin that they looked as if they had been spun by fairy fingers and pile upon pile of underclothes edged with real lace.

At first Tina had expostulated at the expense and then, because no one would listen to her, she had let herself be swept away on the tide of the Dowager's enthusiasm.

"An heiress marrying one of the wealthiest men in England must be dressed worthy of her position," she was told.

Because she was too tired and too miserable to argue, she let it pass. She agreed weakly to every fresh extravagance, to every new suggestion of French gauzes, velvets from Lyons and ribbons from Paris.

Sometimes she thought that she must be enduring a nightmare that she would never wake up from and it was only at nights, when she was alone and knew only too well the shame in her heart that was inescapable, that she knew it was no nightmare but reality.

She hardly saw Lord Wynchingham, his physicians ordered him to rest, besides which he was visited daily by masseurs so that if he appeared at a meal it was but briefly and only to tell the Dowager that he had an appointment and could not even wait for a glass of port.

Sometimes Tina thought it was worse for her when she did see him.

The sudden leap of her heart at his entrance into a room, the way she would find her whole body tense and her knuckles white as she waited for him to speak, the sudden flood of happiness when he smiled at her and the feeling of utter and complete despair when he frowned.

Perhaps it was better not to see him, to imagine that he had already passed out of her life and to face the fact that the future, grim and terrifying, could only be intensified by the sudden rapture of his presence.

But when he did not come and the butler would announce in solemn tones,

"His Lordship's compliments, Your Grace, and he regrets that he has been kept at the Club and will not return for dinner."

The words sounded like a funeral knell and Tina wondered just how she could pass the hours until she could see him again.

It was all crazy and hopeless and yet some unquenchable spark of hope still smouldered in Tina's mind.

Something might happen, something might prevent the final catastrophe.

It was one blessing that she was spared too much of Sir Marcus's presence.

When he protested to the Dowager that he wished to see his future bride, she had shushed his impatience in the most severe manner,

"Stuff and nonsense! You will see plenty of her when you are wed. I will not see her going up the aisle with a trousseau that would ill befit a poor country lass. She will come to you in style or not at all. That is my final word."

"I am marrying Tina, not all these nonsensical frills and furbelows," Sir Marcus protested sulkily.

"A bride is entitled to appear her best and, if she does not have her 'nonsensical frills and furbelows', as you call them, when she weds, she will often have short shrift when she asks for them after the knot is tied," the Dowager said shrewdly.

"I wanted to take you both to Vauxhall this evening," Sir Marcus argued angrily, "and now you tell me that Tina is too tired for such gaieties."

"Of course she is too tired," the Dowager retorted. "So would you be if you had stood on your flat feet having pins stuck into you since cock-crow this morning! Tina has to do me credit on her Wedding Day. I hate these pale brides who look as though they will collapse before they reach the altar and a honeymoon is a strenuous business, especially in the company of such a blade as you, Sir Marcus!"

The Dowager slapped him as she spoke with her ivory-handled fan and then they both laughed a little together, the knowing laughter of the experienced and sophisticated who are always prepared to enjoy a joke at the expense of the innocent.

"You are certainly keeping me under control," Sir Marcus protested, a note of unwilling admiration in his voice.

"It's my last chance," the Dowager parried, "for who will constrain you when I am not there? Not you yourself by all accounts!"

"You should not listen to gossip," Sir Marcus said suavely.

The Dowager's lips tightened and for a moment her eyes were serious.

"I have listened already," she said, "and some of the tales they tell about you are not pretty. You will be kind to this girl?"

"Of course," he answered easily. "I assure you I shall make her happy. In my arms most women find all the blessings that they have ever imagined."

"If by 'most women' you refer to those trollops you have besmirched your reputation with, I am not impressed!" the Dowager flashed.

Sir Marcus laughed and was not in the least put out by her criticism.

"Whatever they may have been like," he said, "they have been only too eager to continue in my company. Women are much the same in bed, Your Grace, wherever they may have been born."

"Not all women," the Dowager snapped. "Some are particular, some have ideals and some, more important still, are good. It is perhaps a word you have not a close acquaintance with."

"I could answer Your Grace more easily if you were of a different sex," Sir Marcus smiled. "Let me say that I can teach an unbroken filly how to behave, a lesson I have always enjoyed, and, if I may boast a trifle, I am a very experienced teacher!"

Sir Marcus bent his handsome head and kissed the Dowager's hand.

As he left the room, he was smiling to himself, but had he looked back and seen the expression on the Dowager's face he might have been surprised.

It was perhaps this conversation that made the Dowager kinder and gentler with Tina than she had been hitherto.

She must have known that Tina had no wish to be alone with her future bridegroom and so she refused all his invitations, however amusing they might sound, to the Pleasure Gardens, to balls, to the Opera House or to Receptions that were taking place nightly among the *Beau Monde*.

Tina would have gone had she been commanded to do so, for it seemed to her that she had lost her last vestige of willpower to resist or stem the oncoming holocaust.

All she could think of was that by marrying Sir Marcus in two days' time she would save Lord Wynchingham from humiliation and ignominy.

She had forgotten that she had to save herself as well from the respectable ill-paid life of a Governess and to refuse to marry Sir Marcus now would not only have sacrificed Lord Wynchingham and disappointed his last chance of paying off his debt, but it would also have embroiled both him and the Dowager in deeper financial disaster when the bills for the elaborate and expensive trousseau began to pour in.

Tina remembered many years before, when she was a little girl, her mother telling her that one lie always led to another.

She thought now how this vast edifice of lies had piled up on the first pretence that she and Lord Wynchingham had entered into so light-heartedly it seemed to her now and so blind to the consequences.

She came back to the house very tired after Madame Rasché had kept her standing for nearly four hours, to find a huge bouquet of purple orchids waiting for her in the hall. It was another of the floral effusions that came daily from Sir Marcus.

She did not even look at it as she turned towards the stairs.

"An expensive tribute from your fiancé, I see," the Dowager remarked drily with a sudden asperity in her voice that told Tina all too clearly that she too was tired and irritable.

"Yes ma'am," she replied.

The Dowager stopped on the second step of the stairway as Tina would have followed her.

"Admire the flowers, read the note," she ordered in a low whisper. "Your indifference must not be so obvious in front of the servants."

Tina turned back into the hall.

She heard the Dowager snort as she went up the stairs alone and guessed that she was in for a lecture later in the evening.

She did her best to look appreciatively at the overblown luxurious blossoms and picked up the note that accompanied them.

She opened it – there were only four words written in the thick aggressive handwriting she had grown to know and hate –

"*Until you are mine.*"

The words seemed to strike at her with a dagger thrust.

Only a few more hours and then she would be his.

It was with an effort that she prevented herself from crumpling the note in her hand, throwing it on the floor and stamping on it.

She glanced upwards, the Dowager was out of sight.

She turned thankfully towards the stairs and, as she did so, at the far end of the passage she saw a footman, carrying a silver salver on which rested a decanter of wine, open the door to the library.

Tina stood still.

"Is his Lordship at home?" she asked the butler.

"Yes, miss, he is in the library," was the reply.

For a moment Tina hesitated and then it seemed that without conscious volition her feet carried her towards the library.

She was no longer tired, no longer listless.

He was there!

She was going to see him!

What did anything else matter?

Sir Marcus, his flowers, the Dowager's anger, the fact that time was running out. She could only snatch at this opportunity of being alone with the man she loved.

The footman held the door open for her.

She saw Lord Wynchingham sitting in the big winged armchair on the hearth, a glass in his hand, his face thin and a little drawn from his illness, but somehow more attractive and less frightening than she had ever known him before.

He looked round at her entrance and she thought his eyes lit up.

"Tina!" he exclaimed.

"Don't get up," she said hastily. "I have just come in with the Dowager – I heard you were here – and wanted to ask how you are."

"Well enough," Lord Wynchingham answered. "The doctors are pleased with me, although perhaps it would have been better if Claude had been a more accurate marksman."

"There was something I was going to tell you," Tina said. "I thought that I saw Claude last night. We were returning home late. The Dowager had driven down to Chelsea to see a tailor who, she had heard, could fashion a riding habit better than anyone in Bond Street. The streets were almost deserted and the sun was sinking when we returned and, as we drew into Berkeley Square, I thought that I saw him in the gardens among the trees."

"Saw Claude?" Lord Wynchingham exclaimed.

"Yes, indeed. I am almost certain that it was him. He was in the shadows and he had two other men with him. He was talking to them and looking towards this house."

"You must be mistaken," Lord Wynchingham replied. "I don't believe that Claude would dare to show his face around the place, not until I am well at any rate. One or two of my friends will lie in wait for him when he does appear. He is not going to get off entirely scot free."

"What do you mean by that?" Tina asked.

"Well, if they don't give him a horse whipping, I shall," Lord Wynchingham explained. "After all he meant to murder me. It was only by a miracle that he did not succeed."

"No. Leave him alone," Tina remonstrated. "Don't try to revenge yourself on him, I beg of you. I don't know why – I am frightened of him."

Lord Wynchingham put back his head and laughed, a dry harsh laugh with no humour in it.

"Frightened of Claude!" he exclaimed. "Well, there is no need to be. He is a fool if ever there was one. The Dowager calls him a worm. There is only one thing to do with worms and that is tread on them."

"No! No! He is not a worm," Tina said. "He is far more like a snake who will go on scheming to get his own way and to destroy you! Oh, please leave him alone. Send him out of the country if you can. Don't put yourself in any further danger."

"Don't fret," Lord Wynchingham said smoothly. "If Claude does kill me, who cares?"

"*I* care," Tina said quickly almost without thinking.

Then, as Lord Wynchingham looked at her and she felt the colour flood into her face, she added hastily,

"I would not wish anything to happen to you or indeed for your cousin to triumph after his dastardly plot to inherit Wynch."

"Wynch, Wynch," Lord Wynchingham moaned, "is that all we ever think about? Is that the reason for all our crimes?"

He put his hand out suddenly and, almost before Tina realised what she was doing, she had laid her own on it.

"Come here close to me," Lord Wynchingham said. "I want to talk to you."

He drew her towards his chair and she found herself sitting on a low stool beside it, looking up at him.

He stared down into her tiny face and then he said with a tone in his voice she did not understand,

"You are looking tired and unhappy."

"No, I am not unhappy now," Tina answered.

It was indeed the truth. The touch of his fingers made her feel as though wine coursed through her veins and that the whole room was alight with sunshine.

"Give it all up," he said gently. "Give up this mad masquerade. Tell them the truth. You will never be happy with Welton, even though he is a rich man."

For a moment Tina closed her eyes.

How easy to agree with him and to say that she loathed Sir Marcus and would give every year of her life to be free of him.

Things had been bad enough when she first came to Berkeley Square, but now, owing to her extravagance, and to the extra money that had been spent on her, things were infinitely worse.

"It's all right," she said softly, "I daresay that we shall deal well enough together and the money is to be handed to me before I leave for the Church. I have arranged it that way so that, as you are to give me away, you can take it into your safe keeping at once."

"I am to give you away?" he exclaimed.

"It is correct, you know," Tina answered. "You are, in fact, my Guardian. It is under your protection that I have appeared in Society."

"Damn it all. I will do nothing of the sort," Lord Wynchingham fumed. "I am not well enough. My physician would forbid it."

"Oh – but please – " Tina said piteously. "I could not face the Church alone – the crowds – the stares of the people and – Sir Marcus waiting. I-I rely on you."

She felt as she spoke that she could not give up those last moments alone with him.

Somehow the Wedding seemed less frightening and less awe-inspiring, simply because she would be driving to the Church in his company, alone in the coach, alone for the last moments before she committed her whole future into the hands of the man she loathed and despised.

"Please say you will," she pleaded again.

Lord Wynchingham shrugged his shoulders and she saw him wince because the movement hurt his wound.

"If it will give you any pleasure," he said ungraciously.

"Thank you," she smiled at him.

"Don't look so damned pleased with yourself," he snapped at her. "You have had your own way, there is no need to smirk about it."

"I was not smirking," she protested, a little bewildered by his harshness.

"You damned women are all the same," he asserted, suddenly getting to his feet and walking towards the window to stand with his back to her. "You make a palaver over trifles, but big things you swallow without a murmur. Perhaps, after all, you want to marry this man?"

Lord Wynchingham laughed sarcastically.

"There are some who consider him handsome and he is rich. That is what really matters, is it not? He is rich enough to supply you with gowns and jewellery that you can wear to fascinate other men, perhaps to lure them into the spider's web of drama and intrigue you surround yourself with. A smug little spider waiting for the poor stupid flies to become entangled! For them there is *no* escape."

There was so much venom in his voice that Tina felt the tears start in her eyes.

She rose and went towards him.

"What are you – saying?" she asked piteously. "Why are you – talking like this?"

"Because you are like all the other women," he returned, "and I thought you were different. Clothes, clothes, *clothes*! That is all you think about, clothes in which to beguile some poor fool to fall in love with you! Clothes to be married in and clothes to dance on his heart in while you marry someone else."

"I think you are mad," Tina said hotly. "You know I have no desire for this ridiculous and elaborate trousseau your grandmother has saddled me with – and yet, what could I say? She believes I am rich – rich enough to pay for it. Once I am married, presumably my husband – will be presented with the bills. Do you really think I care how I am dressed or what I wear? I was happy enough to come here in the dress I made myself. It was only when you all laughed at it that I realised how countrified I must look."

"Your Wedding dress," Lord Wynchingham asked unexpectedly, "what is that like?"

"It is very beautiful," Tina replied lamely, "or so I am told. I have tried not to look at it."

"You tried!" he said sourly. "Sir Marcus will look at it, won't he? Sir Marcus will see you looking radiant, at your best. 'A beautiful bride' they will all say. Are you looking forward to that moment when he puts the ring on your finger and you become Lady Welton? *Lady Welton*. The servants will bow and call you 'my Lady'!"

Tina put her fingers up to her ears.

"Stop! *Stop!*" she cried. "How can you speak to me like this in that hateful voice? You know I am detesting it. You know what we planned and what – we schemed. Sir Marcus was the only one who offered for me. There was no time – to wait for anyone else."

"No time," Lord Wynchingham said almost as though he was talking to himself. "And yet when we first planned it, it seemed as though there would be plenty of time. Time for you to make your choice, time perhaps, for you to find some pleasant, inconspicuous young man. But – no – it had to be Welton with his stinking reputation. He is a notorious lady killer. Welton, who flaunts himself around the Clubs boasting of his conquests."

"I did not choose him, I tell you," Tina interposed. "I hated him the first moment I saw him. I was frightened of him, but there was no one else – no one! Mr. Lampton gave you time to pay. No one gave me time – to find someone more suitable.

"I don't suppose it would have made any difference," Lord Wynchingham said sourly.

He turned from the window to face her.

"What are you doing here?" he asked angrily. "Go upstairs and rest and make yourself beautiful for your bridegroom. Put on your pretty gowns to entice him, enchant him and tell him on no account to fail in handing over the money. You have sold yourself splendidly. One hundred thousand pounds to me, but look what you will have. Sir Marcus's country mansion at Newmarket, his horses, his box at the Opera, his vast estate and his heavy money bags! You will have them all and a great deal of joy may they bring you!"

His voice was like a whip and Tina felt the blood rush into her face.

"You are mean – you are hateful!" she raged at him. "Why are you saying this to me now? Why are you trying to make me unhappy? What else can I do, what alternative is there? I am caught like a rat in a trap and well you know it. Can you not see, I have to go – through with it?"

"Of course you have to," he said.

Again his tone was intolerant so that, with the tears springing to her eyes, she looked up at him shivering, half with anger and half with unhappiness.

"I cannot think what I have done that – you should be so unkind," she said. "I have only tried to help – only tried to do things for you."

Her voice broke on the last word and the tears poured down her cheeks and yet she stood there facing him, her eyes on his, her lips a little open, her hands clenched with the intensity of her feelings.

He was glowering at her, his chin thrust forward and his eyes gazing into hers. He seemed to be seeking, searching, striving to find something within her very soul.

Just for a moment they stood absolutely still as though they had both been turned into stone and then suddenly the tension in Lord Wynchingham seemed to break.

"Damn you!" he cried wildly. "*Damn you*!"

Almost before Tina realised what was happening he swept her into his arms and his lips were on hers.

She gave a little gasp and then she was still.

She felt the hard, almost brutal pressure of his mouth.

She felt herself crushed against him and knew instinctively that while he was kissing her with passion that could not be refused, he was still angry, still resentful and still, in some way that she could not understand, hating her.

But she could think of nothing but the wonder of his kiss.

She felt a flame shoot through her right from the very depths of her body, rising until it seemed as though it consumed her heart and her mind and that finally her whole being was on fire.

She felt as if the world had stopped still and she and Lord Wynchingham were alone, that everything had fallen away from them and they were just man and woman united to each other and belonging only to one another.

'I love you,' she wanted to tell him, but his lips still held hers captive and his arms were like bands of steel and she could not move even if she had wished to do so.

But his kiss had altered – it was possessive yet gentle, hungry yet tender.

The world seemed to be whirling around Tina, gold and glorious and rapturous, until suddenly, with a groan that seemed to shake him, Lord Wynchingham took his lips from hers and pushed her away from him.

She staggered and would have fallen had she not held onto the back of the chair.

"Go!" she heard him cry out. "Go, now – while I can let you. For God's sake don't come near me again!"

"But – but, S-Stern – "

She used his Christian name timidly for the first time.

Her whole face and body were glowing with the wonder of his touch. He had his back to her, his head a little bowed and his shoulders hunched.

"Go!" he said harshly. "Do as I say – *go!*"

She hesitated, wanting to say so much more and yet the command was obvious.

She dared not disobey. Slowly, her feet dragging, hoping for a reprieve, she walked across the room.

At the door she stood and looked back.

Lord Wynchingham was still standing at the window and he looked, she thought with a little pang, like an old and defeated man.

"Stern."

She whispered the name again and, when there was no response, she went from the room and somehow – she was never quite certain how – she found her way to her own bedroom.

There she stood for a moment, her back to the door, her hands to her burning cheeks and she knew, she just knew, with a sudden wild leaping of her heart that he loved her, even as she loved him!

She had not understood why he had railed at her – his anger, his unkindness, the cruel things he had said.

Now she knew.

He had revealed himself unmistakably in the kiss that had started brutally and ended with the softness and the possessiveness of an aching desire that could not be disguised.

"He loves me!"

She said the words aloud and then suddenly was on her knees beside the bed.

"O God, thank you! *Thank you*! He loves me!"

Nothing else seemed to matter.

The past, the future, the present with all its problems, they were all infinitesimal – all small minor irritations beside the overwhelming glory of the fact that he loved her.

Somehow she had never believed that it was possible, never believed that the moment would come when he would want her as she had wanted him and when the ache in her breast would no longer be a lonely isolated burning but something shared.

For a moment it did not even matter that they could not be together in the future. Just the knowledge that she had won him, that his love was hers as wholly and as perfectly as if she had committed her heart to his keeping, was all she asked of life.

"I love him! *I love him!*" she told the empty room and everything seemed more beautiful, because it belonged to him and his heart was hers.

She knew, even in her first rapture that very shortly she would be in the depths of despair because their love could never be the perfect union of two people as it should be and that despair, desolation and misery lay ahead of her.

Yet, for the moment it did not matter.

The only thing that counted was the fact that she was loved – loved by the man she had loved so deeply and so secretly.

"Thank you, God! *Thank you, God!*"

It was a prayer from the heart without even a plea for something more.

And then she saw lying on the bed a gown covered in white muslin.

She had not noticed it in her first rapture when she had come into the room and now, very slowly, she rose to her feet and took off the cover.

It was her Wedding dress that lay there. White silk taffeta over a lace petticoat embroidered in silver and diamonds with tiny sprigs of orange blossom caught cunningly under the panniers and amongst the lace ruffles of the bodice.

Her wedding dress!

Almost blindly Tina stood staring at it.

She knew that what she was about to do was to make a mockery not only of her love but also of all that was sacred and pure.

Marriage was meant as a union of a man and a woman who were prepared to love and cherish each other for all time.

She was cheapening not only herself but also the ideals of all women in love.

She turned towards the door.

She would go downstairs and tell Lord Wynchingham that they could not despoil their lives and break their hearts.

She thought wildly what they would do.

They would run away together – go to France and stay there secretly, content with each other, and then, even as she planned it as a child might plan a Fairytale, she knew that it was impossible.

Their life together could not be built on a foundation of dishonour and cowardice.

She could not bear to imagine Lord Wynchingham eating out his heart in some foreign clime, knowing that he had deserted his family, his estates, evaded his debts and left his creditors clamouring. Better to sell up Wynch and distribute the proceeds among those he owed money to.

Then she knew that this idea was hopeless too.

She had been over all this before and yet she must torture herself again. Mr. Lampton must be paid first, that was a debt of honour, leaving precious little for the rest and to tell the truth now could only lead to scandal and perhaps the Fleet.

Tina turned her face from the door back towards the Wedding gown. Her love, she thought, would give her the strength to go through with this!

At least she had had her moment of utter happiness and for the rest of her life she would remember Lord Wynchingham's kiss and the glory that it had evoked in her.

"I love – you," she whispered, with a sudden break in her voice.

Now there was no elation, no triumph in the simple words, only a dedication of faith.

She crossed to her dressing table, sat down on the low stool in front of the gilt-edged mirror and stared at her reflection.

'I shall grow old,' she thought, 'old and ugly, but I shall always remember the touch of his lips, the feel of his arms around me. The flame rising within me was echoed by the flame rising in him.'

Then the tears came and she cried not desperately but hopelessly as one for whom there is no future, no hope and no salvation.

CHAPTER ELEVEN

"His Lordship has not returned, Your Grace."

"Not returned?" the Dowager's exclamation was almost a shriek. "He was not here last night when I required him, and now we shall be leaving for the Church in twenty minutes!"

Tina turned from the pier glass where she had been looking at her reflection as the lady's maids made the last minute adjustments to her gown and veil.

"His Lordship did not sleep here?" she asked.

The chambermaid, who had relayed the information from a footman, who had heard it from the butler, dropped a little curtsey.

"No, my lady, I mean, miss. Mr. Jarvis said 'is Lordship's bed had not been slept in."

Tina noted the slip in her designation – 'my Lady' – in an hour's time she would be entitled to be addressed in such a manner.

She would be Lady Welton and it seemed as though Lord Wynchingham would not be there to see her wed.

She had not seen him since the night he had kissed her and she had known in her heart that it was because he was afraid – afraid of his own feelings and perhaps hers. Afraid to face the parting they were both being carried to relentlessly by the course of events.

Yesterday had been a day of crises over trivialities. The veil was lost, the clasp of the diamond necklace that the Dowager had given her for a Wedding present was broken and the shoes that matched her most expensive and elaborate gown had not come from the cobblers!

There were a thousand petty irritations to occupy minute after minute and hour after hour of the day.

The Dowager had fussed and fumed and been unaccountably bad-tempered. Abdul had his ears boxed, not once but a dozen times and only a mammoth amount of cakes from the kitchen had been able to quieten his cries.

The servants had seemed flustered and even Mr. Greychurch appeared to lose his habitual calm serenity.

But to Tina the day had had an almost dreamlike quality and like many dreams it seemed to be part nightmare and part of an almost Divine happiness.

She knew in her heart and with every pulse of her being that Lord Wynchingham loved her. She was faced with the fact that, after tomorrow, she would seldom, if ever, see him again.

It was one thing to make a sacrifice for someone one loved, but quite another to be left with the knowledge that, the sacrifice having been made, he would no longer be there to show his gratitude.

Towards evening, because she felt that she could no longer bear not to see him, not to hear his voice even if harsh and abusive, she had gone to the library.

The room was empty but she saw that on the desk lay her Marriage Settlement already signed and sealed and waiting, she imagined, for Mr. Greychurch to collect it and put it away in his usual punctilious manner.

She stared down with almost unseeing eyes at her name and that of Sir Marcus Welton and she saw Lord Wynchingham's signature scrawled, as if angrily or in haste, at the bottom of the page.

There were signs of him everywhere and yet the room was empty.

A glass half-filled with brandy was at the side of his chair. Then she noticed that the door into the garden was open and she thought, perhaps, he had taken a stroll in the evening air, as she knew that he was often wont to do.

Eagerly, because she was so anxious to see him, she stepped through the open door to look around the small garden, with its paved walk and playing fountain, in search of him.

He was not there either, and she walked disconsolately down the narrow path to where, at the far end, concealed from the house by a large magnolia bush, was a small iron gate, which opened onto a passage that led to the stables.

Perhaps he had gone to see his horses. The gate was open and she fancied that he was just a few seconds ahead of her.

She peered down into the shadows of the passage where it ran along a high brick wall that was part of the stables themselves.

There was no one in sight.

As the passage was seldom used, it appeared damp and dark and Tina hesitated before venturing down it in her satin slippers. Lord Wynchingham would be back in a few moments, she thought, and she seated herself in the arbour to wait for him.

She wondered what he would say to her.

Would he, despite his resolution to the contrary, be surprised into showing his true feelings? She had an idea that he would keep an iron control on himself and, with the underlying perception of all women, she believed that he would try to convince her that he was in fact indifferent.

The evening was warm and windless and she waited in the arbour hearing the tinkle of the fountain and the song of the birds as they roosted in the shrubs.

She wondered what life would be like alone with Lord Wynchingham in some tiny cottage in the country, away from this luxury, away from the vast army of servants and retainers and away from the grasping hands of Society that absorbed greedily so much of their time.

She had a sudden vision of long days stretching out before them both, full of sunshine and contentment, when they could be alone, perhaps with their children, their horses and their dogs.

And she knew, as only a woman in love could know, that she would make him happy and content and that he would no longer yearn for the wildness of his rakish bachelor days or the women who had filled his idle hours.

"I love him," she told the little cupid on the fountain. "I love him," she told the birds as they flew to roost over her head.

She lost all count of time.

Suddenly, with a little shiver, she realised that it was growing dark and Lord Wynchingham had not returned. She knew then with a sudden finality that he would not come.

She went slowly and despondently back to the house, thinking perhaps he was assuaging his unhappiness with the woman who had amused him before her arrival, perhaps anticipating that, after her Wedding on the morrow, he would be a rich man again and able to pay, as he had paid before, for the favours of anyone he desired.

Now it seemed strange to her that Lord Wynchingham should not have returned all night.

Could it be that he had felt that the atmosphere of the house was intolerable and the knowledge within himself of his own feelings would make it impossible for him to escort her to the Church?

She felt like crying out in her misery at the thought of not seeing him again.

"His Lordship must be somewhere," she said, her voice rising. "Send a footman immediately to all the Clubs, the houses of his friends and find out if by any chance he has forgotten the time of the Wedding."

"No, do nothing of the sort!" the Dowager interjected.

Tina looked at her with wondering eyes as she added,

"Such questions might cause a scandal. If my grandson does not appear in time for the Ceremony, I shall announce to the world that he is indisposed. I would not have him dragged from some trollop's arms or discovered in unsavoury circumstances that would make him the talk of the town."

"No, no, of course, I did not think of that," Tina said humbly.

"Send his valet to me," the Dowager ordered the chambermaid.

The girl curtseyed and a few seconds later, Jarvis, who had obviously been hovering on the stairs, knocked on the door of Tina's room.

"Come in, man," the Dowager called. "What is all this I hear about your Master not having spent the night here?"

"It's not unusual, Your Grace," Jarvis said apologetically. "But time is creepin' on. His Lordship should be dressin'."

"He should, indeed!" the Dowager agreed. "Although it is the prerogative of brides to be late, no self-respecting bridegroom can expect to be stood up at the altar steps more than fifteen minutes. Have everything prepared and tell the coachman that we shall expect speed from his horseflesh when his Lordship does appear."

"Yes, indeed, Your Grace," Jarvis nodded. "Everythin' is in readiness."

"I cannot understand it," the Dowager muttered.

Unexpectedly she clapped her hands.

"All of you attend to me," she said. "The bride is ready, she does not want any more of your titivating. Leave us now for a few moments and tell the butler to bring me up a glass of wine. I need it."

"Very good, Your Grace."

The maids curtseyed and withdrew, closing the door behind them.

The Dowager was silent for a moment and Tina looked at her wonderingly.

"Well," the Dowager said at last, "tell me what happened."

"W-what h-happened?" Tina faltered.

"Yes, girl. I was not born yesterday. Did he declare himself?"

"I d-do not k-know – what you m-mean," Tina stammered.

"Let's have the truth. There is no time for lies or prevarication. My grandson is in love with you, I have seen it in his eyes this past week and it was there before, I daresay, only I was fool enough not to look for it. What is the matter between you?"

"I cannot – tell you," Tina replied. "It is not – my secret."

"I have only to put two and two together and I don't have to search far to find an explanation," the Dowager said sharply. "With Lampton telling the world that he is expecting a cheque for one hundred thousand pounds and you pretending to be an heiress when you know that you are as poor as a church-mouse, how do the two fit in?"

Tina put her hands up to her face.

"You know that?" she asked.

"Of course I do," the Dowager said, "and I had hoped, yes, I had hoped that somehow you two could come together, but I see that I was mistaken. The boy has run away, I thought better of him!"

There was a bitterness in her voice that made Tina spring to Lord Wynchingham's defence.

"Do you not understand? He is desperate. If he pays Mr. Lampton his debt of honour, all his other creditors will come crowding in on him. They have already been here threatening Mr. Greychurch and he owes thousands, yes thousands, and the only chance for both of us was for me to find a rich husband."

"Well, you have found one," the Dowager retorted sourly, "and now my grandson, though God knows, he cannot have much of my blood in his veins, will not face the music. I thought better of Wynchingham!"

She glanced at the clock over the mantelpiece.

"Come, we must to the Church!"

"I cannot – I *will* not – go without h-him," Tina said in a further panic.

"Have you any alternative?" the Dowager enquired. "I hoped, indeed, I believed that at the last moment he would be man enough to find some solution, but I was mistaken and I was fond of the young blade."

"I love him," Tina whispered almost beneath her breath.

The Dowager would have said something bitter and scathing, but the expression on Tina's face checked the words as they came to her lips.

Instead she rose to her feet, walked to the bedroom door and flung it open.

"Mr. Greychurch!" she called out in a voice of thunder.

The secretary came hurrying up the stairs.

"Yes, Your Grace?"

"Take a coach and go ahead of us to the Church and inform Sir Marcus in a voice audible enough to be heard by most of the congregation that his Lordship is indisposed, and say that I myself will give away my protégée. She will walk up the aisle on my arm."

"Very good, Your Grace," Mr. Greychurch said and hurried to do her bidding.

The Dowager turned to Tina.

"Come, child, you have chosen the path you must tread and at least walk as befits a gentlewoman holding your head high and remember that pride can often sustain one when every other sort of courage fails."

"It is all I have left, is it not?" Tina said quietly, but at the same time her chin went up and she forced the tears back from her eyes as she walked slowly down the stairs in the wake of the Dowager's rustling silk gown and the nodding crimson plumes on her white wig.

In the doorway Mr. Greychurch, still not departed, was holding a big envelope with a red seal.

"Mr. Greychurch, why have you not obeyed my command?" the Dowager enquired.

"I beg your pardon, Your Grace," Mr. Greychurch replied, "but this package has just arrived from Sir Marcus Welton. His Lordship spoke of it to me and it is exceedingly valuable. I must place it in safekeeping before I leave for the Church."

"Give it to me," the Dowager ordered, "and begone with you."

Mr. Greychurch hesitated, but he could not overrule the Dowager's authority.

He handed her the package with a doubtful expression on his face and hurried across the pavement to the waiting coach.

The Dowager turned the sealed package over and over in her hands.

"You drove a hard bargain, my child," she said. "I suspect that this is the money that Mr. Lampton is so patiently waiting for."

"It is indeed," Tina answered.

"Then I will give it to him myself," the Dowager said, "When we return here for the Reception."

She called her maid from upstairs, gave her the package and told her in a whisper, so that she could not be overheard by the attendant footmen, to place it with her jewellery and other valuables for safekeeping.

"And don't leave the bedroom for one second until I return," she admonished. "That is an order. Do you understand?"

The maid promised and the Dowager climbed into the coach, the footmen helped Tina to follow her, lifting the heavy bridal train with careful fingers, while Abdul, seated beside the coachman, rolled his eyes in excitement at the thought of the cakes, jellies and other sweetmeats that were being prepared for the Reception.

It seemed to Tina at this moment as though a sudden numbness came upon her.

She felt as though she ought to be feeling agonised or tearful, hysterical or apprehensive, instead of which her whole body was rigid as if she had been turned to stone.

She could feel nothing.

They drove in silence. It was as if the Dowager, with a reticence strange to her, had said all that there was to say on the matter.

They drove across Berkeley Square, down Bruton Street, over Bond Street and up to the side portico of St. George's Church.

There was a crowd outside, the usual crowd of busybodies interested in watching the Wedding of a stranger.

Tina stepped from the coach and there was a gasp of admiration from the sightseers.

Tina looked round, even at this last moment Lord Wynchingham might appear to rescue her. Even now it might not be too late.

A coach turned the corner of the street past the Church, the coachman cursing the crowds in his way, but he drove on.

She saw the Dowager's satin and lace-covered arm extended towards her. She put out her hand from beneath her lace veil and they moved slowly through the great doorway into the aisle.

She had a sudden glimpse of hundreds of heads turning towards them and of eyes searching her face. Perhaps the congregation was speculating as to why she was being escorted by the Dowager.

Not all of them could have heard Mr. Greychurch's explanation.

Tina cast her eyes down on the floor. One step, another step, on– on – on, up the red carpet.

There was still that lingering belief at the back of her mind that, at the very end, he would not fail her.

They had stopped walking and she felt someone come and stand beside her and knew, without looking, by the very way that her flesh shrank from the contact, who it was.

The service had begun.

The beautiful words of the Marriage Service were being intoned above her head. She tried not to listen, tried not to hear them. At length came the question –

"*Christina Mary Alexandra, will you take this man for your wedded husband?*"

She knew then, with a sudden stab as though a knife had been driven into her heart, that it was too late.

She heard a strange, shy, faltering little voice that she did not recognise as her own, say "*I – will.*"

She heard the sound of possessive triumph in Sir Marcus's words as he took her "*for better for worse, for richer for poorer, till death us do part*".

'In which case I must die!'

Tina almost thought that she had said the words aloud and then had to concentrate her whole strength on keeping herself from swooning.

The register was signed.

They processed slowly down the aisle arm in arm.

And now the hideous reality and horror that she had committed herself to was all too apparent.

She felt Sir Marcus's hands grasping at her body as they travelled alone the short distance from the Church to Berkeley Square.

His eyes were smouldering with a fire that she dreaded beyond words and beyond expression.

Then she heard his voice thick and deep with passion say,

"Only a short time now, my pretty, before we are alone together. Remember I am your husband."

"My gown – my veil – y-you will tear them. We – we cannot arrive d-dishevelled at the Reception!"

It was a fluttering attempt by the captured bird to play for time and the smile on Sir Marcus's face was that of an executioner who knows how helpless and how utterly ineffective are the struggles of his victim.

There was an hour of standing shaking hands, receiving congratulations, hearing the good wishes for 'health and happiness' repeated a thousand times.

Tina cut the cake and somebody, Tina was never sure who, toasted, 'the bride and bridegroom' because Lord Wynchingham was not there to do it.

The Dowager told her that it was time for her to change into her going-away dress and she fled to her bedroom, hearing Sir Marcus whisper as she left him,

"Do not linger, my dear, I am an impatient suitor!"

She stood in her bedroom, her eyes closed, while the lady's maids undressed her.

The feeling of having been turned to stone was passing, instead she knew an agony of apprehension and a fear that made her hands tremble and her heart seem to beat so violently in her breast that she was surprised that others could not hear it.

She was married!

She was Lady Welton!

She heard the maids calling her 'my Lady'.

She knew if she opened her eyes, she would see the shining gold ring on the third finger of her left hand.

"My Lady made the most beautiful bride!"

Far away, far away she heard the Dowager's maid paying her compliments, but made no attempt to answer her.

Only a few moments later the Dowager herself came into the room and Tina turned to her with a look of despair.

"The coach is waiting," the Dowager said and Tina knew that she was being tactful in not saying the words 'your husband'.

"I am – ready," Tina answered.

She felt suddenly that there was no point in procrastinating, no reason to delay any longer.

She picked up her gloves and her little reticule that matched the pale blue satin of her dress.

Almost involuntarily she glanced at herself in the mirror.

She saw the soft blue ostrich feathers framing her face, she saw the sparkle of diamonds at her neck amid the laces that decorated the bodice of her gown and she wondered how she could look so young and so carefree, when she felt old and weighed to the ground with terror of what lay ahead.

She turned towards the Dowager, a little sob in her throat,

"Tell him when he – he comes back that I was – b-brave and that – that I missed – him," she sobbed.

The Dowager nodded and Tina realised that the old lady was fighting tears.

She put her soft cheek against the old and wrinkled one.

"You have been k-kind, so very kind," she murmured.

"If only I could help you, child," the Dowager said in a broken voice.

"No, there is nothing anyone can do," Tina answered. "'Pride', you said. That is what I need – pride!"

She flung up her chin.

"Thank you," she said gently to the chambermaids and went out onto the landing and down the stairs to where her bridegroom was waiting.

There was a crowd of people she said 'goodbye' to and a shower of rose petals, the sting of a few grains of rice as they caught her face.

And then they were in the coach moving away, the horses quickening their pace as they pulled up the hill and onto the flatter ground of Grosvenor Square.

"Well, Lady Welton?"

Sir Marcus was leaning back against the corner of the coach and Tina was thankful that, for the moment, he made no attempt to touch her.

She turned her face towards him reluctantly, but somehow she could find nothing to say and was concerned only with keeping her lips from quivering.

"You are silent," Sir Marcus accused her. "Can it be that you are tired or merely too happy to express yourself in words?"

"I am afraid I am – a little tired," Tina said, grasping at a straw.

"Then there will be no reason for us to stay up late tonight when we reach my house at Newmarket," Sir Marcus said with a note of amusement in his voice.

He put out his hand,

"Come, Tina, we are married. Don't look so frightened. I may beat you, but I shall not eat you!"

He laughed a little at his own joke and then slowly and deliberately, as if he savoured the moment, he reached out his arms and drew her to him.

"You are very lovely," he breathed, "and that shrinking frightened air of yours is enough to drive a man wild with desire. We have a long drive ahead of us, my sweet, let's not waste too much of it in being provocative."

Tina tried to withdraw further into her corner, but the effort was unavailing.

Relentlessly Sir Marcus's hand cupped her chin and turned her face up to his. Just for a moment she had a vision of his eyes glinting evilly, of his mouth hungry and possessive, seeking hers, and then almost as though she had dived to the depths of a dark pool, she felt herself sink down beneath his passion.

He was so strong and she knew that her struggle against him was as ineffective as a sparrow caught in a strawberry net.

She felt the hard brutality of his arms, the impatient searching of his hands, knew herself powerless and helpless and that she would never be safe again.

She wanted to die, but could only tremble and quake and feel as though he drew the breath from her body in some way that dragged her down to the very depths of degradation.

And then, even as she prayed that she might die and this moment might be her last, there was a sudden shout.

The horses came to an unexpected standstill and the coach rocked on its axles.

Sir Marcus released Tina.

They both turned astonished eyes towards the window.

The coach door was flung open and a hand holding a sword appeared.

Before Tina could scream or cry out, a stranger, masked and with a cocked hat pulled low over his face, lunged forward and drove the sword through Sir Marcus's body.

Tina heard someone scream and knew that it must be herself.

"By God – I will have you," Sir Marcus began, but then even as he spoke the blood spurted from his mouth and ran down his chin.

The masked man withdrew his sword and thrust it again and again into the heaving body as it fell from the seat onto the floor of the coach.

There was another scream – a scream of terror.

Tina thought afterwards that she must have tried to stand up.

The other door of the coach opened and two people she could not see flung a dark cloth over her head and pulled her roughly through the doorway.

She would have fallen to the ground had they not held her in their arms and stood her on her feet. They wound a cord round her waist holding the dark cloth in place and pinioning her arms.

Tina screamed again and yet again, but after a moment she stopped. The blanket or cloth she was covered with smelt and the dust from it made her cough.

She felt herself being picked up bodily.

Now she was in another carriage, thrown onto the floor of it and the horses were already moving away.

"Jump on! Don't waste time! *Hurry!*"

Someone was giving commands and, even though she was half-unconscious with the shock of what was occurring, Tina recognised the voice.

It was Claude, she was sure of it! Claude Wynchingham!

She tried, as the coach rattling over uneven roads flung her from side to side as she lay on the floor, to understand what had happened and to foresee what lay ahead.

Claude had killed Sir Marcus, but why and for what reason?

They had no valuables with them in the coach and all their luggage had gone ahead with the servants, who were to arrive at the house at Newmarket before they did.

Claude must be madder and more crazed than even she had believed.

She had thought him mad when he shot Lord Wynchingham, but at least he had a reason for such behaviour, but for him to kill Sir Marcus appeared, on the face of it, a senseless criminal act of folly for which there could be no reasonable explanation.

In the meantime there was her own plight to consider.

The violent way that Claude, or whoever it was, was driving the horses was flinging her about so that she felt as though every part of her body was likely to be bruised before they arrived at their destination.

She was stifled almost to suffocation by the dark cloth that covered her and the musty dusty smell that emanated from it.

After a while Tina must have fainted, for she could think no more and was unconscious of what happened until she felt herself being carried carefully up what appeared to be a very narrow staircase and Claude, she was certain that it was him, was giving instructions to two men who only grunted their replies.

"Careful now. Ease her round the corner, that's right. Set her down on the floor, I will release her in a moment. Now here's your money. Get off at once. If you camp anywhere, camp in the next County, nobody thinks anything if they see gypsies on the move.

Tina heard the men clattering down the narrow and uncarpeted stairs they had come up and now at last she could feel someone fumbling at the cords that bound her.

Suddenly the cloth was dragged from her head as she lay there on the floor and she was looking up into the contorted features of Claude Wynchingham.

For a moment she could say nothing, only stare at him until, because her arms hurt, she began to rub the places where the cord had cut into them, first on her left arm then on her right.

Still she did not speak and Claude stood glaring down at her,

"I have won!" he announced at last.

With an effort, because she was so bruised and her head still felt dizzy, Tina forced herself to sit up on the floor.

"You are mad!" she cried. "What can you hope to gain by killing Sir Marcus?"

"You," Claude answered.

"Me?" Tina stared at him and then slowly and unsteadily she rose to her feet.

She was in the smallest and most strangely shaped room she had ever seen. There was an old couch across one end of it, a table and two chairs and a skylight, which let in the sun, was fitted into the low ceiling.

She felt so weak that for a moment she could not answer Claude and could only stand, feeling the circulation coming back to her arms.

She looked around her then, almost unwillingly, her eyes came back to his face.

He was mad, she could see that.

There was something wild in his eyes that had not been there before, something almost fox-like in the smile that showed his long teeth.

"Yes, *you*," he repeated as she did not answer. "I have won you."

"What for?" Tina asked stupidly, thinking that in his madness he must believe that he really loved her.

"Your money," Claude replied. "I told you I wanted money and now I have got it."

"My money?"

Tina felt a sudden hysterical laughter welling in her throat.

Sir Marcus had been killed for her money! But some instinct warned her not to incite Claude further, but to be calm and gentle with him.

"Listen, Claude," she said quietly. "You have made a mistake. I should have told you before, but it was not my secret. I am not an heiress. I have no money. The Dowager was confused when I first came to London and believed that I was my cousin's child, not my father's. My father was a poor man, he was a soldier and he saved Lord Wynchingham's life but he had no money – none at all – and that was why your cousin presented me to Society so that I should find myself a husband! But I am – penniless."

To her consternation Claude flung back his head and wild almost diabolical laughter echoed round the tiny room.

"Penniless!" he shouted. "That's a hum – penniless!"

Gripping her fingers tightly together because she was so frightened by his behaviour, she forced herself to say,

"But it's true, Claude. You have to face it. I have no money. None at all."

Claude laughed again and was almost doubled up with amusement.

"Penniless, she says!" he managed to gasp at last. "Penniless!"

"But I am," Tina protested.

"You *were*," he corrected her. "You were, my dear, and I only found that out after I had made a fool of myself in offering you marriage. Yes, I found out. I am not as stupid as people thought. 'Poor Claude,' they said. And now they are going to laugh on the other side of their faces. Not 'poor Claude' any longer, but 'rich Claude!'"

"I don't – understand," Tina quavered. "Will you not you explain – it all to me?"

"Of course I will, my dear," Claude answered. "I will explain it to you very simply. You are going to marry me and you are going to marry me now. I am going to leave you here while I go and fetch a Priest."

"But Claude, what are you going to gain by that?" Tina asked, knowing with an absolute certainty that he had it all planned out and that in arguing with him she was hitting her head against a brick wall.

"Listen – to me, Claude! *I have no money*!"

He started to laugh again and this time Tina felt she could bear it no longer.

She stamped her foot.

"Stop it!" she cried. "Stop that horrible bestial laughter and listen to me. You killed a man, she could not bring herself to say 'my husband', and the Dragoons will be looking for you. You will not be able to escape them. Can you not understand, Claude, you are in danger? If you want to save yourself, you must run away. You must – hide somewhere."

"Nobody will find me," Claude said, "and if they do, I will be able to buy my pardon, buy it with your money, my dear, the money of my wife."

Tina gave a little exasperated sigh.

She was frightened. He was terrifying!

At the same time Claude and his obsession about her money was being irritating beyond words.

"I have no money," she repeated slowly as one would speak to a child.

"Go on thinking so," he said almost tauntingly. "It will be all the easier for me. We are going to be married and then we are leaving for the coast. It is all arranged. You don't have to worry your silly little head. A ship is waiting to take us to France. We will live there and be rich and comfortable and we will have everything I have always been denied. It is not going to be poor Claude any longer. Not now."

Tina shrugged her shoulders.

"Have it your own way," she said, "but I will not marry you."

"Oh, yes, you will!" he answered.

He pulled from his coat pocket a long, evil-looking stiletto, such as travellers to Italy brought home from their journeys.

"Do you see this?" he asked, as Tina backed away from him with sudden apprehension in her eyes. "If you don't marry me without making a scene and a fuss, I shall mark your face with it – a great line on either cheek, a slit on your mouth, a cross on your forehead. I might even ornament your nose, my pretty, and then who would be interested in you? Claude, of course. Claude, because he will have both his hands on your money bags and therefore your looks will not worry him. You can either be pretty and married to Claude or ugly and married to Claude. It doesn't matter to Claude."

He chuckled again in a mad inane manner and Tina, with her back against the wall, knew that there was nothing she could say.

He was clearly deranged and she thought wildly that the only thing would be to let him go and hope perhaps that she could barricade the door against him and that someone would come to her rescue while he was gone.

As if with the shrewdness of the unbalanced he had read her thoughts, he chuckled.

"Scream until you scream your heart out, no one will hear. Do you know where you are?"

"No," she answered, "do – tell me."

"There is no harm in your knowing, because you cannot get out," he replied. "You are in the Temple at Wynch and no one in the whole place goes near it if they can help it because it is haunted. Haunted, my dear Tina, by a ghost, a ghost called 'Claude'."

Tina had a sudden memory of herself staring from Lord Wynchingham's window across the garden and up the long green walk that led to the beautiful white Grecian Temple.

This was where Claude must have been hiding.

"And now I will leave you," Claude said, putting his stiletto back in his pocket. "The Priest I am bringing is a Portuguese and speaks very little English, very little indeed, but, if he should refuse to marry us through anything you should say, well, it is then that I shall destroy your pretty face, carry you to France and marry you there."

He chuckled evilly.

"Claude has thought it all out."

He walked one step towards the low door.

With a last effort Tina moved quickly towards him and put her hand on his arm.

"Listen, Claude, will you believe me when I swear to you that I have no money. It was only a hoax, like a game, to make Society interested in me. I am penniless. I swear to you that is – the truth."

The mad laughter she had heard before seemed to well up in Claude's throat, but he controlled it and mockingly sweeping her a bow, he said,

"Widow and heir to the vast fortune of the late Sir Marcus Welton, I salute you. You will not, I promise you, be widowed long, for you have before you a most ardent and impatient husband, one Claude Wynchingham."

As he finished speaking, he went through the narrow doorway.

Tina heard him lock the door on the other side and then she heard his footsteps rattle down the narrow staircase and another door at the bottom close and the sound of a key turning in the lock.

"Widow of Sir – Marcus – Welton!"

She put her hands to her temples.

But of course! She had never thought of it.

Claude was right. She was a rich woman! A very rich woman!

And he, in his madness, had not only realised it, but plotted to use it to his own advantage.

This could not be happening to her! It could not be true!

To be married to Claude or to be marked for life – to be taken from here by him across the Channel to France. She gave a little cry and the whole horror of what was happening swept over her.

The moment when Sir Marcus had slumped forward in the coach, the sword thrust through his heart, the painful, bumpy journey to this forgotten and isolated place where Claude could do with her what he wished.

She knew that he had told her that no one could hear, but she began to scream.

"Help! Help! *Save me*!"

Suddenly the misery and horror of her position swept over her so that she lost control of herself.

"Save me, oh, Stern, save me! Save me!"

She cried out the words, screaming them with all the strength of her lungs, then beat ineffectually with her bare hands on the locked door.

"Help! Help! Someone help me!"

She knew that it was hopeless, still she went on shouting, beating with her hands and stamping with her feet.

Then with a sharp crack the floorboards she was standing on gave way, rotten with age, and her foot sank beneath them.

The sudden pain in her ankle seemed the last straw to bring her misery and unhappiness beyond all bearing.

She made no attempt to extract her foot. She only sat down on the floor and started to cry hopelessly, the tears of a child who had been shut away in the dark of a child who is frightened and utterly and completely alone.

Then, as she cried, it seemed to her that the last rays of the sun shining through the skylight were reflected back at her from her captured foot.

She stared at it through her tears – stared and stared again.

CHAPTER TWELVE

Lord Wynchingham signed his name in an angry irritated manner on the Marriage Settlement and Mr. Greychurch leant forward to sand it.

Lord Wynchingham then rose to his feet and stood staring down at the document with a strange expression on his face.

Sir Marcus Welton had been generous – very generous indeed. There was no doubt at all that, as far as her financial needs were concerned, his wife would be a very fortunate woman.

"I think that is all, my Lord," Mr. Greychurch said. "I will have these documents sent by a groom to your Solicitor for safekeeping."

He picked up the document, shook away the sand and was about to leave the room when Lord Wynchingham said sharply,

"Put it down! Leave it where it is!"

"Your pardon, my Lord, but I promised – "

"I am not concerned with your promises, Greychurch," Lord Wynchingham replied. "Do as you are told and leave the document where it is."

Mr. Greychurch pursed his lips, a characteristic habit when he was hurt in his feelings.

"If that is your wish, my Lord," he said stiffly and walked from the room, the very picture of affronted dignity.

Lord Wynchingham was quite unaware of Mr. Greychurch's sensitivity. He was still staring down at the Marriage Settlement, and suddenly he knew, with the absolute certainty of a man who has reached his journey's end, what he must do.

He would tear up the document, he would send it back to Sir Marcus and he would take Tina away with him.

He had for the moment no idea where they would go or what they would do.

He could not see further than the simple fact that he could not live without her.

He must have known this, he thought now, for over a week, perhaps longer, but he was utterly convinced of it from that moment last night when he had kissed her in anger, fury and jealousy.

He had felt her lips respond to his and knew that they were both consumed by a leaping flame of passion and desire that would not be denied.

He had fought against this love.

God knows how he had fought, but it had defeated him.

He would take her away. They would be fugitives from his debts.

They would be scorned and derided by Society because he was unable to pay his dues of honour to Lampton, but it did not matter.

The only thing of any consequence was that they loved each other.

He thought for a moment of Wynch and swept it aside as though that too was of little import beside the light he had seen in Tina's eyes and the response he had felt on her lips.

He felt a sudden surge of joy within himself and thought with a whimsical smile that he had once supposed he knew all there was to know about love.

And yet this was so different, so utterly and completely different from anything he had ever experienced before, from anything he had ever dreamt love could be like.

He was impatient to tell her what he had decided.

He knew, not with conceit but with the certainty of love, that she too would be prepared to sacrifice everything for him.

They would have to flee the country and perhaps later, when the scandal and the hue and cry had died down, they could creep back to live in some small fishing village in Cornwall or some sleepy hamlet deep in the countryside, where no one would worry about them and no one would guess their secret.

'Tina, *Tina*,' he found himself whispering her name almost beneath his breath.

He knew then that the wonder and excitement within himself must be shared.

They must make plans, they must depart tonight and leave the storm to break tomorrow when Sir Marcus and the rest of the world discovered that they had gone.

Lord Wynchingham turned from the desk towards the fireplace to pull the bell, but as he did so he had the uncomfortable feeling that he was being watched.

It was so strong that he looked round, half expecting to see Mr. Greychurch or one of the footmen awaiting his recognition of their presence, but the room was empty save for himself.

Then he glanced through the window and saw what he thought to be the head of a man peer round the bushes at the far end of the garden.

He stared in surprise and with an instant feeling of irritation.

He had given orders, not once but many times, that never, in any circumstances, were the servants or stable boys to come into the garden. The gardeners did their work when everyone else in the house was asleep.

The head was withdrawn and he thought for a moment that he had imagined it, then, suddenly, running across the garden there came a young boy.

It was no one he had ever seen before. He was not wearing the livery that all the grooms in his stables were provided with.

Before he could demand an explanation, the boy cried out,

"Oh, my Lord, come quick. There's bin a terrible accident! Come, come at once!"

"An accident – where?" Lord Wynchingham asked sharply.

"In the stables, my Lord. Oh, it be real bad, there be no time to explain. Please come."

Lord Wynchingham flung wide the French window and ran into the garden.

He wanted to ask further questions, but the boy was already running ahead of him.

He noticed vaguely that he had bare feet and thought it strange that a ragged urchin of this sort should be in his well-kept and exceedingly expensive stables, but he followed him quickly through the bushes that screened the entrance to the passage that led down to the stables.

The boy was already halfway down the narrow alleyway and then, when Lord Wynchingham turned to follow him, he heard a movement behind him and half-turned.

Before he could see anything, a crashing blow on the head brought him stumbling to his knees.

He made an effort to cry out, but another blow knocked him senseless and he went down into a deep darkness –

It must have been a long time later when he felt himself coming very very slowly back to consciousness. There was a long tunnel with a faint, very faint light, at the end of it that he must struggle up.

He was aware of an almost intolerable pain in his head, which, for a moment, precluded any thought.

They were moving him. His head was being shaken and the agony was almost past bearing.

A long time later he became aware of other things, that his hands were tied and so were his feet.

He was lying on the floor of a carriage that was being driven at breakneck speed over a very rough road.

He must have groaned from a sudden bump that shook his head into a darting pattern of stabbing pain, because a rough voice, with a strange accent that he could not place, said,

"Did 'e make a sound?"

"I doubt it," the other man replied. "I thought you 'ad killed 'im, you 'it 'im so 'ard."

"What's it matter if I did?" the first man said surlily. 'Is Nibs 'as said 'e's got to die anyway."

Lord Wynchingham forced himself not to open his eyes and not to move. He knew that to do so would draw attention to the fact that he was alive and listening.

The coach suddenly lurched and swayed as they took a corner too sharply and the two men who had spoken were flung about on the back seat.

"'E'll 'ave us over," one of them swore-.

"Mad, that's what 'e is, if you asks me," the other man said. "I never trusts these *gorgios*."

Something clicked in Lord Wynchingham's memory and he recognised the word and the accent.

The men in the coach with him were gypsies and he remembered speaking to them as a child, when they came to Wynch, which was one of their habitual camping places, year after year.

The local people were afraid of them and gave them water or bought their clothes pegs only because they were too scared to say 'no'.

But he and Claude had been fascinated by the camp, the dark- eyed women with their braided hair, the children tumbling about half-naked on the grass, the piebald ponies and the painted caravans that were usually grouped in a circle round the fire over which bubbled a pot of savoury stew.

'Yes, gypsies,' he thought. 'But why should they wish to do me harm?'

Before he could answer his own question the men spoke again.

"I dunna like this," one said. "It'll bring bad luck."

"You're being well paid for it, ain't you?" the other asked.

"'E didn't say nuthin' about a-killin' 'im in the first place," the other gypsy replied.

"Forget it," the second man answered. "It's a job and we need the money."

There was silence, save for the rattling of the stones on the bottom of the coach, the grinding whirr of the wheels and the clatter of the horses' hoofs.

The way the coach was being driven was almost suicidal, Lord Wynchingham thought, and hoped that they were not his horses that were being whipped into such a pace over such bad roads.

Waves of pain from the wound in his head made him feel half-unconscious.

It was almost a shock when the coach came to a sudden halt.

"Where be we?" one of the gypsies asked.

"I be not sure," the other replied and then added, "I knows! 'Tis the old mill, the one they says be 'aunted. You remember we went for a swim there once, but the water were too cold."

"Aye, I remember," the other said.

Lord Wynchingham remembered too and he knew exactly where they had brought him and now he could guess why.

The old mill was about three miles from Wynch!

It was in a desolate uncultivated part of the estate, far from any of the farms. The mill itself had not been worked for many years.

There was a deep, dark, shadowy mill pool in the bottom of which, it was said, demons lurked, who periodically claimed the sacrifice of some young man or beautiful young girl to prevent them casting evil spells on any who visited the mill.

The local people shunned the place, which was small wonder in view of the fact that there had been a number of suicides there and even the farm hands avoided passing it on their way to work.

Lord Wynchingham's heart sank.

He knew if this was really where he had been taken, there was small hope of his being rescued by any casual passer-by or of his cries for help, if he was able to make any, attracting attention.

An innate sense of self-preservation in the face of what he knew to be great danger made him keep his eyes closed and he forced himself to lie helpless and inert on the floor of the coach, even when the gypsies climbed over him to reach the door.

Then he heard his cousin Claude's voice and knew that what he had suspected almost from the first moment of consciousness was true.

"Get him out!" he heard Claude ordering. "Carry him into the mill, I'll show you where to put him."

The two gypsies picked Lord Wynchingham up roughly, bumping his head on the door in getting him out of the coach. It was with the greatest difficulty that he managed not to wince or exclaim at the pain it caused him.

With his eyes still tight shut he heard them clump through the door and out of the sunshine along a dark damp passage and then down some rickety wooden stairs.

He knew now with a sudden fear where they were taking him. It was to a small dark dungeon-like room that in the past had been used only by the men who had to repair the wooden wheel of the mill or the axle it turned on.

He remembered as a child going there with Claude and how they had tried to play prisoners. But somehow the silence, the damp and the feeling of being locked in had been too frightening and they had run away from the mill and back to the security of Wynch.

Lord Wynchingham tried feverishly to remember more about the room. Was there any other exit except through the door and through the small opening onto the wheel?

Before he had had time to think, the room had been reached.

"Put him down."

The gypsies deposited him on the stone-flagged floor and Lord Wynchingham felt the cold strike instantly through his clothes onto his body.

The gypsies then pulled the ropes roughly from his hands and feet.

"Now you know what to do," he heard Claude say and there was a note of elation, almost of triumph, in his usually somewhat effeminate voice.

"Yus, sir, we does," one of the gypsies answered.

"Well, don't forget any of the things I have told you," Claude said. "You will come back here late tonight."

"No, sir, not at night," the other gypsy interrupted and Lord Wynchingham guessed that he was younger and therefore more afraid.

"Scared are you?" Claude sneered. "Well, the demons will have enough to placate them with this fine gentleman you are giving them as a sacrifice so they won't want either of you. You're not important enough."

"Maybe, but 'twould be best not to do it at night," the other gypsy said stolidly.

"Very well, dawn, but not later, there might be someone about," Claude conceded. "And remember what I told you. You take off his clothes and put them on the bank. It will look as though he has been swimming and you will not steal them. If you steal them, you won't get a penny piece from me."

There was silence while he waited for his words to be digested and then he went on,

"And no knives, you understand. If he moves, struggles or even if he is conscious, give him another blow on the head, but no knives. I don't want any marks on his body. Is that clear?"

"Yus, sir, we understand," the older gipsy nodded.

There was the chink of money and Lord Wynchingham guessed that Claude had drawn out his purse.

"Here is half of what I promised you," he said, "and a half will be yours when you finish the job."

The gypsies did not say 'thank you' and Lord Wynchingham remembered that they never thanked for gifts or for money. It was unlucky. He heard someone step nearer to him and realised that Claude was standing there looking down at him.

"I knew I should win," he said in a strange, almost crazy voice. "Now, my dear coz, it is I who will have everything and you – you will have the demons."

He chuckled and there was something in the sound that told Lord Wynchingham that Claude was mad, completely and absolutely mad.

Claude must have turned on his heel.

There was the sound of his footsteps going up the wooden stairs and then the gypsies followed him from the room.

They locked the door and Lord Wynchingham heard the heavy key turn in the lock, then it was withdrawn and there were only their footsteps fading away in the distance.

He lay where he was, without moving, until he heard the carriage drive away.

There was absolute silence for several minutes. Then, and only then, did he cautiously open his eyes and after a long wait, just in case someone was peering in at him, he raised himself first on his elbow and then to a sitting position.

His head was agony.

He put up a finger and found that whatever he had been struck with had drawn blood, so that his hair was matted and a big scab was forming over the wound.

The movement even of sitting up made him feel faint and he waited for some time before gradually the pain subsided a little and then he staggered to his feet.

The room was even smaller than he had remembered it. It must have shrunk with the years, but it was just as dank and sinister and the door into it was made of solid oak and he knew, without even looking, it would be impossible to pick the lock without the right kind of tools.

The only other exit was the opening onto the machinery of the wheel, but he saw that over the aperture, not much bigger than a small window, bars had been nailed only a few inches apart from each other, new bars fastened at each end with strong nails that would defy any ordinary man's strength to remove them.

He knew then with a kind of helplessness that, with the shrewdness and cleverness of a madman, Claude had prepared this all too well.

He could see the whole picture. The hue and cry that would arise from his not appearing at the Wedding would first be confined to London and then the Dowager, perhaps, would insist on sending a messenger to Wynch to see if they had any news of him.

After that it might be weeks, perhaps months, maybe even years, before his clothes were found beside the millstream.

There would be no question of his body coming to the surface. It was one of the reasons the people believed in the demons that the bodies of those who were drowned never reappeared.

For perhaps the first time in his life Lord Wynchingham was really afraid.

He could see that the cards were heavily stacked against him.

He sat down on the step that led from the doorway into the room. That at least was of wood and not so old as the flagstones he had been lying on.

His head ached intolerably, but his brain was no longer clouded or dazed and he was able to think clearly and coherently.

He saw that he was caught like a rat in a trap. Claude had been extremely clever and, as far as he could see at the moment, there was no possible way out.

He stood up and tried to shake the door and with all his strength attempted to force the iron bars apart, but that, he knew before he started was quite hopeless.

Then he sat down again and realised that nothing was going to happen until dawn, when his executioners would come for him.

Should he attempt to fight them? Although he had not seen them, he guessed that they were both strong and wiry and would be quite equal to grappling with and defeating one man.

Claude had also mentioned knives and Lord Wynchingham knew enough to realise that, if they were attacked, they would not hesitate to disobey his orders and use knives while he himself was weaponless.

He thought it over and the more he thought, the more he was convinced that there was only one possible thing for him to do.

As the night passed, he sat there thinking, planning and scheming and all the time his body cried out for Tina.

Why had he not spoken to her sooner?

Why had he left it to the last moment?

Why had he not been brave enough to acknowledge the dictates of his own heart when he had first known that she was indispensable to him?

It was easy to see now that their plan, which they had thought out so cleverly with a partnership that they thought would work, was hopeless because they had both forgotten the human factor.

Love had defeated them. Love had mocked and laughed at all their schemes and left them both vulnerable and helpless.

For Tina's sake, if not for his own, he could not die like this.

If Claude was mad, he thought, he himself was madder still.

To have imagined for one moment she could put up with a dissolute beast like Sir Marcus!

And to have believed that all the money in the world could assuage his feeling of guilt or his unhappiness without her.

As the night drew on, he grew calm with the resolute determination of a man going into battle.

When it was nearly dawn, he laid himself down on the cold stone floor, exactly as the gypsies had left him. He closed his eyes and waited.

He had to wait a long time. The gypsies were obviously taking no chances with the demons and the sun was riding high in the Heavens before Lord Wynchingham heard the crunch of their feet outside on the gravel and the sound of their coming down the wooden stairs.

He thought that they made an unconscionable noise and realised, when they entered the room, that there were not two but three of them.

He was glad then that he had not put his other plan into action of trying to jump on them from behind the door.

They were chatting together in their own language and he could not understand what they were saying but, in an instant, he felt their hands on him and knew that they were going to strip him in accordance with Claude's instructions.

He forced himself to lie limp and helpless, but they were pretty expert at their job and Lord Wynchingham guessed that he was not the first man that they had knocked unconscious and robbed.

Two of them lifted him naked off the floor while the third, obviously carrying his clothes, hurried up the stairs.

They waited for a signal and when it came, a long low whistle, they carried him up. He felt the sunshine, warm and somehow comforting, on his body.

He did not dare open his eyes, but from his memory of the mill he tried to visualise exactly where they were carrying him.

They went left, avoiding the wheel, for which he was grateful and then onto the side of the pool where the bushes had grown wild and high.

"Put his clothes down there," one of the gypsies ordered and Lord Wynchingham recognised him as the man who had been with him in the coach.

"Now!"

It was a signal to the man who was carrying his legs and he felt them swing him with all their strength and then fling him into the pool.

He took a deep breath and now the icy-cold water closed over him.

He felt himself going down, down and now there was a sudden suction as if of some whirlpool lurking in the very depths.

He had anticipated this and he started to swim strongly under water towards the bank he had just been thrown from.

The suction was still there, he could feel it and it warned him to go no deeper and yet, knowing the gypsies were watching, he must not reveal his presence.

He swam on, forcing himself as deep as he dared and keeping away from the centre of the pool.

His lungs were nearly bursting and the pain in his head threatened him once again with unconsciousness before he found what he was seeking, the underwater part of the old millwheel.

It was right ahead of him and he grasped it thankfully. One second more and he could have swum no further.

Clinging to the wheel with both hands, Lord Wynchingham twisted himself behind it and raised himself cautiously in the water.

The breath in his nostrils was a life-giving elixir and for a moment he could think of nothing except the fact that he could breathe and live.

Then, because he was very well aware of the danger that still threatened him, he moved lower in the water until only his eyes were above the surface, and looked around for the gypsies.

He was, as he had hoped, hidden behind the broken wheel and, perhaps thirty yards away, on the bank where he had left them, he could see the gypsies.

They were staring into the pool, looking towards the centre and had obviously no idea that he had eluded both the demons of the whirlpool and themselves.

Lord Wynchingham gave a little sigh of relief and slipped further into the shadows of the millwheel.

The water was bitterly cold. He felt his teeth beginning to chatter and hoped that the gypsies would not be long in leaving.

He was right in that assumption and even as he watched they turned, the elder one looking over his shoulder first to the right and then to the left and moved swiftly and, Lord Wynchingham imagined, with a quietness of Indian trappers, away towards the wood on the other side of the mill.

The gypsies were almost out of sight and Lord Wynchingham was thinking thankfully that he could come out of the water, when one of them re-appeared.

He ducked his head low behind the wheel again, but the gypsy was not looking in his direction. He was only a young boy, perhaps the third gypsy who had not been present when he was kidnapped.

He picked up the pile of clothes that lay beside the millstream, tucked them under his arm and ran after the others.

Lord Wynchingham had an insane desire to shout after him, to call out 'stop thief' and then remembered that, whatever happened, one thing he must not do at this moment is to draw attention to himself.

He waited nearly five minutes and then, shivering and blue with cold, he swam to the bank and climbed out into the sunshine.

He would have liked to rest for a few minutes and let the sun warm his body, but it was too dangerous.

Instead he hurried into the bushes, shook himself as dry as he could and then set off in the opposite direction to that which the gypsies had taken towards Wynch.

He looked at the sun, guessed that it must be getting on for nine o'clock and with a little groan began to run.

Nine o'clock and Tina would be married at eleven!

They had planned the time most meticulously so that the Wedding Breakfast could be at noon and the bride and bridegroom get away in plenty of time to reach Newmarket before nightfall.

He could have hit his head against a rock when he thought how he had acquiesced in the arrangements that seemed so sensible.

Why had he not suggested an afternoon Wedding? It would have given him time.

He ran until he was forced to slacken his pace, not because he was winded, but because his feet were such agony.

Not since he was a child had he walked without shoes and the rough scrubland, full of stones and thistles, made each step a purgatory.

Time was passing and he pushed on.

There were no houses, not even a cottage in this part of his estate. The agricultural land was all on the other side and the only time he walked over this particular part was when he was shooting.

Stark naked, burnt now by the sun, stung by the flies, and his feet cut and bleeding, he struggled on with only one idea in his mind. To get to Tina to save her!

He did not allow himself to think that it was, in fact, impossible.

It was already too late for him to go to London, even on the fastest horse in his stables.

He was obsessed by one thought and one thought only and that was to reach her and he would not admit that it could not be done.

Three-quarters of an hour later he crossed a field that had been planted with wheat and saw, in the centre of it, a scarecrow.

He went towards it and found beneath the tattered coat a pair of very old breeches, stuffed with straw. He dragged them off the scarecrow and put them on, thankful that at least he would not arrive at his own house in the embarrassing position of being as naked as the day he was born,

On, on. Never before had he realised how vast his estate was or how much more might have been done for it in the way of roads and cottages.

He vowed to himself that, if he was ever granted a chance, these things should be done, more people should be employed, there should be more houses and better conditions for those who trusted him.

It was just a dream that would never be realised, but he promised himself, or rather he promised Wynch, that if he was ever in a position to do anything he would do it.

Still he went on, his head aching, his feet smarting and bleeding.

He had no time to think of them.

It was Tina who mattered. Tina who, through his stupid selfish fault, was being sacrificed!

It was with a sigh of relief that he saw ahead of him the road to London, which passed through the middle of his estate.

On this side it was rough, mostly uncultivated, land he had just passed through. On the other side was Parkland surrounded by a brick wall.

He was about to cross the road when he saw in the distance a carriage approaching.

He thought quickly. If he was to ask assistance, perhaps they would carry him straight to London or to Wynch, where he could mount one of his own horses.

His horse would be the best for, after all, he would look a strange figure arriving to stop the Wedding of his Ward with nothing on but a pair of old, torn and rain-washed breeches.

He put out his hand ready to step forward towards the coach, and then some premonition of danger made him draw back.

There was a bush beside the road and he moved quickly behind it.

'They would not stop, anyway,' he muttered to himself. 'They would think I was a tramp or a footpad.'

It was only an excuse, and he knew it, an excuse, because something stronger than common sense told him not to hail the coach.

He saw now that the coach was being driven by a man who was using his whip unmercifully on two horses which, with flying manes, were moving down the road at an almost incredible speed, but, as they flashed by, a shower of stones flew up from the wheels and a cloud of dust obscured them.

But before they passed Lord Wynchingham had recognised the driver.

It was Claude, his lips drawn back from his teeth in an almost diabolical grin, his eyes glinting strongly with the madness that was apparent even in that flashing second.

Lord Wynchingham did not wait for the dust to subside before he crossed the road and vaulted over the wall on the other side.

Where was Claude going and why?

He could not understand and yet, vaguely, some presentiment told him that it concerned Tina.

Tina was in danger.

He must he must save her!

He started to run again, faster, faster, certain now, with a kind of sick horror within himself, that Claude having, as he thought, murdered one person, was perhaps in his evil mood seeking another victim.

"Tina! *Tina!*"

Lord Wynchingham whispered her name beneath his breath as he ran down the avenue beneath the great oak trees, hurrying towards the rooftops of Wynch, which he could now see rising above the trees,

And planning which horse in his stables could move the fastest and in his mind he was already ordering it to be saddled.

He would just give himself time to be dressed and then he would be after Claude.

"*Tina!*"

Her name had almost become a prayer but suddenly, as he speeded up his already quick pace, he caught his foot in a rabbit hole and, because he was travelling so fast, turned head over heels.

He felt himself catapult through the air and then, as he fell, his head struck against the root of one of the oak trees.

It struck the same place where he had been knocked out the night before and now, once again, the sudden streak of agony shot through his whole body and darkness swallowed him up –

*

Lord Wynchingham opened his eyes to find himself in his own bed.

He was wearing a fresh white nightshirt and with his first movements of consciousness he knew that his feet had been bandaged.

The housekeeper at Wynch, Mrs. Harding, was standing beside the bed and he saw the anxiety on her face and turned from her to see the worried expression in the eyes of old Saintley, who had been butler at Wynch since his grandfather's time.

"What has happened? Where am I?" he murmured.

"Oh, your Lordship, you are alive!" Mrs. Harding responded, the tears coming into her eyes. "We don't know, your Lordship, we don't know what happened. We found you in the drive, in a terrible state you were and we have sent for the physician and he should be here very shortly. But your Lordship must not move because there is a fearsome wound on the back of your head."

For a moment Lord Wynchingham lay staring at her and then he remembered.

"Move? Of course I have to move," he cried. "You don't know what is happening. Get me my clothes, Saintley, and be quick about it."

He staggered as his feet reached the ground and with a supreme effort he pulled himself together.

"Your Lordship is not well!" Mrs. Harding exclaimed. "You must not be gettin' up, you must not really! Oh, your Lordship, lie still and wait for the doctor."

"I'll wait for nobody," Lord Wynchingham said in what he hoped was a resolute voice, but which even to his own ears sounded rather weak and ineffectual. "Brandy, that's what I want, brandy! Give me a drink, Saintley, for God's sake! Mrs. Harding, get me something to eat!"

"Of course, your Lordship. Your Lordship must be hungry, I never thought of that."

She bustled from the room, obviously thankful to have something to do, while Saintley, as if by magic, produced a decanter filled with brandy and poured Lord Wynchingham out a glass.

His instinct was to toss it back as he would ordinarily have done, but some half-forgotten wisdom warned him that it would be far too potent on an empty stomach.

So he took a few sips and demanded his clothes forcibly and added a string of oaths that made Saintley shudder, when he saw the thickness of the bandages on his feet.

"I'll never get my boots over those. Take them off, you old fool. I don't want to be cosseted, I only want to get to London."

"Your feet were raw and bleeding, my Lord," Saintley said quietly, "but if your Lordship insists on dressing, I have a pair of your father's boots. You always took a size smaller than his late Lordship."

"Then get them, get them at once," Lord Wynchingham urged him.

It was an almost superhuman effort to dress, but, with an occasional sip of brandy to help, he managed it.

When Mrs. Harding appeared, followed by a footman bearing a tray of food, he made himself eat a few mouthfuls, simply because, otherwise, he knew that he would be too weak to go on with his journey.

Saintley came back with his boots and somehow they got them on over the bandages and now, although he was pale and there was a bandage round his head, Lord Wynchingham was almost himself.

"Is my horse ready? " he asked Saintley as he swallowed another mouthful of food from the overladen tray.

"At the door, my Lord," Saintley told him.

He was used to the vagaries of the aristocracy and he was too well trained, from pantry boy to butler, to argue with any decision his Master might make, but, because he was genuinely fond of his young Lordship, wild though he might be, he did suggest tentatively,

"It might be wise if a groom accompanied your Lordship."

Lord Wynchingham flashed him a smile as he went towards the door.

"Thank you, Saintley, but I assure you that no groom or jockey, for that matter, could travel as fast as I am going to."

As he spoke, he glanced at the clock over the mantelpiece and stopped dead.

"That is not the correct time, is it?" he asked. "I thought when I looked at it just now it must have stopped."

Saintley drew a monumental silver watch from the pocket of his waistcoat.

"The clock, I regret to say, my Lord, is precisely five minutes fast," he said. "The correct time is a quarter to four."

"*God!*" Lord Wynchingham exclaimed. "It cannot be! I reached here this morning! I could not have taken much more than an hour and, perhaps, a half, to come from the mill!"

"No one discovered you, my Lord, until early in the afternoon," Saintley replied.

"But I cannot have lost all that time, all those hours," Lord Wynchingham cried. "Oh, my God! What will happen now?"

He turned and rushed from the room. Saintley heard his steps hurrying down the stairway and shook his head.

"His Lordship is not well enough to racket about with a wound like that on his head."

The horse was waiting outside the front door.

Lord Wynchingham could see it through the open doorway, pawing the ground and tossing its head, a magnificent stallion with a touch of Arab in its breeding.

"I must go to London!" he muttered. "I must find out what has happened."

But he remembered that if the clocks were right and the Wedding plans had not miscarried, Tina would already be on the way to Newmarket.

He suddenly made up his mind to do something different.

He turned to one of the footmen waiting in the hall.

"Bring me my duelling pistols," he ordered.

"Very good, my Lord."

The box was brought to him and he took them both out.

It would not take him very long to prime and load them and, mounting his horse, he galloped not in the direction of London, but to the habitual camping ground of the gypsies.

He guessed even before he arrived there that they would be gone. There were the smoking ashes of what had been a fire, but the caravans had disappeared.

He sat on his horse looking around him with a sudden feeling of anti-climax, his pistols heavy in his coat pocket and the feeling that even they could bring him any nearer to Tina.

Then, as he sat there, he saw, hidden in a little dip in the ground, that one of the caravans was left.

It was a small unobtrusive one, but had a well fed horse to draw it.

Lord Wynchingham rode towards it.

There was a woman sitting on the driving seat, the reins in her hand, but she was alone. He guessed that she was waiting, although for whom and why, he had no idea.

She had not seen him for she was looking in the opposite direction, but then through the bushes, loping along in the easy, comfortable gait of men who run long distances, came two men.

They sprang onto the footboard of the caravan and without a word, the woman whipped up the horse.

"Stop!"

Lord Wynchingham was across their path before they had any idea of his presence.

He saw the startled fear on their faces. He saw the apprehension in the dark eyes of the woman as they all stared at him as he slowly drew his pistols from the pocket of his coat.

"Where have you been and what have you been doing? Tell me the truth or you will not live to tell me another lie."

He was threatening them dramatically, and even as he spoke he was surprised at himself.

Yet some intuition told him that it was the only way.

"We have been a-doin' nothin', mister."

"You lie, I want the truth."

"They didn't know they was a-doin' anythin' wrong," the woman interposed shrilly. "The gentleman only asked 'em to carry off the young lady for 'im. 'E didna say anythin' about murder. We told 'im we were peaceable folk. 'E only said as 'e wanted 'em to take the young lady."

Lord Wynchingham felt a sudden relief sweep over him.

"And where have you taken her?" he asked gently.

"To that little white place up on the 'ill," one of the gypsies answered.

He pointed behind him and Lord Wynchingham slipped his pistol back in his pocket and dug his spurs into his horse's sides.

He did not look back at the gypsies scuttling away.

He was travelling as fast as his mount could carry him, back towards Wynch, back to where he knew that he would find Tina.

It must have taken him less than ten minutes to reach the Temple, but it seemed to him as though ten hours had passed before he flung himself off his horse and found his way to the back of the Temple where there was a small door that led to the tiny upper chamber, which one of his ancestors had built because he liked to lie there at night and look at the stars.

It took Lord Wynchingham only a second to unlock the door, the key was on the outside, before breathlessly he was running up the narrow staircase.

He unlocked the door at the top and just for one terrible moment the thought struck him that he would find Tina there but she would be dead.

The door swung back and he saw her sitting on the floor, only a foot away from him.

Her face was stained with tears and there was an expression of terror in her eyes as she first looked at him, which was swiftly replaced by one of such radiance that he felt himself almost blinded by the beauty of it!

Then he was on the floor beside her, his arms around her.

"Oh, Tina! *Tina!*" he cried. "Thank God I have found you. I have been mad, crazy and stupid, but at last I have come to my senses. Oh, Tina, I cannot live without you and I have no desire to live at all unless I can have you. It doesn't matter what the world thinks, it doesn't matter about the money. We shall be together and I love you so much. Please, Tina, say you love me! Say you will have me!"

He must have been kissing her as the words tumbled incoherently from his lips as he found her mouth beneath his and he could taste the salt of her tears.

"Oh, Stern! Are you sure you love me enough?"

"I love you more than anything in the whole world," he answered. "I am such a fool that I did not realise it till now, but oh, Tina. I love you! Say you love me."

"I love you too," she whispered. "I have loved you for a long time, and oh, Stern, everything is all right — everything."

"Of course it is, if you love me," he answered. "But come, let's get away from here quickly. They will try to stop us, but nothing, nothing in the world can stop us now."

He put his arms round her and held her so close that she could hardly breathe.

For a moment she surrendered herself to the glory that was enveloping her and the happiness that was almost too wonderful to be borne, until, with an effort to behave rationally, she said,

"Listen, Stern."

"There is nothing to listen to," he said roughly. "You can tell me what has happened as we go. I know that Claude has kidnapped you. Well, he did the same to me and what is more, he tried to kill me! I was afraid. Oh, Tina, how afraid I was that he might have killed you!"

She gave a little gurgle of laughter.

"He did not want to kill me. He wanted to *marry* me — that was why he killed Sir Marcus."

Lord Wynchingham stared at her in astonishment.

"Claude killed Sir Marcus!"

Tina nodded.

"Yes, after we were married. He is mad, quite, quite mad and has gone now to get a Priest, because he knows that as his widow I inherit Sir Marcus's money."

"He is insane!"

"Yes, of course he is and what is so terrible, Stern, is that it was all quite unnecessary, the killing of Sir Marcus or even the fact that I had to marry him or for Claude to try and kill you. You see – look! You were living with it all the time!"

"What are you talking about?" Lord Wynchingham asked, his eyes on her face, as if he could never see enough of her.

Almost reluctantly he looked to where she was pointing and to where her foot was still embedded in the broken floorboards and then he saw, glittering and shining, innumerable pieces of gold and he knew instantly, as Tina had known, that here was the treasure of Wynch, hidden in the most unlikely place where anyone could search for it.

He stared down in stupefaction and was conscious, not so much of relief, excitement or even pleasure, but of the fact that Tina was there beside him and her lips were very close to his.

He drew her back again into his arms.

"Oh, Tina!" he murmured. "It ought to matter, and it doesn't. We have been through too much for money to count any more. I thought that you were married and I had lost you. I thought that you were dead and you are alive. I am content with that! I can think of nothing else. Do you realise we are together, together at last. You love me. Oh, darling, my little love, tell me again that you love me."

And Tina tried to say it and wanted to say it, but it was too late.

Their lips met in a kiss that made them forget everything, except that they were man and woman and they wanted and needed each other until the end of time.

'I love you,' she whispered in her heart and was swept away by the ecstasy and wonder of his touch.

OTHER BOOKS IN THIS SERIES

The Barbara Cartland Eternal Collection is the unique opportunity to collect all five hundred of the timeless beautiful romantic novels written by the world's most celebrated and enduring romantic author.

Named the Eternal Collection because Barbara's inspiring stories of pure love, just the same as love itself, the books will be published on the internet at the rate of four titles per month until all five hundred are available.

The Eternal Collection, classic pure romance available worldwide for all time.

1. Elizabethan Lover
2. The Little Pretender
3. A Ghost in Monte Carlo
4. A Duel of Hearts
5. The Saint and the Sinner
6. The Penniless Peer
7. The Proud Princess
8. The Dare-Devil Duke
9. Diona and a Dalmatian
10. A Shaft of Sunlight
11. Lies for Love
12. Love and Lucia
13. Love and the Loathsome Leopard
14. Beauty or Brains
15. The Temptation of Torilla
16. The Goddess and the Gaiety Girl
17. Fragrant Flower
18. Look, Listen and Love
19. The Duke and the Preacher's Daughter
20. A Kiss For The King
21. The Mysterious Maid-Servant
22. Lucky Logan Finds Love
23. The Wings of Ecstasy
24. Mission to Monte Carlo
25. Revenge of the Heart
26. The Unbreakable Spell
27. Never Laugh at Love
28. Bride to a Brigand
29. Lucifer and the Angel
30. Journey to a Star
31. Solita and the Spies
32. The Chieftain without a Heart
33. No Escape from Love
34. Dollars for the Duke
35. Pure and Untouched
36. Secrets
37. Fire in the Blood
38. Love, Lies and Marriage
39. The Ghost who fell in love
40. Hungry for Love
41. The wild cry of love
42. The blue eyed witch
43. The Punishment of a Vixen
44. The Secret of the Glen

45. Bride to The King
46. For All Eternity
47. A King in Love
48. A Marriage Made in Heaven
49. Who Can Deny Love?
50. Riding to The Moon
51. Wish for Love
52. Dancing on a Rainbow
53. Gypsy Magic
54. Love in the Clouds
55. Count the Stars
56. White Lilac
57. Too Precious to Lose
58. The Devil Defeated
59. An Angel Runs Away
60. The Duchess Disappeared
61. The Pretty Horse-breakers
62. The Prisoner of Love
63. Ola and the Sea Wolf
64. The Castle made for Love
65. A Heart is Stolen
66. The Love Pirate
67. As Eagles Fly
68. The Magic of Love
69. Love Leaves at Midnight
70. A Witch's Spell
71. Love Comes West
72. The Impetuous Duchess
73. A Tangled Web
74. Love Lifts the Curse
75. Saved By A Saint
76. Love is Dangerous
77. The Poor Governess
78. The Peril and the Prince
79. A Very Unusual Wife
80. Say Yes Samantha
81. Punished with love
82. A Royal Rebuke
83. The Husband Hunters
84. Signpost To Love
85. Love Forbidden
86. Gift of the Gods
87. The Outrageous Lady
88. The Slaves of Love
89. The Disgraceful Duke
90. The Unwanted Wedding
91. Lord Ravenscar's Revenge
92. From Hate to Love
93. A Very Naughty Angel
94. The Innocent Imposter
95. A Rebel Princess
96. A Wish Come True
97. Haunted
98. Passions In The Sand
99. Little White Doves of Love
100. A Portrait of Love
101. The Enchanted Waltz
102. Alone and Afraid
103. The Call of the Highlands
104. The Glittering Lights
105. An Angel in Hell
106. Only a Dream
107. A Nightingale Sang
108. Pride and the Poor Princess
109. Stars in my Heart
110. The Fire of Love
111. A Dream from the Night
112. Sweet Enchantress
113. The Kiss of the Devil
114. Fascination in France
115. Love Runs in
116. Lost Enchantment
117. Love is Innocent
118. The Love Trap
119. No Darkness for Love
120. Kiss from a Stranger
121. The Flame Is Love
122. A Touch Of Love

123. The Dangerous Dandy
124. In Love In Lucca
125. The Karma of Love
126. Magic from the Heart
127. Paradise Found
128. Only Love
129. A Duel with Destiny
130. The Heart of the Clan
131. The Ruthless Rake
132. Revenge Is Sweet
133. Fire on the Snow
134. A Revolution of Love
135. Love at the Helm
136. Listen to Love
137. Love Casts out Fear
138. The Devilish Deception
139. Riding in the Sky
140. The Wonderful Dream
141. This Time it's Love
142. The River of Love
143. A Gentleman in Love
144. The Island of Love
145. Miracle for a Madonna
146. The Storms of Love
147. The Prince and the Pekingese
148. The Golden Cage
149. Theresa and a Tiger
150. The Goddess of Love
151. Alone in Paris
152. The Earl Rings a Belle
153. The Runaway Heart
154. From Hell to Heaven
155. Love in the Ruins
156. Crowned with Love
157. Love is a Maze
158. Hidden by Love
159. Love Is The Key
160. A Miracle In Music
161. The Race For Love
162. Call of The Heart
163. The Curse of the Clan
164. Saved by Love
165. The Tears of Love
166. Winged Magic
167. Born of Love
168. Love Holds the Cards

Paper Flowers
Face ???
Flowers - Rose
Fruit

Printed in Great Britain
by Amazon